John S. Sauz

Mark Gildersleeve

John S. Sauzade

Mark Gildersleeve

1st Edition | ISBN: 978-3-75242-756-1

Place of Publication: Frankfurt am Main, Germany

Year of Publication: 2020

Outlook Verlag GmbH, Germany.

Reproduction of the original.

Mark Gildersleeve.

A Novel.

BY JOHN S. SAUZADE.

I.

Although of much importance as a manufacturing place, Belton is noted chiefly for the beautiful water-fall to which the town, in fact, owes its existence.

Here the Passaic, interrupted in its placid flow by a rocky barrier, takes an abrupt turn, and plunges in a narrow sheet of foam adown a deep chasm, formed in one of Nature's throes ages ago, and then with wild swirls rushes angrily over a rocky bed, until spent and quiet it skirts the town, and winds away appeased and pellucid—despite the murky drain of dye-houses—through woodlands, fields, and pastures green. Ere reaching the cataract, however, the river is tapped by a canal which serves to feed the flumes that run the many mills of Belton; and through this race-way the diverted waters speed on their busy errand, starting cumbersome overshot, undershot, breast, and turbine wheels into action, that in their turn quicken into life the restless shuttle and whirling spindle.

From the cliff, at the head of the cataract, one may completely overlook the town, a cheerful hive, compactly built, and consisting chiefly of long brick factories, with little belfries, and rows of small white wooden dwellings. The whole is neat and bright; no canopy of coal-smoke obscures the blue sky, and but an occasional tall chimney or jet of vapor is seen, for here steam is dethroned, and the cheaper motor reigns supreme.

The river side, the cliff, the falls, in short the water-power belongs and has belonged for generations to the Obershaw family. In days of yore, when Whitman Obershaw ran a saw-mill, and tilled a clearing hereabout, his worldly possessions, it is safe to say, were not such as to assimilate his chances of salvation to the facility with which a camel can go through a needle's eye, and it was reserved for his son, John Peter Obershaw, to reap the benefit of the accident that had put his ancestors in possession of the site of Belton. And when you consider the present magnitude of the place, its many mills, and the enormous yearly rental of the water-power, you will not be surprised to learn that the costly stone mansion on the cliff, with its imposing front, its beautiful grounds, conservatories, and lodges, is the residence of the Hon. Rufus Heath, son-in-law and heir of John Peter Obershaw, who built it.

There is a mural tablet in the apse of St. Jude's, Belton, inscribed to the memory of

JOHN PETER OBERSHAW,
OF THIS TOWN,

Through whose munificence this Church
WAS ERECTED,
A.D. 1840.
HIS CHRISTIAN VIRTUES ENDEARED HIM TO ALL.

An epitaph which bore out the proverbial reputation of its kind in being essentially a lie—a lie in black and white, for old Obershaw had no Christian or even Pagan virtues to speak of, and was rather disliked by all for a selfish, avaricious, nonagenarian. Perhaps the only commendable act of his life was the erection of the small, but handsome church in question. Yet, even this was looked upon as but the placatory offering of a prudent worldling, about to appear before the final tribunal, and anxious to propitiate the great Judge. Moreover, those who knew the most about it asserted that the church would never have been built, nor a dollar spent towards it, had it not been for Rufus Heath, who, during the last years of his father-in-law's life, had the entire control of the estate, owing to the latter's age and incapacity. Doubtless these assertions were true, for neither dread of God or demon could ever have wrung an unremunerative stiver from old John Peter Obershaw's clutching fist, as he belonged to the orthodox school of misers—the class who live but to accumulate, and find all their pleasure in that sound, wholesome vice which prolongs life, and betrays not to a fool's paradise.

To the last he was steadfast to his idol. For years previous he was confined to his room by paralysis, dead to all affections save love of money, and vegetating in an easy chair stuffed literally with gold; for the senile miser, like a magpie, slyly secreted coin in every nook and corner of his chamber. In this second childhood, it was necessary to quiet him by giving him money to toy with, and musty accounts and deeds, which he pored over with the vacuity of an imbecile. To the end the ruling passion swayed him. At the last moment, when the taper of life was about giving its expiring flicker, he asked his attendant to bring him a surveyor's map of his estate. "And, James, tell ... tell Mr. Heath I want to see him ... see him at once. Must buy Van Slyke's farm if he'll sell it right ... sell it right. But he wants too much ... too much. No ... no ... can't give it. No ... no; haven't ... got the money. Soon as I am well, well ... and strong, I'll go out and have a look at it ... look at it. Soon as I am well, and go out ... go out. But can't 'ford to pay much. No ... no. Van Slyke's farm'll square the addition. But, I can't pay much ... can't 'ford it;" and a nervous twitching of his pale thin lips, as he mumbled to himself, showed teeth still sound, though worn down like an old mastiff's. He was a man of large frame, gaunt, bowed with age, and the dried yellow skin of his face resembled wrinkled parchment. When the map was brought to him, he stared vacantly at it with faded eyes that looked like dull agates, then relapsed into a still slumber with the map gripped in his long, talon-like, bony fingers, as if some one would steal it from him. Aroused by the entrance of his son-in-law, he again mumbled—"Where's the map … map? Heath, see Van Slyke 'bout the farm and don't let him … let him cheat me. I ain't quite … quite so strong now, and … and they'll cheat me. Ah, they're a close, sharp set.... Soon as I am well I'll go … I'll go...."

The last words were uttered in a faint whisper; no further sound came from the moving lips; the death film crept over his eyes, and he was gone. He had lasted well and long, for avarice is a powerful antiseptic. The dry heart burns to the socket, and the selfish miser was blessed with an euthanasia that a saint might have envied.

The nearest physician, Dr. Wattletop, was swiftly summoned, only to return discomfited, as he expressed it, by that omnipotent leech who carries his lancet at the end of a snath.

The fall of so heavily laden a body into the great ocean of eternity created, to use a homely simile, an unusual splash, and occasioned no little commotion in Belton.

"Why, sir," said Mr. Madison Mumbie, the eminent paper-maker, addressing Dr. Wattletop, in the agitation of the moment, "Why, sir, Mr. Obershaw's wealth is e-normous! Probably the richest man we had in the State. Yes, sir" (with a sigh), "I regret to say it, we have lost a gentleman, and a Christian, who leaves at least two millions of dollars. Yes, sir, two millions at the lowest calculation—he leaves all of that!"

"Leaves!" repeated the doctor. "Aye, there's the rub. Now, if he could only have taken the two millions with him, there would have been something in it, wouldn't there?"

This view of the case did not strike Mr. Mumbie, who was himself rather inclined to accumulate, as cheerful or encouraging, and he went his way in a meditative mood.

Mr. Mook, the gentlemanly undertaker, in walking twenty rods from the residence of the deceased, was accosted by not less than a dozen anxious inquirers eager to learn the slightest particular relating to the sorrowful event. To whom Mr. Mook, with that mingled air of neatness, despatch, and meek resignation to the decrees of Providence, which characterized him, replied in a serious and very proper way. The information imparted was invariably received by the questioners with expressions of deep interest and sympathy, as if they had lost a near and dear friend. It is sad to add, though, that one individual, George Gildersleeve, the noisiest quidnunc in Belton, was on the contrary rather discourteous and disparaging in his inquiries and comments. George is a man of substance, and proprietor of the Archimedes Works. A burly fellow of middle age, with chest and loins like an ox, coarse mouth, hale complexion, and sandy hair shorn close over an obstinate head. Rich and purse-proud, he proclaims himself a plebeian, and in keeping therewith is generally seen divested of coat and hands in pockets. Thus he appeared in the doorway of his counting-room as Mr. Mook came down the street, and passed the Archimedes Works. Decorous and mournful Mook affected not to see Gildersleeve, dreading him as a bore and button-holder; but the stratagem was futile, and bluff George, hailing the undertaker as "Commodore," brought him —speaking nautically—"to."

"First-class obsequies, sir, have been ordered. Most elegant rosewood casket, new pattern silver handles. Everything in the most rekerchey and approved style. Funeral on Wednesday," Mook replied, in a tone of mild reproof, in answer to Gildersleeve's query as to when he was going to put old Uncle John to bed with a shovel.

Mr. Mook took pride in his profession. He was the inventor and patentee of a burial casket, that for "ease, elegance, and comfort," as he admiringly described it, was equalled by few and surpassed by none.

"Well, well, Commodore"—it was a habit of Gildersleeve's to dub his friends and acquaintances with incongruous titles, whether prompted thereto by affectionate impulses or a peculiar sense of humor, we are not prepared to decide; sufficient to say that the undertaker was invariably addressed as "Commodore" by the master of the Archimedes Works; similarly, Mr. McGoffin, the highly respectable, though illiterate shoe-maker, was styled "Judge;" Dr. Wattletop, "Major," etc., etc.

"Well, well, Commodore," said Gildersleeve, leaving his door-step and planting himself on the sidewalk so as to bar the way and hold the undertaker to converse, "so we go. If the man with the pitchfork don't get old Uncle John, what the deuce is the use of having a man with a pitchfork, eh?"

Mr. Mook coughed behind his hand, and tried to look as if he hadn't heard the remark, as he said, "Great loss to Belton, Mr. Gildersleeve."

"Great loss!" repeated Gildersleeve. "The old cuss! Why, confound him, he drove his only son, Johnny Obershaw, to sea when he was but fourteen years old, by his infernal meanness, and the little monkey was lost overboard less than a month after; and now here's Rufe Heath, that I recklect when he hadn't two coppers to jingle on a tombstone, slips in, bags the whole pool, and puts on more airs than a French barber. Now I'll tell you what it is, Joe Mook, you know me well enough, and you know that I can show as lovely a little pile of rocks as the next man, and you know, too, that I sweat for it. Yes, sir, by the hokey! on this spot (with a flourish towards the works), where my grandfather shod Gineral Washington's horse in a rickety old shanty that you could have capsized with a kick, I began when I was knee-high, with a hide apron on, swinging the sledge and paring hoofs late and early. Yes, sir! late and early, warm or cold, I stuck to it, and no thanks to any one, until you see what I've come to! And is there any airs about me? I think not; and there's many a man in this place that's as proud as a peacock, that I could buy and sell twice over. But I can say this, and you know it, that I've always been, and always intend to be, as independent as a hog on ice. That's me!"

And that *was* he. For if Mr. George Washington Gildersleeve prided himself on anything, it was on being free from "airs," and independent as a hog on ice —a comparison, it must be confessed, not particularly happy, and that conveyed an entirely unintended impression. However, it came pat to him, and he flung it defiantly in the teeth of the world. Mook had heard those sentiments before, hence he was not vividly impressed by them, nor altogether pleased with the diatribe against his present patrons. Still, he was not prepared for their sakes to remonstrate, and perhaps offend a future customer, for the undertaker, "thankful for past favors," as he stated in his advertisement in the *Belton Sentinel*, "and soliciting a continuance of the same," seemed to think himself exempt from the common lot of humanity, and set apart to take under all Belton forever. So he gave a non-committal shake of the head, as he contemplated the pavement, and then, profiting by a pause in Gildersleeve's harangue to escape, glided with soft steps away to his avocations.

The funeral was an imposing one. Many of the mills were closed—all, in fact, that could conveniently stop working. The Archimedes Works, though, remained in full blast, as the proprietor, true to his independence, did not feel himself any more called upon to close his shops for old John Peter Obershaw's death, than for that of any other mere acquaintance. Gildersleeve, however, as a concession, was at the interment, with his coat on too, somewhat subdued, perhaps, in tone and demeanor, but keeping up, nevertheless, an animated political discussion with a fellow-citizen as they stood in the churchyard. Nine-tenths of the population of the town gathered to witness the funeral. There had not been so much excitement in the place since the day of the "Grand Triumphal Entrée" of "Peabody's Combination

6

Menagerie and Hippodrome." The people lined the streets through which the procession passed, and filled St. Jude's, where the services were held. No less than three ministers were in attendance, and a bishop extolled the virtues and success of the decedent in a way to persuade the auditors that they mourned a well-spent life. Then the church bell tolled a requiem knell as to the family vault the corpse was borne along, attended by pall-bearers, who had been consistently selected from among the wealthiest acquaintances of the family. The Hon. Rufus Heath followed as chief mourner, with his young daughter; then came his son and daughter-in-law; and lastly, a multitude of relatives and friends.

So passed away this old man, leaving behind a vast fortune, that had brought him but the gambler's joy—but the arid pleasures of the gold glutton, subsisting on the fumes of money; the odorless fumes whose cold astringency withers the emotions, dries the heart, and leaves man with but the instincts of the vulture and fox.

John Peter Obershaw left no children to survive him. His only son, as Gildersleeve had said, was lost at sea, and his daughter, Mrs. Heath, had preceded her father on the long journey years before. As he owed much of the augmentation of his wealth to the judgment, vigilance, and superintendence of his son-in-law, it was not surprising that the estate was found devised to him, the only being who had ever secured the favor and entire confidence of the old miser. Town tattle hinted at "undue influence" and "imbecility." There might have been more in this than idle gossip, but as no one was interested other than the devisee's children in making any investigations, he inherited without opposition. A great accretion of wealth this to Rufus Heath, who stepped thus quietly into the shoes of the late owner of Belton, for that town was in reality little more than an appanage of the Obershaw family. The evidences of this were patent on every side. A walk through the principal street showed you Heath Hall, where political meetings to distract, and balls and concerts to delight, the denizens took place; Obershaw House, a tavern of dimensions vast, where the lodging and dining rooms were too gorgeous to be comfortable, and only the bar commodious and consolatory; the Belton Bank; the Passaic Insurance Company; the Savings Institution, with its bee-hive sign —in all of which Rufus Heath's claim of ownership, or sovereignty, gave further indication of the wealth of the Obershaw estate. In short, you could not turn without being reminded how fortunate and important a man was the present heir, whilom a poor lawyer's clerk and now owner of the truly Pactolian waters of the Falls of the Passaic.

II.

The villa on the cliff would probably have excited but little attention in any country where chateaux or palaces abound, but it was looked upon by the simple people of Belton as a magnificent dwelling. After a stranger or tourist had seen the falls, he was invariably driven by the ciceroning hackman, desirous of lengthening the ride and increasing the fare, to view Mr. Heath's residence, that being considered next in importance as a noteworthy object. It was built of a gray stone, on a site that commanded a fine prospect of the town and of a long stretch of river. There was no attempt to preserve architectural unity in the structure; in fact, it exhibited rather an incongruous medley of orders. The front was partly Italian, with a circular portico supported by slender Ionic columns. The rear was Elizabethan, pieced out with an extension for a picture-gallery; on one side were oriel windows, and the other was flanked by a keep, with turret and embattled parapet, which gave the edifice rather a frowning appearance, as if the host were prepared for any emergency, and could treat visitors with bountiful hospitality, or a narrow cell in the donjon, as he saw fit and felt disposed. The interior was in keeping with this pretentious exterior. A stately staircase led up from a wide entrance hall tessellated with marble tiles, on either side of which were dining and reception rooms. These and the boudoirs and bedchambers were all resplendent with gilt and elegant frescoes. The surrounding grounds, or "park," as they were called, were spacious. There were terraces with marble urns, fountains, velvet lawns, interspersed with brilliant beds of flowers, and rows of shapely evergreens. In short, no expense had been spared to construct a habitation capable of impressing an ordinary beholder with the wealth and importance of the dwellers therein, and if corroborative evidence were needed, the porter at the lodge would carry conviction by referring to the elegant iron railing inclosing the grounds, which he asserted, with emphatic pride, "cost more'n twenty thousand hard, ringing silver dollars! a fortune for any one."

Do not suppose that old John Peter Obershaw was in any way responsible for all this pomp and splendor. Spending money, much less extravagance in any shape, was totally foreign to his habits or tastes; and he had been led into the outlay requisite for all this grandeur insensibly and unwittingly. We say insensibly and unwittingly the more positively, as the aged invalid could not be said to have had any sense or wit of his own, during the last years of his long life, and was completely under the dominion of his son-in-law, who planned and built the villa in accordance with his own ostentatious ideas.

The morning after the late owner of this princely residence had left it for the narrow quarters of a churchyard vault, the new one arose early and descended from his bedroom for a short walk in the fresh morning air. A very handsome man of fifty or so, with a compact figure, keen gray eyes, high receding forehead, slightly bald, and hair prematurely silvered. Perceptible on the firm surface of his pale, close-shorn face, were the lines of decision and shrewdness, and that seal of pride conferred by the possession of wealth and authority—a chilling expression commonly called aristocratic, and which is simply refined vanity. Musing with downcast eyes, hands clasped behind his back, and head uncovered, to and fro on the terrace paced Mr. Heath. Before descending, he had opened the door of his father-in-law's room, and looked in. The huge stuffed arm-chair was still there in its accustomed place, but vacant; the padding ripped up—done to look for secreted coin. His staff lay in one corner, a worn hickory stick, his companion for years,—but the old man was gone. He had been for years but an inert dweller, verging on imbecility, an incumbrance, and yet what a void he had left! How silent and empty the chamber seemed! Mr. Heath closed the door softly, and went gravely down the stairs. He was glad to breathe the refreshing air and feel the sunshine. As he paced, he would occasionally stop and glance over the sloping lawn, and towards the river whose shining current bore thrift to the town and tribute to him. All these possessions were now his, absolutely and entirely his. Without longing for it, he had expected and looked forward to this day. He remembered, when a poor clerk, how he had coveted the wealth of the proprietor of Belton Falls, as he watched him, meanly clad, haggling with some shop-keeper over a few coppers. He remembered his joy when a stroke of luck put him in possession of the capital necessary to carry out a scheme whose consummation had enabled him finally to attain his present position, first, by securing Mr. Obershaw's confidence, and eventually, a less difficult feat (favored as he was by an uncommon share of good looks), the hand and heart of his daughter. And now they were both gone, and he was left loaded with wealth; wealth unmeasured—wealth to flatter every wish and further every ambitious project. The fruit was ripe and had fallen. He bit it, but no luscious juice rushed to the bare papillæ; the taste was insipid and dry as ashes! Every realization is but an after-taste, but this was almost bitter. The morning sun spangled the dewy grass, and darted brightly through the tree boughs. Birds carolled sweetly, and all nature rejoiced, but his spirits seemed to sink under the increased weight of riches, and he felt burdened. For an instant an unaccountable depression seized him, and he hardly heeded a gardener who approached to speak. The man noticed his master's pre-occupation, and waited patiently and respectfully until his attention was drawn towards him. He wanted to know if Mr. Heath would like to look at a beautiful exotic that had just bloomed that morning. Mr. Heath mechanically assented, and followed the gardener to the greenhouse. Usually he was much interested in the fine collection of plants in the conservatory, but now he listened dully to the man's enthusiastic praises of the rare flower, and looked at it with indifference. Without replying to the gardener, he walked away slowly, musing as he went on that sermon so often repeated but never heeded —the vanity of earthly possessions. "Dross, dross, it is so," he soliloquized, "but how long it takes to learn the lesson! How many envy me; how many whose first thought on seeing me, whose first wish, is to be as I am! What a supremely happy and blessed man I must be! Ah, the monks are wise.... But fame—the incense of popular applause—a name to live in future generations; something that the grave cannot extinguish, and death take away, that is the goal to strive for! Aye, ambition is the only passion worthy a master mind."

He re-entered the house and went to his library. The sight of his accustomed work-room seemed to banish the shadow on his countenance. "Blessed— blessed labor, what a balm thou art!" he apostrophized as with a sort of eagerness he threw himself in a chair, seized a pen, and followed a new train of ideas.

A singular fit of despondency this in one basking in the smiles of Fortune, and who had so steadily enjoyed her favors; for the capricious dame had marked Rufus Heath for a favorite long ago by a significant gift plainly indicative of her partiality. This gift, or stroke of luck, was the winning at his start in life of a lottery prize, which sudden affluence, judiciously invested, had led to the splendid culmination now apparent.

———————————

Mr. Heath was in his library, a large room adjoining his bedchamber, which also answered the purposes of a study, and was furnished with leathern-covered chairs, and surrounded by closely filled book-cases of polished walnut, surmounted at intervals with marble busts of the giants of intellect. A long table in the centre of the room was covered with maps, manuscripts, and works of reference. At one end Mr. Heath sat intently writing. His early habits of industry he still carried almost to excess. Idleness filched but few moments from him, and by a thorough system he managed to perform an amount of labor that would have been deemed prodigious in a close student. The work that engrossed the most of his time, the opus magnus, was the preparation of a pandect wherein the constitutions, statutes, and enactments of the various States of the Union would be digested and reconciled into one harmonious code of laws. The mere gathering and collating of material for this purpose involved a formidable amount of labor, and when in addition to this we consider that he supervised the accounts of the estate and kept up a voluminous correspondence with statesmen and politicians in all parts of the country, we may imagine that he had but few spare moments.

Behind him on the wall hung the symbol of his weakness—an illuminated achievement intended to represent the arms of the Heath family. Should a visitor's attention be attracted by this heraldic device, the host was only too happy to explain the mystery of crest and quarterings, and to dilate on his lineage, tracing its common origin with that of a distinguished English ducal family. For Rufus Heath, in his heart of hearts, despised a republic and had no faith in the stability of its institutions. His ideal of a government was an oligarchy, with him and his like as oligarchs. Outwardly he professed the stanchest republicanism and devotion to equal rights.

So absorbed had Mr. Heath become in his occupation that he heeded not his daughter as she came to ask him to breakfast. She entered the study softly, and almost timidly, for she held her father in a certain awe and dreaded to disturb him. It was only when she laid her hand lightly on his shoulder that he discovered her presence. "Father, good-morning," said she, seeking to press her lips to his cheek.

"Ah! Miss Edna. Is that you?" he replied, impassively, and slowly disengaging her arm from his neck. "Good-morning. Leave me, child; I will be with you in an instant."

There was no unkindness in the tone, but there was no warmth. The few words that had passed between them revealed enough to indicate to an observant witness the history of a daughter's heart, eager for the affection of a parent insulated from domestic ties by egotistic worldliness.

Mr. Heath laid aside his pen, passed to his chamber, and arranged his toilet preparatory to the morning repast. He then descended the stairs as if a chamberlain preceded him; entered the breakfast-room with a stately nod to those present, and took his seat at the table gravely, and with an apology for his tardiness. After a scrutinizing glance around, a preparatory pause followed, and then, bending low his head, he invoked the Divine blessing. The meals in that family were not at any time those cheerful family gatherings that diversify existence so pleasantly, but serious proceedings, conducted with severe propriety, the head of the house being exceedingly punctilious on that score. On this morning, naturally enough, a greater solemnity prevailed, and the breakfast was passed almost in silence. Mrs. Applegate, a widow, and elder sister of Mr. Heath, presided. She had been installed housekeeper on the death of her brother's wife, and occupied the post at table that should have devolved upon young Mrs. Heath, but that lady was too indifferent, and disinclined to any exertion to fill it. She was a Creole by birth, the daughter of a Yankee machinist who had married the very wealthy widow of a Cuban planter. This machinist, Sam Wolvern, previous to going to the West Indies, had learned his trade in Belton, and after the death of his wife returned there to live. Dying soon after his arrival, he left Mr. Heath sole guardian of the person and fortune of his only child, Mercedita Wolvern. So well did the guardian manage his trust, that he succeeded, in due time, in transferring his ward and her fortune to the custody of his son. This occasioned some unfavorable tattle, but as Mercedita Wolvern, a pale, feeble girl, had no will of her own, it may have been justifiable in somebody else's having one for her, if matters had turned out well. Unfortunately they did not, for her husband, with all the arrogance and vanity, and none of the brains of his sire, was possessed of sundry vices, which rendered him anything but an agreeable life companion. A spoiled boy, indulged and toadied, he easily fell into the snares that beset rich men's sons, and grew up a worthless and dissipated man. His father designed him for the legal profession, but "living like a hermit and working like a horse," was not at all to the taste of young Hopeful. Hence, in the hope that an early marriage might reform him,—to say nothing of the pecuniary advantages of such a match,—his father had given him poor weak Mercedita, and her fortune, to wife. And a wretched connubial existence she had of it, for Jack Heath added drunkenness to his other unamiable traits, and was hardly sober from one day to another. This, of course, created much uneasiness in the father's mind, who naturally hoped that his son would at least perpetuate the family name with dignity, if he were incapable of shedding lustre on it.

"Where is John?" inquired Mr. Heath of his daughter-in-law, as he noticed his son's absence from the table.

"Sleeping, I presume, sir," replied the young wife; "I heard the clock strike one before he came in last night."

"What! again? And last night of all nights!" escaped from the father's lips. Ordinarily his pride prevented him from showing displeasure at his son's misconduct, in the presence of others, but that John should have so far forgotten himself as to indulge in a debauch on the very day of his grandfather's funeral; that he should have gone in his mourning clothes to the town bar-rooms, his usual haunts, and swaggered tipsily along the streets, a spectacle of shame, furnishing food for scandal for a month—for the Heath family were considered in the light of public personages, and every act of theirs was commented on by all Belton—this, all this, touched Mr. Heath keenly. His daughter, who was seated beside him, noticed his clouded brow, and asked him with anxiety, if anything ailed him?

"No, nothing, child," he replied, and turning to the colored servant in attendance bade him summon John at once. Edna, the daughter, had but just returned from boarding-school, where she had spent the greater part of three previous years; hence she knew but little of her brother's habits, and imagined that a lack of respect on his part was all that had disturbed her usually imperturbable father.

It's the old Obershaw blood in him—the coarse tastes which he inherits from his grandfather, reflected Mr. Heath with bitterness. The old man had the same propensity, but avarice smothered it in him. With a sigh he turned toward his daughter for consolation. His looks dwelt on her, and it seemed as if it were the first time he had ever noticed her beauty. How lovely she has grown, thought he. A true Heath—if she were only a boy! Still, why should she not aspire, and reflect honor on me? I shall be Governor of this State, next a foreign mission, an ambassadorship. All she would need is the opportunity. Did ever coronet grace a fairer brow? My daughter a countess or a marchioness—is there anything impossible or improbable in that?

While Mr. Heath was in the midst of his fanciful cogitations, the object of them was eating in a matter-of-fact way, and in utter unconsciousness of the ambitious views she had awakened. Nevertheless, there was everything to justify her father's pride and hopes; for Edna, a girl of seventeen, had a graceful figure, a cheek as delicate as a rose-petal, soft steel-blue eyes with dark lashes and brows, hair the hue of ripe wheat, and that indescribable sweetness of expression in which American maidens surpass all others. Her plain, black dress, relieved only by a white collar and wristbands, did not in the least detract from her appearance, but, on the contrary, enhanced her clear complexion to brilliancy. So her father thought, and his heart swelled with new-born pride in the possession of such a child. There was an unusual tenderness in his voice when he questioned her, "Edna, what are you going to do this morning?"

It was a purposeless question, meant simply to attract her attention towards him.

Edna turned her face towards her father with an inquiring look, for the query was a very unusual one. "I intend to call on Ada Mumbie; I left my crochet-work there on Monday, and am going after it. Have you any errand for me, sir?"

"No, daughter. Crochet-work is certainly important business, and should not be neglected," replied her father with a smile. "I hope, however, you have other and better ways of employing your time."

"I trust so, sir," said Edna.

"I wish, my child, you would adopt the plan of writing me a letter every day,

14

or every other day will do. It matters not how short it may be—a few sentences will suffice. But I want it done as well as you know how, and have you bestow thought upon it. Let it consist of a criticism on some book you have read, or some picture you have seen. For instance, you might begin to write criticisms on the pictures in the gallery in succession, varying them, however, with such opinions of other matters, persons, or objects as may strike your fancy. But what I want are your ideas and none other, expressed in the best language you are capable of. You will do so, will you not?"

"Certainly, father, if it pleases you."

"Well, but I don't want you to do it solely because it pleases me. I want you to acquire a taste for such employment. I was looking over some of your letters from school the other day, and I was very well pleased with the style, but I noticed a lack of thought. True, you are still young, and can hardly be expected to evince much of that, but I want to cultivate your mind in that respect, and now is the time to begin. Bear in mind, skill in epistolary writing is a great accomplishment; especially so in a woman," continued Mr. Heath; then turning to his daughter-in-law he said, "Mercedita, I have an appointment at the bank at ten. I shall be back at eleven. Tell John I shall expect to find him in the library waiting for me at that hour. I have business for him. I want some copying done. Mr. Frisbee has more than he can attend to now;" and Mr. Heath rose to leave. As he opened the door to go out he stopped for a moment, reflectively, with his hand on the knob, "Edna."

"Yes, father," replied the young girl, rising and going towards him.

"When you return from your visit, come up into the library. I shall select some works I wish you to read. Don't fail, my dear;" and Mr. Heath, before leaving, imprinted a light kiss on his daughter's forehead. She received it with an expression of pleased surprise. It was the first time he had ever favored her in that way. So unwonted a demonstration of tenderness on the part of her brother even caused Mrs. Applegate to pause in the act of pouring out her fourth cup of tea, and stare at the scene. "Edna seems to be in favor this morning," she remarked when Mr. Heath had left, "but John, I am afraid, Mercedita, has greatly offended his father, and is very much in disfavor."

"O Mercedita!" added Edna, "do beg him to apologize to father at once, and try and make amends. Just think how troubled father must be at grandfather's death, and that Jack should add to his grief is too bad. Do, please, entreat him, Mercedita, to—"

"I do not pretend to have any influence whatever over John. I might have, if he had any consideration for my feelings; but as I am sure he has never shown the slightest, of what use would my remonstrances or pleadings be? He may follow the path he has chosen without any interference from me," answered the young wife with an affected indifference.

"Father expects him at eleven," said Edna, "and I hope Jack will be punctual. I wouldn't have father continue angry at him for the world. I wonder if James has told him? I'll go and see;" and she hurried off, in her anxiety to reconcile her father and brother.

"I think, Mercedita, if you took John in the right way," said Mrs. Applegate, "you might do a good deal with him. He is as good-hearted a person as ever lived. He's whimsical, to be sure, and perhaps we all indulged him a little too much when he was a boy. I'll not deny that. But then, you know, a little coaxing will go a great ways."

A shrug of the shoulders was the only reply the young wife deigned to make to this advice, and Mrs. Applegate continued: "Now, I've had a good deal of experience in these matters, and I recollect very distinctly, when Mr. Applegate and I were first married, he was as full of whims and notions as could be, and naturally it was a source of trouble in more ways than one to me. Mr. Applegate utterly detested cats for one thing—couldn't bear 'em; indeed, he had such a great detestation of them, that I verily believe it actually affected his system; though, to be sure, he was consumptive, and subject to constant attacks of dyspepsia. I've heard of many such cases. Not long ago I read in the papers an account of some distinguished person—I forget the name, now, though it's a familiar one—let me see, I think it was Alexander the Great, or it might have been Luther, I won't be certain which; but at all events it was some well-known and distinguished person who was thrown into convulsions every time he saw a black rabbit—no, not a black rabbit, but a drawn sword. It was another well-known person who was affected in a similar way by a black rabbit. Now this goes to show—"

What this went to show we are unable to say, for at this point, Mrs. Applegate's instructive, though somewhat irrelevant discourse, was interrupted by the entrance of Jack Heath, who was evidently in no amiable frame of mind, and under the influence, probably, of the whimsical state alluded to by his kinswoman. He took his seat in sulky silence, and then began to scold the waiter. He found fault with everything—the steak was too cold, the eggs too hard, the tea too hot, the toast too dry, etc. The two ladies looked on without venturing a remark. From the dull, sodden look of his eyes, and his carelessly brushed hair, Jack's rest and peace of mind had evidently been badly disturbed. He was large and unduly corpulent for so young a man, being barely two-and-twenty, although he might have passed for ten years older; and on his fat face the freshness of youth had given place to the inflamed flush of the toper. After a few mouthfuls he could contain himself no longer, and vented his spleen in a grumbling tirade. "Seems to me there's a devil of a row here about nothing. Can't have a bit of comfort in this house. Come home tired and want to have my sleep out, and along comes James drumming away at my door as if the house was on fire; says the old man sent him—then Edna, she must come bothering me to get up. Confound it, some of you women are at the bottom of it all, I'll bet. Been complaining to the old man, have you?"

This last was directed with a scowl to his wife, who, without condescending to reply, arose from her chair and wrapping her shawl close about her, swept out of the room indignant, leaving Mrs. Applegate to confront Jack's temper alone.

"A young feller's a fool that gets married," continued Jack, addressing no one in particular.

Mrs. Applegate, feeling this apothegm to be rather a reflection on her sex, and one which ought not to pass unchallenged, ventured a mild qualification. "Well, John, it depends very much whether the fellow, as you call him, is of a domestic disposition or not. Now, there is great difference in people, and especially in married couples. There was Mr. Applegate, for instance; I'm sure no one could have led a happier life, and he often used to say to me, 'My dear—'"

"I say," repeated the nephew, dogmatically, "that a young feller's a fool that gets married. That's all. And he'll find it out sooner or later, I'll bet he does. To have a woman always tied to you, that goes whining around and complaining if a feller comes in late, or has been on a little jamboree with a friend and gets a little set up. I'd rather be hung and be done with it."

"Dear me, John, I wouldn't go on so about it," said his aunt, placatingly. "To be sure I don't ever remember of Mr. Applegate's going on a jam—jamboree, as you call it, as he was always afraid of dampness and night air; but then you must admit that it isn't the pleasantest thing in the world to be wakened out of a sound sleep, or to sit up waiting for some one to come home, particularly if you are anyway delicate; and young people should bear in mind that the easiest way is always the best."

Mrs. Applegate added a few more mollifying sentences of the same general application, until Jack, having by this time finished his breakfast, seemed to be appeased, and remarked in rather more peaceful tones, that he "was off his feed," a statement which might well cause an onlooker to wonder how much provender Jack consumed when he was "on his feed." Then pulling out a case, he struck a match and lit a cigar, remarking as he did so to his aunt: "Old man wants me in the library punctually at eleven, does he? Think I see

17

myself. Not to-day, thank you. If I'm there I guess he'll know it. As the Frenchman said, 'I've got to fry some fish,'" and off he lounged to the stables.

III.

The Hon. Rufus Heath, in requesting his son's attendance in the library that morning, had reckoned without the "Horse-show." For that day was the concluding one of the County Agricultural Fair, which, though held ostensibly in honor of sundry overgrown vegetables and patchwork quilts, derived its principal attraction from the "Grand Exhibition of Blood and other Horses," which terminated it. The exhibition consisted in a number of fast nags showing their points, and competing for prizes on a race-course conveniently near the fair-grounds. To attend these "trials of speed" was far more to John Peter Heath's taste, than to be immured in his father's library copying tedious documents. Hence he did not deliberate long over the paternal mandate, and was soon spinning away comfortably behind his trotting mare to the fair. He stayed there the greater part of the day; swaggering over the grounds with a knowing air; noisily backing horses by bets with stable-men and blacklegs, and losing some of his wife's money which rather soured him, for Jack had a decided streak of stinginess in his character, and disliked extremely to part with money that had not ministered to his selfish gratifications. So, to console himself for his ill-luck, he repaired to a public-house hard by, and cracked bottles of wine with boon companions until the remembrance of his losses supervened, and he became obstreperous; swore he had been cheated; grew abusive; drew off his coat to fight anybody, and but for the interposition of the landlord, might have received a severe pommelling. In this condition he mounted his vehicle to return home. The spirited little mare, having been kept so long waiting at the tavern door, had become restive, and it was with some difficulty that she could be held by the hostler while Jack got into the wagon. He gathered the reins, flung a dime to the man, and the mare released, sped off like an arrow.

The sun was setting as Jack crossed the bridge over the Passaic at the north end of town, and the toll-gatherer noticed that the driver was (as he had often seen him before) in liquor. Jack Heath was not at any time a very pleasing object to look at, and still less so when in his cups, for his tipsiness bore an expression of defiant arrogance that boded no good to intermeddlers. Thus, flown with insolence and wine, along he went, lashing his horse and driving recklessly up the principal street of the town, in utter disregard of the wayfarers, whom he roughly ordered with an oath to get out of his way. Just at that moment a young man, with a slight limp in his gait, was crossing the street, who seemed in no haste to accelerate his pace at Jack Heath's bidding. A well-dressed young fellow he was, of about twenty, with a dash of pretension in his appearance, and a light in his eye that betokened a spirit not likely to brook dictation. Jack, unfortunately, was not in a condition to discriminate, and as he approached the pedestrian, yelled, with a curse, "Ki-hi —cripple! Out of the way, or I'll run over you!" No sooner were these words uttered, than the young man, pale with anger, raised a light cane he carried, and struck fiercely at the horse's head. The nervous animal, frightened at this sudden attack, sprang off sideways, dashing the light jagger against the curb, and sending its occupant headlong to the earth. Such an excitement in the quiet street! The disaster occurred directly opposite McGoffin's "Shoe Emporium," and that honest tradesman ran out, leaving Miss Winter (a highly respectable maiden lady whom he was about measuring for bootees) to expose in her agitation and stockings her somewhat large and bulbous feet to the brutal gaze of a gathering crowd. The colored barber from over the way hastened to the spot with a razor in his hand, followed by a half-shaved client with lathered, face and bib on, and then in quick succession loungers from the "Tanglefoot Saloon" and corner grocery. Meanwhile, the cause of all this trouble, whom we may as well introduce to the reader at once as Mark Gildersleeve, forgot his resentment on seeing the plight of his insulter, and hurried off for a physician, under the impression that; perhaps, Jack Heath was killed. There he lay in the kennel, stunned, with a cut on his sconce and a contemplative crowd about him. Discussions arose as to whether he was dead or dying, and a glass of brandy was put to his lips as a test; it probably being deemed conclusive that if he did not drink, or at least taste the beverage, he must be very nearly in the former condition. As he did neither, his case looked hopeless, and some one suggested removing him to the apothecary's shop; but Mr. Snopple, the photographer, a little fat man who diffused an aroma of collodion about him, protested strenuously, reminding the by-standers that it would be a violation of the law, and render a person liable to prosecution to disturb the body until the coroner came and an inquest was held. Advice not altogether disinterested on the part of Mr. Snopple, who, in his professional zeal, saw at once an excellent opportunity for an effective picture, and did not wish the group disturbed while he hastened off to his studio for a camera. Unfortunately for the advancement of art, before he returned, George Gildersleeve, the ubiquitous, appeared on the scene. Here was a man of action. He took one hand out of its pocket, felt of Jack and pronounced him "right enough," and then addressing the crowd said, "Lay hold here, boys, some of you, and toss him into this cart and get him home. He'shefty."

And "hefty" he was, sure enough, and it took some tugging from strong arms to lift the dead weight of his bulky form into a grocer's cart near at hand, for the racing jagger was badly broken, and the mare had scampered off with the thills.

By this time Mark Gildersleeve had returned with Dr. Wattletop, and the latter accompanied Jack to his home, where the fears of his relatives were speedily allayed by his being pronounced not seriously injured, but uncommonly drunk.

When Dr. Wattletop returned to his domicil he found Mark Gildersleeve awaiting him. "How is he, doctor?" eagerly asked the young man.

"Oh bless you, he'll do. The devil takes care of his own. Born to be hung, you know, and so forth. A simple contusion—plastered it up—he'll be all right when he gets sober. He's just ugly enough, too, to appear worse than he is, and frightened his sweet little sister out of her wits. The others, though, didn't seem to mind it so much, and no wonder. But what makes you so anxious about him? When you came after me, you looked so pale and agitated hopes arose of a profitable patient. They're not so plenty now as they might be, and I welcome them with joy and gratitude," said the doctor, tapping Mark familiarly on the shoulder.

"I feel so relieved, doctor; I was afraid he might be seriously hurt. He provoked me, and I retaliated. Had I noticed or known that he was drunk, perhaps I would not have minded him. He fell so heavily that I feared he might have broken his neck."

"He might, I grant, but he didn't. More's the pity, perhaps, for his friends and family. Especially for that poor wife of his, whom he will certainly kill in time, if he don't kill himself first. But, so you were the one that caused all this row, eh? You didn't say anything about that before. How dared you, rash youth, raise your ire against the heir-apparent? Fear you not the wrath of the prince-regnant? Know ye not that for thrift to follow it is as necessary now, as ever, to fawn to wealth and position? Anchylosis, my boy, invariably affects the pocket, mind that!"

"If it were not for—" began Mark, with a determined look, which he suddenly checked, to add with a quiet smile, "No one knows better than you, doctor, what little store I set by thrift, or any considerations of that kind. I trust my ambition aims higher than that."

"Fresh and admirable adolescence! Roseate age, when the glistening soap-bubble, Fame, hath more charms than substantial shekels! So be it, and well it is so, for without those soft illusions the aridity of existence would be insupportable, the world a desert and life a blank. And now, my boy, while I wash my hands bring out the chess-board. I'll give you a bishop to-night, and unless I am interrupted by some silly biped seeking admittance to this sphere of trouble, or some still sillier one reluctant to leave it, we'll have a snug hour or two of enjoyment. So, votary of Caïssa, to chess—to chess."

Soon the polished dome of the doctor's capacious head, and the curly black pate of the young man, were bent in intense study over the checkered field of mimic battle. In silence passed the moments until a scratching at the door announced a visitor. "Ah, Dagon! Open the door, Mark, and let him in, please," said the doctor.

The young man complied, and a large black Newfoundland dog walked gravely in towards the doctor, and rested his head on his master's knee to be caressed. "True friend—faithful heart! Mark, three winters ago that dog saved my life. I was called out the night of the great snowstorm to go to the Furnaces, and but for Dagon your most obedient wouldn't be here. I've told it you before, I believe, so I'll not repeat the circumstances, but I love to dwell on them. Last spring he drew a child out of the canal; he would allow himself to be cut to pieces for me, and yet they say he has no soul! The Turks say the same of women. Are we any wiser? They say, too, he has no reason. Look at his expressive, sagacious eye. The gibbering idiot has a soul, the vilest miscreant reason; but this noble animal has neither, 'tis said, and man's vanity invents instinct! O man—man, what a conceited fool thou art! Check, eh? Ha! a bold move, my boy."

The doctor's speculations were cut short by a brilliant stroke on the part of his adversary, and as the game is becoming more absorbing, and the players less communicative, we will leave them, to digress a little.

Dr. Basil Wattletop had been an English army-surgeon, and as such had spent much of his time in foreign parts. How he came to drift into Belton, no one knew positively, although there was a legend that he had stopped there one day, on his way from Canada, to view the cataract, and had remained in the town ever since. Be this as it might, there he was and had been for many years, enjoying a lucrative practice, as he doubtless well deserved, for he was a skilful practitioner. An odd-looking man he was, a bachelor of very uncertain age, yet hale and vigorous; in person short and rotund, like the typical Briton of mature years, with thin wisps of brown hair brushed around his bald crown, and large searching dark eyes set in a long, grave, rubicund face. In attire inclined to carelessness, but scrupulous as to polished shoes and immaculate linen, wearing collars perilously starched over a throttling black stock, the buckle and tag of which prominently ornamented his nape. Partial indeed was he to this stock, despite the sway of fashion. In moments of caprice he would replace it by swaddling his short neck in a black cravat of many folds, the knot of which invariably slipped around and under his ear, giving him a losel and dissipated air.

His benevolent disposition had made him popular with the people of Belton, and many a poor body had reason to thank the good physician not only for gratuitous attendance, but for the wherewithal to buy indispensable remedies and comforts. We say had reason to thank him, for they seldom ventured to do so, certainly not a second time, for the doctor was exceedingly impatient of any manifestations of gratitude, and generally received them with a cynical or tart comment.

One weakness the doctor had in common with many of his countrymen—devotion to the social glass and flowing bowl, and when he had indulged over freely he was a changed man. Then his ordinary blandness forsook him, and he became pompous and choleric. He buttoned his coat tightly over his chest, carried his cane under his arm, and gave a defiant cock to his hat. Beware then how you contradicted him; beware how you defended that absurd heresy, homoeopathy; and above all, beware how you disparaged, even in the remotest degree, her Majesty of England, God bless her! as he would add, reverently lifting his hat. His loyalty and pomposity increased in proportion to the depths of his potations, but, whether in rigid obedience to a self-imposed law, or owing to the resistant power of his brain, he never appeared to exceed a certain well-defined limit; and no one had ever seen the doctor overcome, or known him to be in a worse state than that peculiar one indicated by a highly burnished nose, tetchy dignity, and exaggerated self-importance. The doctor was generally in this condition three evenings in the week, beginning at about four o'clock post-meridian, and so far from its being considered prejudicial to the exercise of his professional duties by his patients, many of them religiously believed that his sagacity was keener and skill greater at those times than at others.

The doctor was an enigma to the Belton folk. While they all respected him for his good qualities, many were offended at his sarcasm, puzzled by his paradoxes, or displeased at his oracular utterances. A few even pronounced him an "infidel" and an "atheist." Opinionated George Gildersleeve objected to the doctor's opinionativeness, and rated him a "pig-headed John Bull." As to the charge of atheism, who could have believed it that had ever seen the doctor at service, as he stood reverentially burying his red face in his stiff hat on Sundays in the fifth pew from the chancel, in the middle aisle of St. Jude's?

"Atheist, bosh!" said the doctor; "the old Latin proverb, *Ubi tres medici duo athei*, is simply nonsensical. Who comes so closely in contact with the mysterious ways of God, and realizes so thoroughly his own ignorance and impotence, as the physician? No—no, a corner of the veil has been uplifted to us, and we stand appalled and humble."

Mark Gildersleeve was almost an adopted son of the old physician, who had taken the youth in affection and proved an invaluable friend to him, chiefly by directing a course of reading and study. A priceless benefit this to Mark, whose advantages for instruction had been slight, for he had lost his parents at an early age, and been left to the care of his half-brother George, or rather to his half-brother's wife. It would have been difficult to find more dissimilar beings than these two brothers. George was the true son of Eben Gildersleeve, the tough old smith who could forge the best horse-shoe in the county; while Mark inherited the character and tastes of his mother, Eben Gildersleeve's second wife, a woman of beauty and delicacy, a rustic Venus mated to a village Vulcan. George was boisterous, given to bully and boast, and hid his purse-pride in an affected contempt for the world's opinion. Mark, on the contrary, was reserved, and rendered morbidly sensitive by a slight lameness resulting from an injury received in childhood—a mere blemish, though, in an otherwise well-knit and graceful form. For all his reserve the lad had a resolute and ambitious spirit. Gifted with quick perception, and a natural aptitude for mathematics, he had become, although almost self-taught, proficient as a mechanical engineer. After a common-school education, his brother, in accordance with the theory that the only road to success was through a diligent use of the flexors and extensors, set him to work in the shops, but it was not long before he was found to be more useful in the draughting room. Young as he was, Mark had introduced some valuable improvements in his brother's works, although that independent fellow was not over-ready to acknowledge it. On the contrary, he rather berated the young man behind his back, for a fop who cared for nothing but dress, or a fool who was occupied with dreams and poetry instead of devoting himself to his business. Mark, it must be admitted, sinned a little in that way, although not to an extent to justify his brother's railings. Full of enthusiasm and high aspirations, he scorned mere money-making, and as he earned enough to satisfy his wants he bestowed no further thought in that direction. This was a source of displeasure to George. "Confound the fellow," he would exclaim in the barber-shop, perhaps, or at Bird's livery stable, "Confound the fellow! he's no slouch, but as smart as they make 'em, and if he'd only stick to his work he'd be a rich man in time. I never had much of a head for figures, but it comes nat'ral to him. If he's a mind to, he can do more work than any other two men you can scare up, and if he aint a-mind, you can't coax or drive him. He'll go off and jingle away by the hour on a piano, like a girl, or play chess or read novels half the night. Why, he's even got a banjo up in his room that he strums away on like a nigger minstrel" (alluding to a Spanish guitar that Mark had bought, probably with the romantic intention of practising seguidillas). "Look at me," George would add as a clincher; "the only music ever I made was with a riveting hammer on a boiler, or a sledge on an anvil, and am I any the worse for it? Not much, I think, and here I am, as independent as a hog on ice! Don't owe a man a dollar in the world, and though I don't roost in as big a house as Rufe Heath or Pop Mumbie up on the hill yonder, they'll take my note at the bank as quick as either of theirs if I should ask it, which I don't, as I pays as I goes; and what's more, I can dust any of 'em on the plank-road any day of the week, with as pretty a pair o' flyers as there is in the State, and if you don't believe it here's the soap to back it for any amount from fifty to five thousand!"

And he would conclude customarily by drawing out a well-stuffed wallet, and slapping it energetically, with a defiant look at the by-standers. That wallet was George's *ultimo ratio*, and when pushed in an argument, or at loss for a reply, he would flourish it at his opponent, with an offer to wager any sum on the moot-point; a rebutter which, if it did not carry conviction, enabled George to close the issue in a triumphant manner. There was a story current to the effect that he had once startled a tableful of Methodist clergymen, assembled to take tea at Mrs. Gildersleeve's during a conference, by proffering to the decorous men a bet on the correct interpretation of a disputed passage in St. John; but this lacked confirmation, for George, if he had but little respect for any one else, had a great deal for his wife, and as such an act would have shocked her exceedingly, it is not at all likely that it took place.

The sagacious reader has doubtless come to the conclusion that the Gildersleeve family was composed of rather incongruous members, and yet, for one comprising such opposite characters, its harmony was remarkable. They occupied a small two-story dwelling with a flower-garden attached, in a side street, not far from the Archimedes Works. A large, bright brass door-plate bore in very loud letters the name: GILDERSLEEVE—as if there were none other of that name in the universe, or as if this was *the* Gildersleeve *par excellence* of all who were fortunate enough to bear that honest patronymic. Aside from this, the residence presented a very quiet and modest appearance. The interior was plainly furnished, but neat as wax. In the little parlor were old-fashioned mahogany chairs and sofas dark with age, but polished, and protected with snowy tidies. In one corner was Mark's piano, and on either side of the chimney-breast hung portraits in oil of Mr. and Mrs. Gildersleeve, taken when they were first married, and looking wooden in port and flat as to perspective, faced on the opposite side by photographic likenesses of the same at a mature age. Then between the windows was a colored photograph of Mr. Gildersleeve in his costume of foreman of a fire company, with red shirt, leathern cap, and trumpet; and still another representing him in his regalia as a Sir Knight of the Sancho Panza Commandery of the Knights of the Golden Fleece. George had a passion for counterfeit presentments of himself, and in the album on the centre-table might have been found a number of others, taken in various attitudes and in various expressions of obstinacy, by that distinguished artist, Alonzo Snopple, Esq., who kept duplicates in his "studio" and never failed to call visitors' attention to them as remarkable pictures of a remarkable self-made man. "Fine head," he would say, "very fine head—rare combination of intellect and force—especially force. Strongly marked lineaments, well adapted for Rembrandt effects. Observe the lights and shadows, that well-defined nose, etc.;" and George seemingly was not indisposed to allow the public every opportunity to familiarize itself with the representation of such a masterpiece of nature in the way of a head. Besides his love of portraiture, he was given to keeping fast trotters and game-cocks, and in the stables at the Works were stalls devoted to a span of the speediest Morgans for the owner's private use, and in the stable yard strutted a certain breed of "orange-piles," whose pugnacious qualities were almost as well known as those of the celebrated fowls of the Derby walk; the dauntless game-cocks, that:

"symbolize their lord."

These animals enabled George to indulge occasionally in a little sportsmanlike relaxation, and spice his toil-earned wealth by a few chance dollars won from fickle fortune.

Mrs. Gildersleeve was an industrious little housekeeper with an equable temper, and an unbounded and unquestioning faith in her husband; scarcely less so, too, in her brother-in-law Mark, whom she had brought up from childhood and looked upon as a son—an affection reciprocated by the young man, who loved her as if she were his mother, and with reason, for she could not have been more devoted had she really stood in that relation to him. The only thing that ever cast a shadow on her uniform serenity and cheerfulness, was the remissness in their religious duties of the two beings the nearest and dearest to her. She had more than once mentioned this subject to the Rev. Samuel Sniffen, and this good man had striven zealously to bring these wayward sheep into the fold, but with small effect; for George Gildersleeve seemed flint, and his brother quicksilver. Nevertheless, Mrs. Gildersleeve had gained ground and progressed so far in her endeavors at reclamation, that her husband invariably accompanied her to meeting every Sabbath morning and afternoon, while Mark escorted her to the evening service, the mornings and afternoons of that sacred day being devoted by the erratic youth to St. Jude's. It was an edifying sight to behold George at meeting. The stolidity with which he received the earnest and vivifying sermons of the Rev. Samuel Sniffen—as if they imparted teachings which the rest of the congregation would do well to heed, but which did not concern him in the least—was the despair of the excellent minister. The hardened sinner had even shown, on frequent occasions, a tendency to nap through exhortations of the most vehement and fervid character. What was to be done with such a soul? The only answer he would vouchsafe to the friendliest and most persuasive counsel was, that his wife was good enough for both of them, and he felt insured as to the future, as she no doubt would have influence enough to "pull him through" in any event. "She'll take care of me, you bet," he would add; "she's good enough to save a half a dozen;" and in this conviction of security nothing could shake him. Brother Sniffen then wisely concluded that as it seemed a hopeless task for the patient to obtain sanctification through faith, he would induce him to try the efficacy of good works, and in this laudable endeavor called upon him constantly for contributions to the support and propagation of the Methodist Episcopal persuasion, and as George always responded liberally to all such requests, he stood well with the good people of that sect, in spite of his stiff-neckedness.

Mark was more tractable. He was willing to do almost anything to please his sister-in-law except, perhaps, giving up his attendance at St. Jude's. And whence, it may be asked, arose this preference in the young man for that particular temple of worship? Did he hunger after the spiritual truth as dispensed by the rector, the Rev. Spencer Abbott? Alas! we fear not. Did he deem his tenor voice an indispensable adjunct to the church choir? Strict truth compels us to say nay. Mrs. Gildersleeve, for her part, attributed his partiality for the Episcopal service to Dr. Wattletop's influence; but the worthy lady's perspicuity was entirely at fault, and the motive that impelled her brother-in-law to such an assiduous attendance at St. Jude's was not any preference for a liturgy, or leaning for the tenets of that church; in fact, we regret to say, it was not any religious conviction whatever, but simply and solely—love! Love for the sweetest profile ever imagined; the profile that he was continually sketching on the draughting sheets or tracing-paper; that distracted him while at work; that drew him to St. Jude's, but drew his attention away from the excellent sermons of the young and worthy rector. And the possessor of that profile was—Edna Heath. She, of course, was attentive to the sermon as good girls always are, and utterly unconscious of the glances directed at her from the organ-loft, where Mark poured forth the pantings of his sighing soul in song. Utterly unconscious, too, of the influence she exerted over that youth's ideas and aspirations; how she had inspired him with vaulting ambition, and given him a corresponding distaste for his calling; how, for her sake, he desired to become famous, and, of all things, to be a poet! In this frame of mind, this fervent exaltation, the church seemed a haven of bliss to him, and his worshipping, we grieve to say, was directed chiefly to the idol who sat in the double pew in the transept nearest to the chancel. All his longing for fame was solely to lay it at her feet, and win not only her favor, but her admiration. He scarcely desired the one without the other; for once she had pitied him, and that pity had left a sting which could only be healed by the salve of admiration. How and when this uneffaced wound was received, we shall divulge in the succeeding chapter.

IV.

Years before, when our young people were children, a juvenile party was given one evening at Mr. Heath's, in honor of his son's birthday. The children's schoolmates were invited, and Mark Gildersleeve among the number. Miss Edna, in white with a big blue sash, was naturally enough an object of much devotion to the young gallants in roundabouts and pumps, who certainly evinced good taste, as the little belle was lovely as delicate bloom, bright eyes, and rich curls could make her. Poor Mark was dismal enough while the dancing was in progress, as his sensitiveness in regard to his lameness, and his Methodist relative's scruples had prevented him from learning that accomplishment; hence, he would have passed but a dull evening, had it not been for Edna, whose kind little heart prompted her to select him as her partner in "Come, Philanders," "Oats, peas, beans, and barley," etc., when those games came on the carpet. This partiality on the part of Miss Edna naturally engendered much jealousy in the breasts of her numerous admirers; and one, a malicious urchin, with the instincts of an Iago, plotted to make Jack Heath his avenger. Jack, an overgrown, lubberly boy, swelling with the importance of his position, and the possession of a gold watch and tail-coat, was diverting himself by teasing the girls and playing tricks on the younger lads. Young Iago suggested having some fun with Mark. Said he, "I will go and get Willie Hull and Mortimer, and we'll all hustle him, eh, Jack?"

"All right," said Jack; "he's a mean sneak, anyway. He thinks himself so smart. He's no business here. Edna sent him an invitation; I wouldn't."

The boys surrounded Mark and jeered him. "Where are your gloves?" inquired Iago, Junior, pointing to Mark's bare hands. The poor boy colored, for the other lads wore white kids, while he had none—an omission due, most likely, to his sister's ignorance of the requirements of fashionable society.

"Oh, what a pooty cravat! Look here, ain't that a pooty one? Don't you wish you had one like it? What lots of money it must have cost, eh?" cried Jack, in affected admiration, as he pulled the boy's rather gaudy neck-tie.

"Let me alone," said Mark, indignantly.

"Suppose I won't," continued Jack, "what are you going to do about it, limpey?"

Stung by this cruel taunt, Mark's eyes flashed, and on the instant he struck his insulter full in the face. Jack, for the moment, was bewildered by this sudden and unexpected attack, but soon recovering himself, rushed at Mark, threw him down, and fell on him. Over they rolled in their struggles, but Jack, being older and heavier, soon had the best of it, and kept the other under. The girls screamed, and Professor Banghoffen sprang from the grand piano to separate the combatants. This was no easy matter for a pursy man, and a kick in the stomach from the writhing legs caused him to recoil, pant, and consider. The colored domestic, however, soon came to his assistance, and between them they succeeded, after much puffing on the part of the professor and the fracture of his spectacles, in stopping the fight. The contestants were not much hurt, but stood glaring at each other with rumpled hair and flushed countenances. The children nearly all blamed Mark, but Edna, greatly to his surprise, took his part with much warmth. She had overheard the provocation, and now stood by him with a very indignant and determined air.

"I've a good mind to tell father, Jack, how you have behaved; I think it is real shameful. Mark is your guest, and it is very—very mean indeed, and real wicked to tease him as you did; and you ought to be thankful in your prayers that you are not lame as he is, and ought to pity him, and be kind to him, instead of teasing him so unkindly."

"You seem very fond of him all of a sudden," sneered Jack; "Guess he must be your beau. Better kiss him, hadn't you?"

At this sally the boys laughed, and Edna, covering her blushing face with her hands, burst into tears and went away sobbing. "You ought (sob) you ought (sob) ought to be ashamed. I'll (sob) I'll go (sob—sob—sob) and tell father (sob, etc.)."

Mark felt as if he could have pitched into Jack with increased vigor; but he refrained from any demonstration, and as this last incident broke up the party, went home with a spark in his bosom that was destined to kindle into a flame.

Mark arose early the next morning, and before going to school stopped to see Dr. Wattletop.

The doctor was still abed, for he had been up nearly all the previous night; nevertheless, he rose cheerfully at the call, broken rest having become a second nature to him, drew on a dressing-gown, and went into his consulting-room, where he found Mark waiting.

"Well, my lad, what is it?" inquired the doctor, who was unacquainted with his visitor.

"Doctor, I am lame, and I want you to cure me," said Mark.

"Lame, eh? How long have you been so, and what caused it?"

"Ever since I was a child. I was knocked down by a runaway horse and run over by a wagon. My ankle was broken, I believe."

"Hum—um. Take off your shoe and stocking. Lie down on that sofa, and let me look at your ankle."

Mark did as he was bid, and the doctor drew up a chair and sat down by him to examine the defective joint. The boy's black eyes were fixed with a searching gaze on the doctor's face, as if to read his thoughts, but there was nothing to be derived from the grave, sphinx-like countenance. The eager, inquisitive look of the lad, however, did not escape the physician's notice.

"What is your name, my boy?" inquired the doctor.

"Mark Gildersleeve, sir."

"Ah, you're Mr. Gildersleeve the iron-master's son, are you?"

"No, sir, his brother."

"His brother, eh! Who attended you when you received the injury?"

"Dr. Pokemore, sir."

"Dr. Pokemore, eh! He is your brother's family physician, is he not?"

"Yes, sir."

"Who sent you to me?"

"No one, sir. I came myself."

"Why did you not go to Dr. Pokemore?"

"Because he said I could not be cured."

The doctor after some reflection gave a doubtful nod, and said, "If anything can be done it will only be after a painful operation."

"I'll stand anything, doctor, if you will only cure me. You may cut me, or do anything you like, only make me walk like other boys."

The doctor took from a case of surgical instruments a bright bistoury, which he caused to glitter before the boy's eyes, as he felt its edge.

A plucky little fellow, thought the doctor, (struck by the unflinching look of determination in the boy's countenance,) and seems to be in earnest. "You say that you have been this way from infancy; why are you so anxious to be helped now?"

"Because—because—they worry me about it," replied Mark.

"Worry you—that's very unkind. Come, tell me all about it. I suspect there's a little history behind this, and you must make me your confidant."

Led on by the doctor's kind way, Mark exposed the wound his pride had received; related the story of his fight with Jack Heath (omitting, however, any mention of Edna's interference), and again begged the doctor to remove the impediment in his walk, asserting his willingness to submit to any operation, however painful, that might be deemed necessary to effect the object. Pleased with the boy's frankness and resolution, and desirous to help him, the doctor again examined the maimed ankle. A slow, fixed pursing of his lips expressed doubt, and the boy's countenance fell. There was a glimpse of hope, though, in the doctor's words, who told Mark that although he could not say anything encouraging now, he would talk the matter over with his (Mark's) brother, "And if he is willing, I will take you to New York with me, where we can consult the best skill, and if there be a probability of helping you, it shall be done."

A fine head, thought the doctor, passing his hand over Mark's broad forehead; there should be something there. "Stop a bit, Mark; what do you intend to be when you grow up, my boy?"

"I don't know, sir."

"What would you like to be, then?"

"I'd like," replied Mark, after some hesitation, "I think—I'd like to be a hero."

"A hero, eh! Come, that's modest and laudable. But what kind of a hero, pray?"

"Like—like Jack Sheppard."

"Jack Sheppard, umph! Why so?" said the doctor, rather surprised at this example and selection.

"Oh he was such a smart, brave fellow! They couldn't keep him in prison," replied Mark, wagging his head in admiration.

"But didn't he drive his poor mother crazy by his conduct, or something of that sort?" inquired the doctor. "That wasn't brave or smart, I take it, but rather mean and contemptible for a hero, wasn't it?"

"Yes, that was mean and bad," echoed Mark, reflectively; "I think I'd rather be a Crusader."

"Better, much better. But where did you hear of Jack Sheppard?"

"Jerry Cook lent me the book, and I am reading it."

"Fond of reading, Mark?"

"Yes, sir."

"Well, tell me what you have read."

"I've read 'The Three Spaniards,' and 'Rinaldo Rinaldini,' 'Illustrious Highwaymen,' 'Three-fingered Jack,' and—"

"I see—I see. Now, my boy, as you are fond of reading, I'll lend you a book to read that's worth all the books that were ever written, except, perhaps, the plays of Shakespeare. It is called 'The Adventures of the Ingenious Knight, Don Quixote of La Mancha.' Now, after you have read it, I'll lend you the plays of William Shakespeare, and after you have read those, you will have read the very best product of human intellect in the way of fiction. I do not expect that you will understand those books fully; it may take you all your life to do that, but if you can get but an idea of their contents, or rather, acquire but a taste for them, it will be sufficient for the present."

Mark thanked the doctor, and trudged away, delighted, with the Don Quixote under his arm. This was the beginning of an intimacy, and close friendship between the two. As he had promised, Dr. Wattletop took the boy, with his brother's consent, to New York, and consulted the best chirurgical authority on his case; but, as the doctor had feared, without being able to obtain any encouragement as to the possibility of relieving him from the imperfection in his gait. Mark, for a time, was greatly disappointed at this result; but finally this feeling wore away, and grateful for all the kindness shown to him by the doctor, became attached to him, and was never more happy than when able to reciprocate with some slight service. The doctor's slender stock of literature was soon devoured by the boy, but as the books were choice, they bore re-reading and study. They consisted chiefly of poetry and a few standard novels. Histories there were none, the doctor in regard to these being of Walpole's opinion, "Lies, my boy, lies, mere records of men's prejudices and self-glorification. Sound, wholesome truth is found in a good poem or noble novel."

Thus did Mark imbibe his taste for the ideal, and thus was his mental growth fashioned by the eccentric physician. His moral training, too, was not overlooked by this teacher, but the code inculcated was a simple one, and merely this: "Be just. There is but one virtue—justice," asserted Dr. Wattletop; "men resort to makeshifts, such as generosity, or charity, but they are but confessions of their shortcomings in respect to justice. If men were not unjust, there would be no need of generosity, or charity, and forgiveness would be either uncalled for, or a crime."

There was doubtless a deal of the stoic in these teachings, but it was on such philosophy that Mark was nourished.

As for his boyish passion for Edna Heath, that grew apace, but accompanied with the bitter remembrance that the sympathy she had shown him was prompted simply by commiseration. He was made none the less unhappy also, by noticing that since the eventful party Edna was not as cordial as formerly, but inclined to be distant; for the little beauty thought, perhaps, that she had been too pointed in her sympathy and desired, like older maidens, to set matters aright by an excess of reserve in the future. Very soon after this, however, she was sent to a seminary at Burlington, and during an interval of several years made but short and infrequent visits home. In this way the intercourse between the two gradually became less familiar, until now, Edna having attained young lady-hood, it was formal, and restricted to what is called a bowing acquaintance. Mark finally imagined he detected an intention on her part to repel him, and met it by assuming an attitude of corresponding hauteur. Still, the secret passion burned within his breast with steady fervor. It was his greatest joy to see her, although he never did so without those bitter words recurring to him: *You ought to be thankful you are not lame as he is, and ought to pity him.* Each word a thorn pressed to the quick! Meaning to be kind, how cruel she had been! How much sharper those words had stung than the mean taunt of her brother! *that* he could forgive and forget, for it came from one he despised, but could he ever forgive or forget the wound inflicted by her expressions of pity? Nothing but a complete and voluntary retraction on her part could compensate for that, and he resolved to toil with energy, and patience—to strain nerve and brain—to undergo, and brave everything until he had achieved distinction enough to excite her admiration, and wonder that she could ever have deemed him an object of compassion. Ridiculous, self-tormenting resolutions these will appear to common sense; yet were they but the natural impulses of a proud, sensitive, and we may add rather conceited youth, full of the illusions of life, and pushing every sentiment to extremes.

V.

Now that the intelligent reader is better acquainted with our hero's history and aspirations, he will at once conceive that Mark was rather alarmed for more reasons than one at the possible consequences of his second altercation with John Peter Heath, as related in a previous chapter.

Dr. Wattletop had relieved his fears in relation to any serious injury's resulting to the brother; but, reflected Mark, what will the sister think of it, and how has the affair been represented to her? Most likely, I am held up as a ruffian, who brutally and causelessly assailed her brother. Shall I submit, and let the future explain, or had I better seek an interview, and set myself right? I must do it, and I'll do it at once, was his decision—a decision he arrived at the more readily, as it afforded him an excellent pretext to see and converse with the object of his secret and constant adoration. But, on consideration, fearing that such a step might be misinterpreted, he concluded reluctantly to address himself to her father, and offer a frank explanation of the occurrence. It required an effort to come to this decision, for Mark dreaded Mr. Heath's patronizing politeness, and invariably avoided meeting him. But he conquered his repugnance on reflecting that that gentleman was fortunate enough to be Edna's father, and, moreover, that there was a likelihood of meeting and conversing with that young lady in compensation. In view of the latter probability, he prepared himself by making a more than usual neat and careful toilet, and by the time he was ready to start, his thoughts were far more occupied with Miss Edna's eyes, than with her brother's broken head. Off he started for the "Cliff," but soon his courage failed him, as he imagined the reception he was likely to meet with. Twice or thrice he stopped, hesitated, and only continued after much cogitation. Resolutely he walked past the gate-lodge, and up the avenue that led to the house. He rang the bell with a thumping heart. It was the first time he had crossed that threshold since he had been to Jack Heath's birthday party, and he remembered the colored servant who now ushered him into a reception room, as the same one—with a gray poll now, however—who had assisted the pianist in stopping the fight on that memorable occasion. Mark sent his name up to Mr. Heath, with the wish to be allowed a few moments' conversation with him. That gentleman, evidently, was in no haste to see his visitor, for he kept him waiting a long time. Meanwhile, Mark amused himself by staring at the pictures on the wall, and looking over some books that lay on the pier-table, when he heard light tripping footsteps coming towards him, and, turning suddenly, beheld Edna standing in the doorway in a startled attitude—a charming picture of a surprised maiden, lithe figure poised forward, with slightly parted lips, and fine, large eyes opened in full wonder. "Oh, I beg pardon—excuse me, I thought it was father;" and advancing, she added in a frank, pleasant way, "Why, this is Mark Gildersleeve."

All the blood in Mark's body rushed to his face as he bowed and explained, rather awkwardly, that he had called to see her father.

"I'll go and call him," said Edna; but as she was about leaving the room, Mark arrested her with an eager exclamation, "Stay, Miss Heath; do not leave yet, I beseech you. One moment—I beg of you—Pray tell me, is your brother severely hurt?"

"Not seriously so. He slept quite soundly last night. He very fortunately escaped any great harm. His horse ran away with him—upset the wagon he was riding in, and he fell—"

"I know it all, Miss Heath. It was my fault."

"Your fault," repeated Edna with surprise.

"My fault, I regret to say. But please forgive me. I came to explain and apologize. Your brother provoked me, and I was carried away by anger. Had the consequences been serious, I should never have forgiven myself. I am sorry—very sorry, Miss Heath. You were so kind as to take my part on a former occasion, when we were children. I have never forgotten it. (Edna colored at the reminder.) Please do so again. I know you are too just and too kind to blame me, if you knew all the circumstances."

Edna, who knew nothing of Mark's share in the misadventure, was much mystified by his appeal, and rather confused by his demeanor; for emboldened by the opportunity, the young man had advanced towards her in a supplicatory attitude, while his gaze expressed far more of admiration than contrition. She stood with a light blush tinting her features, not knowing how to receive so demonstrative an address, when, fortunately, the appearance of her father permitted her to withdraw, and caused her admirer suddenly to subdue his rather dramatic manner.

"This is—Mr. George Gildersleeve's brother, if I am not mistaken," quoth Mr. Heath with, easy condescension, and extending a finger to Mark.

"Yes, sir," replied the young man. "I came to inquire about your son, feeling it my duty to do so."

"Better this morning—much better, in fact."

"So I was glad to learn from Miss Heath. It is but proper that I should tell you, sir, that I was unfortunately the cause of the accident," said Mark.

"Indeed—indeed," said Mr. Heath loftily, "I wasn't aware."

36

This was a fib, for he knew all about the affair, and that his son had been the aggressor.

"I came," continued Mark, "to offer any explanation that might be required, or to do anything in my power to—"

"None is needed, sir; none is needed. The matter is fortunately of no consequence," interrupted Mr. Heath, who was not desirous of discussing the unpleasant event, for he was vexed and somewhat ashamed at this fresh exhibition of his son's misconduct. "I am obliged to you for calling, and can safely say, that my son has no grave injury whatever—none whatever."

Mr. Heath had not asked his visitor to be seated, and as he paused in a significant way after every sentence he uttered, Mark took the hint and his departure.

Seldom had Mark been so happy as after this visit. The effect of the frigid, almost discourteous reception given him by the father, was completely effaced by his short but delightful interview with the daughter. To be near her, and to converse with her, was compensation enough for any annoyance. Moreover, he had discovered to his joy, that while he had fancied himself almost forgotten and unthought of, she had on the contrary recognized him as an old friend, and even remembered the occasion, long since passed, when she had assumed with childish frankness the part of his ally and defender. The bitter side of that incident faded away for the moment, and his happiness was unalloyed. He cared little for the opinion of father or brother. Marriage with Miss Heath had not yet entered the scope of his aspirations. His aim was to acquire her close friendship, and above all her esteem and admiration. For this he resolved to live and strive. A modest ambition truly, but might not friendship, esteem, and admiration blossom into love? And to that complexion also, were not Edna's feelings, insensibly perhaps, tending? For it was not from any sense of displeasure that she withdrew so summarily from Mark's presence; on the contrary, she carried away a very agreeable impression of him; so much so, that his pleading face involuntarily presented itself to her repeatedly during the day. "I never before noticed," thought she, "how much better looking Mark Gildersleeve has grown to be. He certainly has beautiful eyes—so very expressive, and such pleasing manners, and there is something so gentlemanly and refined about him too." Evidently, the hoodwinked archer-boy had sped a shaft in her direction.

Mark, certainly, had made the most of his opportunity. Casting aside all his usual reserve, he had thrown as much eloquence and magnetism as he could, in a pair of black eyes that proved to be not ineffective. At least the ice was broken. But after the first moment of elation had passed, came the disturbing idea of the obstacles he might have to encounter in the way of future success. As has been mentioned, he only desired such as he might win through personal distinction. Doubtless there was a large share of vanity in this determination; but vanity was the weak side of the Gildersleeves, half-redeemed, though, in Mark, as it never manifested itself in any offensive way. In social standing, he was not considered the equal of Miss Heath; for in our republic, gradations in society are as sharply defined as elsewhere, with the difference that with us wealth more frequently draws the line. Mark understood this, but such was his contempt for mere money-getting, that the enthusiastic youth, would even have preferred to resign any attempt to gain Miss Heath's favor, if to accomplish it the acquisition of wealth were necessary. His estimate of the young lady's character, however, was too high to admit for a moment of the supposition that she could in any way be influenced by mercenary motives. No money could buy what he aspired to possess—to wit, her admiration. Fame alone could win that; and were this the age of chivalry, how eagerly would he don casque, mount the barbed steed, and tilt his way to death or distinction! But in this prosaic age few paths are open to ambitious youth. He was a draughtsman—an engineer. Howsoever eminent one might become in that profession, it still remained a commonplace one. He did not think Edna had any especial admiration for Brunel, or Stephenson, or even Watt. In his calling genius itself could hardly efface the stains of labor, and obtain the consideration accorded to mediocrity in the genteel professions. In medicine, or law, one might with far more facility attain celebrity; but he had no taste for those vocations. He had dabbled with paint, and executed some very indifferent daubs, until in disgust he had thrown away the palette and brush. Then the versatile youth had coquetted with Euterpe, and practised on every instrument, from the harmonica to the organ. In vocal music he was more successful; but poesy, the art of all arts, was the one he longed to cultivate and excel in. He loved the poets, and believed himself animated with a spark of their celestial fire. If genius were patience, why might one not become by constant effort, if not a Shakespeare, say a Keats, or a Tennyson? Phrenologists taught that every faculty could be modified, and its power increased by exercise. Knatchbull, a foreman in the Works, who had been a Chartist in his own country, and possessed a remarkable head, told him that he had succeeded, under the advice of a phrenologist, in so changing his character that plaster casts of his cranium taken at different periods showed corresponding modifications in the prominences. This practical example of what persistence might do was encouraging; and so Mark, stung by some stray bee from Mount Hymettus, wrote quires of plain verses, which he thought very fine and destined to stir the world of letters, but which were simply transpositions of ideas and similes of the master poets with which his mind was saturated.

Could poets have been made other than by the hand of Nature, Mark would certainly have become one, for he strove with an indefatigable ardor that nothing could dampen to succeed; but the divine afflatus so charily bestowed was lacking, and he thrummed the lyre without evoking strains immortal. What phrenzy and foolscap were wasted—what moonlight walks indulged in, and sylvan groves haunted, to meditate and seek inspiration! How often he sauntered around the margin of the Passaic, watching the leap of the cataract and rise of its snowy mist, as its low thunder lulled him into delicious day dreams. Far into the night would he linger reclining against the bole of some tree, gazing with straining eyes towards Mr. Heath's villa, whose gray walls loomed in the moonlight like a feudal castle, to catch, perhaps, a glimpse of a shadow that might appear occasionally behind the curtains of a lighted room that he knew to be Edna's. Often had the faint sound of music or mirth, that reached him from the open drawing-room windows, filled him with envy and jealousy, as he thought of the Rev. Spencer Abbott and young Mumbie, who were constant visitors at the villa. Then, dismally homeward would he wend his way, go to his room, and spend the silent watches of the night racking his brains to commit his thoughts to paper. Quires, nay reams, were covered with superfine tropes and metaphors, as he strove to coin words that the world would not willingly let die. He ventured to show his lucubrations to Dr. Wattletop, but the reception they met with was neither flattering nor even encouraging. "My dear boy, drop all this," was the advice given. "Not only are you wasting precious time, but your taste and mind are becoming vitiated by the namby-pamby trash of modern rhymesters. If you must plagiarize, do it from Pope, or Milton, or Gray. Study them, or the master Shakespeare. Remember, as Coleridge said, poetry must be either music or sense, and I cannot say there is much of either in your verses. Get at the kernel. But after all, the study for a poetically inclined youth is medicine, singular as that may seem to you. If the desire be to awaken sublime ideas, investigate the abstruse problem of life. Follow the noblest calling, the art of healing, and seek to penetrate the arcana of Nature. I wish I could induce you to become one of us. Our profession greatly needs ardent and intelligent recruits, else we shall be overrun with quacks in every shape. Look at the frightful progress of that modern humbug, homoeopathy. There is no error, however absurd, but will find supporters and disciples, and nowhere can there be a nobler field for the exercise of the highest talent than in combating and routing those egregious and pernicious pretenders to science, who, with the absurd brocard, that 'like cures like,' impose on the simple and gullible. Now I am anything but illiberal —if anything, I err on the opposite side. Whatever my convictions may be, I am willing to give a patient hearing and investigation to any theory or system bearing a show of probability, that is advanced in a truthful, earnest, and humble spirit. I do not forget that alchemy was the mother of chemistry, and astrology of astronomy; that Harvey met with bigoted opposition, and in short that it becomes the seeker to be humble; but when I see a fellow like this Keene here—this hatchet-faced Yankee from Connecticut, who probably a year ago was peddling wooden clocks, going around Belton with his ridiculous pellets, and presuming to be a physician, I am provoked beyond endurance, and feel sometimes as if I could give the fellow a horse-whipping. Well, well, the fools are not all dead yet."

"I hope, doctor, you don't class me among them," said crestfallen Mark, with a feeble smile.

"No—no—my dear boy," replied the doctor, patting his *protégé* affectionately on the shoulder. "Not by any means. I was merely alluding to the facility with which the generous public is gulled. As for you, Mark, I think there is the stuff in you for something, if not for a bard. I dislike to see you chasing jack-o'-lanterns. Think of it; there are but a certain quantity of poetic ideas, and they have all been thought out and put into English words long ago. Fresh attempts result only in tricking them out in fantastic dresses, and with poor effect. Modern critics may sneer at the old favorites, but what have your rhymesters of to-day produced equal to the 'Universal Prayer,' 'Gray's Elegy,' or 'The Deserted Village'? No, no, lad; love the old poets, from Homer down, but don't attempt to soar with them to the empyrean. Stay with us on *terra firma*; invent a new cut-off, or condenser, and let anapest, dactyl, and trochee alone."

This advice was not relished by Mark, and like most distasteful advice, was not followed; if anything, it proved a spur to his literary exertions. Occasionally his effusions found their way into print, and shone in the Literary column of the *Belton Sentinel*, accompanied by a notice from the editor, who alluded to the talent of his young fellow-townsman in terms of unmeasured praise. Said that influential sheet on the appearance of *The Broken Abacus*:

"In spite of a press of matter, we determined to make room, in our issue of to-day, for another poem from the pen of our gifted young poet, Mark Gildersleeve, which will be found on the third page. The favor with which the 'Withered Chaplet' and 'The Spear of Ithuriel' were received, encourage us to print the present verses. They are hexameters, and remind us in their flowing rhythm of the earlier efforts of Longfellow, while in gorgeousness of imagery and luxuriance of diction, they equal some of the finest passages in Keats. Altogether, we congratulate Mr. Gildersleeve on this exquisite production, whose symmetry and polished beauty can only be fitly compared to a capital of Pentelican marble from the chisel of Phidias."

Dr. Wattletop, though, said "Bosh" to this, when he read it, and it could not be denied that he was a competent critic. He, also, had trod the primrose path of literature in leisure moments, not as a poet, but as an occasional contributor of essays to magazines and reviews. There was a literary club in Belton, composed of young men who loved to indulge in debates and other intellectual gymnastics. Mark, as might be supposed, was an active member, and, indeed, at one time president of this association. Besides deciding the momentous topics of "Whether men of thought, or men of action, have done the most for civilization," or "Whether the execution of Mary Queen of Scots was justifiable or not," and other questions of similar perplexity, the society gave lectures, or rather lectures were given, to quote the posters, under their auspices, during the winter months. At their solicitation, Dr. Wattletop was induced to prepare and deliver a lecture on "Eccentricity," a theme which he was well qualified, at least from experience, to treat of. He diversified it with many humorous anecdotes of Porson and Abernethy, and it met with much applause, and elicited very flattering encomiums from the *Belton Sentinel.* So successful, indeed, was it, that efforts were made to have the doctor repeat it in neighboring towns, but he excused himself on the plea of want of time. Then proffers of money were made to induce him to comply; this only served to incense him, and an indignant refusal was the result. He was inclined to blame Mark a little in his displeasure.

"Mark, you rascal, all this is your fault. I never would have given that confounded lecture but for you. It ill becomes a man of my years and profession to waste the time he owes to his patients, in relating stale jests to a grinning audience. I don't know what I could have been thinking of. In future, spin your nonsense as much as you like, my boy, but don't ask me to join you —at my age, too! My remnant of life is too short, and time has become too precious to me, to be squandered in that way."

As well in that way, and better than in another he was prone to; and unfortunately, he was getting rather too much on his hands, just then, of the article he deemed so precious. For Keene, the hatchet-faced homoeopath, had relieved the doctor of a vast deal of practice, and left him with overmuch unemployed time on his hands. Dr. Wattletop explained the increasing popularity of the heterodox practitioner in this wise: "The infernal quack seduces the children with his sugar-plums, and the mothers are silly enough to yield to their preferences; once introduced in the family, of course it is pleasanter, if one needs physic, to appease the conscience with a make-believe medicine than to take a bitter though wholesome remedy. How are you to meet this folly and weakness? Between these sugar-plums, and water-drenching, and clairvoyant cures, the profession, I say, is going to the devil— yes, sir, going to the devil! Come, Dagon, let's be off, old boy;" and with his dog jogging beside him he would betake himself to a walk, which, after a circuit of a mile or so, invariably terminated not to the infernal regions, as one would naturally infer, but to what the Belton "Band of Hope" would have designated as half way to it, viz.: "The Shades." This was a little tavern at the far end of the town, kept by an Englishman, and frequented solely by "old-country" people (of whom there were many among the mill-hands), who resorted thither to indulge in Welsh rarebits and old ale. You ascended a few steps, pushed open a swing-door, and found yourself facing a little bar attached to a small quiet room with a sanded floor. There were wire screens in the windows on the street, and the walls were ornamented with fine engravings of the All England Eleven, the Cambridgeshire Hunt, and portraits of Nelson, Wellington, and Queen Victoria. The host was a "Brummagem" man, suspected, from his blunted nose, of having been a pugilist, but as he was a surly man of uncommunicative disposition, the suspicion had never been verified. There were a half-dozen tables in the room, and at a particular one in a corner Dr. Wattletop took his place, and Dagon his (beneath the table), with undeviating method, about three days in the week, unless prevented by professional duties. Mutely, then, the blunt-nosed man brought a beaker of gin and sugar, and the *Albion*, or *Illustrated London News* to the doctor, who in silence consumed the gin and perused the paper, his interest in the latter centring in the "Gazette," whose announcement that Major Pipeclay was promoted, vice Colonel Sabretasche retired, or that the ——th Foot were ordered to Bermuda, or that some old chum had gone to his long home, recalled recollections of by-gone days, and furnished food for reflection. After the third beaker he laid aside the paper, and was now become intensely grave and imposing, sitting bolt upright with his cane between his knees, and gazing in a very uncompromising way into vacancy. The scot settled without exchanging a word, the doctor buttoned his coat tightly, grasped his cane firmly, and sternly began his return homeward. His way led the length of Main Street, and seldom was any one bold enough to accost him then.

Once, at such a time, Mr. Mumbie crossed his path (it was shortly after the delivery of the doctor's lecture on Eccentricity), and ventured to greet him with a smile and extended hand: "Good-day, doctor."

"Sir to you," replied the doctor, halting in a military attitude.

"Fine afternoon, doctor."

"Very fine indeed, sir. Ha! very fine."

"Doctor, you'd hardly believe it, but to-day is my birthday," said Mr. Mumbie, assuming a triumphant air as if he were imparting a surprising piece of news.

"I see no reason to doubt it," replied the doctor, curtly.

"Yes, sir, that is so," rejoined Mr. Mumbie with decision; "I'm a much older man, let me tell you, than you take me for."

Dr. Wattletop looked as if he were prepared to take Mr. Mumbie for any age whatever, for that gentleman presented what might be styled an anachronistic appearance. He was a large man, offering at first view a protuberant expanse of waistcoat, supported by somewhat unstable legs. His head was an oblong one, covered with a curly glossy brown wig, that contrasted singularly with thick gray eyebrows, and dyed whiskers on flabby cheeks flanked by two large ears.

"Yes, sir," repeated Mr. Mumbie, "I'm a much older man than you take me for. You know Mrs. Mumbie is much my junior, and that I never made up my mind to marry until late in life—that accounts for it."

"Accounts for what?" inquired the doctor, beginning to be bored.

"Accounts for the—the discrepancy I spoke of. Now, here's a knife," and Mr. Mumbie drew from his pocket a jack-knife, the bone-handle of which was yellow with age, "here's a knife that I have carried about with me since I was a boy. It was given to me as a birthday present. Just notice the date I scratched on the handle—Nov. 16th, 1814. Just think of that. I've carried it for going on fifty years—yes, sir, fifty years. I doubt if there's many men, or in fact any man, can say as much; and what changes have taken place since then! But I'm a man of strong local attachments. I had an umbrella, doctor, when I was first married that I had used steadily for twenty-six years—think of that! I suppose I would have had it yet, but Mrs. Mumbie, unfortunately, was prejudiced against that umbrella, and one day it disappeared. I never saw it again." This was said solemnly, and Mr. Mumbie looked as if he were about to pay the tribute of a tear to the manes of the departed umbrella.

The doctor's patience becoming weary, he was about to turn on his heel to leave, when Mr. Mumbie resumed:

"Doctor, I ought to thank you for the pleasure you afforded me the other evening. I haven't had such a treat in a long time. 'Pears to me you might make lots o' money going about delivering that lecture. It was capital. You did get off some of the funniest anecdotes I ever heard, and I assure you I was really very much entertained."

"Entertained, sir! Dammit, sir, do you take me for a mountebank?" exclaimed the doctor, swelling with rising indignation.

It required very many apologies and explanations on Mr. Mumbie's part to allay the ire of the physician, who continued, after parting with his interlocutor, to mutter to himself as he went along: "Entertained him! Am I, Basil Wattletop, a buffoon? Does he attempt to patronize me? The insolence of these Yankee upstarts is really something perfectly amazing! It's almost beyond belief." Unfortunately, his dignity that day was destined to be subjected to further ruffling, for as he neared the Archimedes Works he caught sight of the proprietor thereof, who was lounging as usual on the door-step of his "office," with his hands in his pockets. No man, we will venture to say, that kept his hands as often pocketed, ever earned so much money as George Gildersleeve; but if his hands were idle, his eyes were busy and everywhere. A more vigilant pair of optics never lodged in a human head. "Now, that fellow," soliloquized the doctor, alluding to George, "has sense enough to know that he springs from the lees. He don't attempt to ape his betters or to patronize them, and his rudeness and ignorance are far less offensive than the insufferable pretensions of that snob Mumbie—um—um."

"Hold up, Major," broke in George, hailing the doctor stentoriously. "Step over here a moment. Foreman of my finishing-shop split his thumb to-day in a lathe, and I want you to look at it."

The doctor was in doubts whether to respond to an appeal so unceremoniously conveyed. He decided, however, after a short debate with himself, to cross over to the counting-room and examine the injured man. The hurt being dressed and pronounced but a slight affair, he was about to leave when George Gildersleeve must needs engage him in a discussion, which gradually drifted into the delicate subject of the comparative merits of Englishmen and Americans. At this time there were sputterings in Congress, and in the newspapers, in regard to a fresh "outrage" perpetrated by the navy of Great Britain on our flag, and the general expression was that we were not "going to stand it."

George for his part certainly was not, and said so plainly: "Look here, Major, do you see that?" (pointing to an old horse-shoe nailed over the fire-place.) "Right here was my grandfather's forge, and right about here's where he shod Gineral Washington's horse just awhile afore he fought the great battle of Trenton, and that's one of the cast-off shoes, and I wouldn't take a thousand dollars for it. Well, sir, the man that rode that horse that my grandfather shod, flaxed you Englishmen out of your boots; and I tell you we've plenty more that can do it now, and they'll do it again, if you Johnny Bulls don't behave yourselves; now mind."

Dr. Wattletop, being in that condition when he was excessively patriotic, prejudiced, and punctilious, was so utterly dumbfounded by this tirade, that for a moment apoplexy was imminent. Luckily, contempt supervened, and with a smile of scorn and withering irony, he repeated, "Washington—

Trenton—great battle of Trenton, I believe you said? Do you seriously call that a battle? Why, my man, do you know what a battle is? At the so-called battle of Trenton the total loss, according to your historians, and their statements are evidently grossly exaggerated—the total loss in killed on both sides amounted to five-and-twenty, including a drummer, who received a black eye in the shindy; five-and-twenty killed! all told—all told!"

George Gildersleeve shook his head incredulously at this statement, and the doctor continued: "Now, if you will take the trouble to instruct yourself a bit, you will find out what Englishmen can do. Read, for instance, an account of the battle of Waterloo. Talk of Homeric heroes! What's Achilles and the well-greaved Greeks to the Iron Duke and the Guards?—what's Ajax Telamon to Shaw the Life-guardsman? tell me that—tell me that?" Shaw the Life-guardsman was the doctor's favorite hero, and he never failed, when the occasion offered, to bring him in as the compeer of all the paladins of old, from Hector to Roland.

"Ah! there was fighting such as the world ne'er saw before," continued the doctor, kindling with enthusiasm. "Not the famous Macedonian phalanx nor the Roman legion held their ground so stoutly as the squares of British linesmen when the steel-clad squadrons of cuirassiers broke against them in vain."

"That was all very well when you fought them Frenchmen and Greeks. But when you tackled us, you found a different sort of people to deal with, I reckon. Old Put, and Jackson, and Gineral Scott, were too much for you, old man," returned George, with a shake of the head that ought to have settled matters.

Dr. Wattletop's nose glowed with a fiercer heat, and if looks could have scorched a man, Gildersleeve would have shrivelled on the spot; but the chances are that even the glances of that pleasant dame Medusa would have fallen harmless on the pachydermatous master of the Archimedes Works.

"Why, confound it, man, you talk like an ass. Should her Gracious Majesty, the Queen of England, ever deign to notice the vaporings of your politicians, and take it into her head to resent them, she'd send the Channel fleet over here and knock your blasted country into flinders in no time, and dammit, I wish she would!" and with that volley the doctor turned on his heel, and left abruptly, to work off his choler by an additional tramp of a mile or two.

"How are you to convince a pig-headed, obstinate man like that?" said George, turning to his book-keeper. "He's so prejudiced that he won't listen to reason, and must have his own way."

VI.

While all the efforts of man, long-repeated, to change the baser metals into gold have proved futile, it is no less certain that gold, in revenge, has been successful in transmuting man. The power of its moral alchemy is seen in individuals like Rufus Heath. Poor, he would have remained a fawning toady, but wealth transformed him into a haughty, arrogant aristocrat at heart. No Somerset or Rohan was ever more so. Starting in life without other capital than a moderate education, tact, and industry, his first aim was to acquire wealth. His tastes were luxurious and refined, and to gratify them wealth was necessary. So to succeed he was plastic and serviceable to his employers, and assiduous in courting useful friends. A good name is a great stepping-stone, and to secure this he was correct and respectable in his conduct and demeanor. "Correctness," in fact, was his religion and code of morality. Of course, right and wrong were relative terms, and it was not to be expected that any one should live up to the exact letter of the law. A margin was allowable.

Nevertheless, decorum and all outward observances were due to society, and indispensable. Acting on this principle, there was no more popular and respected young man at twenty-one, in Belton, than Rufus Heath, nor one with brighter prospects. Counsellor Hull, his patron, declared that the young lawyer promised to be an ornament to the profession; and when the Counsellor was called to the bench, Rufus Heath succeeded to his practice. Exempt from gross vices, and gifted with an elastic conscience, the thriving lawyer successfully pursued his calling, until his marriage with Miss Obershaw crowned his pecuniary prosperity. Now the influence of riches made itself manifest, and it almost seemed as if the precious metals had been injected into his veins. He stiffened, became cold and imperturbable, laid aside his urbanity, and his ill-concealed pride and contempt for the less prosperous betrayed itself. And now that he had tasted all the joys that affluence can give, and tasted them unto satiety, he craved the flattering unction of distinction. Ambition was now his god. He was a politician, but a successful one only so far as he had been assisted by his wealth and family connections. He owed it to these powerful auxiliaries that he had spent a term in Congress. But he had gained no prominence there. He lacked oratorical ability, and without it, it is scarcely possible to attain eminence in a republic. His daintiness, moreover, caused him to recoil from contact with the masses, and though he strove to overcome this repugnance when the occasion called for it, he had never entirely succeeded. Perseverance, intrigue, and a lavish expenditure of money, were the means he relied on to ascend the first steps of political preferment. Once fairly launched as a public man, he doubted not his ability to make his way and mark as a statesman or a diplomat. To become Governor of his State was his present aim, and he had laid his plans to secure the nomination from his party as a candidate at the next election. To this end a host of emissaries, with money at command, were at work throughout the State. The *Belton Sentinel*, the organ in the county of Mr. Heath's party, advocated his interest with tremendous energy, persistency, and abundance of adjectives. Finnegass, the editor, was a poor printer, whose shop, presses, types, and all were mortgaged to Rufus Heath. This well-known fact furnished an unfailing quantity of sarcasm to the *Passaic County Argus*, the opposition sheet, that invariably alluded to Finnegass as the "minion" or "serf," either "pampered" or "truckling," of the "aristocrat on the cliff." These amenities were treated by the editor of the *Sentinel* with complete indifference, until once (stung into retorting by some particularly sharp gibe) he referred to the *Argus* as an "obscure sheet of no circulation, edited by a low, ignorant felon." Obscurity and "no circulation" were accusations too atrocious to be borne, and the editor of the *Argus* flung them back, with indignation, in the teeth of his defamer. This brought out sworn statements of copies issued by the two presses, and much evidence on both sides was published; for the rival editors were ready to go to any lengths to exculpate their respective papers from so heinous a charge as obscurity or want of "circulation." As for the personalities, they were treated as mild banter, tending to enliven the canvass, and stimulate partisans.

At this time, to quote the after-words of the *Belton Sentinel*, "the horizon of political affairs was darkening, and the clouds that confined the storm destined to shake the fabric of our Union to its foundation, were gathering ominously." The different parties were in a ferment. The Whigs no longer existed—they had given way to an organization originated by the Free-Soilers, and styling themselves Republicans. There were, however, a large number of old Whigs wedded to their prejudices, with a distaste for affiliation with the Democrats and a greater repugnance to a party tainted in any degree with Abolitionism, who looked upon the new movement as an ephemeral ebullition. These individuals, calling themselves "Conservatives," imagined that it required but an effort on their part to still the waters of political strife, and decided to constitute themselves "bulwarks," and "arks of safety." Among these was the Hon. Rufus Heath. Like all men of his stamp, he was utterly opposed to any disturbance of the established order of things. He was perfectly well satisfied with them as they were. As for radicals or reformers, he hated their very name. Such people sprang from the vulgar herd, and were only bent on mischief. His ideal of a proper government was a constitutional monarchy supported by an oligarchy of wealth, and to this form he believed the republic was gradually tending. He was not unobservant of the increasing prestige of birth. Position in the army, navy, or state was gradually tending to perpetuate itself in certain families. The bearers of historic names wielded a certain influence, which increased with time, and would eventually and under certain circumstances crystallize into decided power. Here were the germs of an oligarchy, which needed but a law of entail to perfect itself and institute a class of hereditary legislators, or house of peers—the bulwark indispensable against the agrarianism inherent in a democratic form of government.

In order to exchange views on the condition of the body-politic, and devise means to combat the evil influences then prevailing (to say nothing of advancing his own personal plans), Mr. Heath took advantage of the presence in the vicinity of a statesman who had occupied a very exalted position in the commonwealth, to ask him to meet at dinner sundry other influential and distinguished citizens, and confer on the important subjects in question.

The preliminary step was to send for Mr. Mumbie. Mr. Heath had an imperial way of summoning people to him, and his mandates were generally obeyed with alacrity—always so when addressed to his good old neighbor and toady, Mumbie; who, although suffering from an attack of rheumatic gout, hobbled as quickly as his swollen feet would permit him, in prompt response to the call.

"Mumbie," said Mr. Heath, "I suppose you have heard that there is a great deal of talk about my running for Governor at the next election?"

Mr. Mumbie had not heard of it, nor had any one else; but he looked and nodded as if it were a familiar and constant topic of conversation with everybody.

"Well, I have not yet made up my mind whether I will consent to run or not. However, that is neither here nor there at present, nor what I wanted to see and talk with you about. Senator Rangle is your brother's wife's cousin, I believe, and you are on a familiar footing with him, are you not?"

"Yes, sir," said Mumbie, listening attentively.

"So I thought. Now Rangle and I are not on the very best of terms. He accuses me, I believe, of having used my influence against him in the Legislature, when he sought a renomination—said I wanted the place myself, and so forth. He is mistaken in that. However, I am willing to pass it over, as this is a time when personal feeling should not interfere to prevent men from acting in accord on vital questions of state. Here is the point. I have asked ex-President

—— to meet Judge Hull at dinner Thursday week. Several other prominent gentlemen will be present, and matters of importance may be discussed. Now, Mumbie, you can assist me in this way: call on Rangle, state to him that as my friend you regret that there should be any divergence of opinion between us; that from your personal knowledge I have never held any but the highest opinion of him; and so on. You might then introduce the subject of the proposed dinner, and state that you know that I would be pleased to have him make one of the company. On your report, if everything is satisfactory, I can forward him a formal invitation. Now, my dear Mumbie, you will help me in this little matter, and I can rely on your discretion, I know."

"Certainly, Mr. Heath, certainly. I shall be delighted to undertake the job;" and Mr. Mumbie hastened off, big with the importance of his mission, and happy as if he had received an order for ten thousand reams of foolscap, paid for in advance. His task was an easy one. The senator was flattered by Mr. Heath's advances, and in no way averse to partake of his dinners, whose celebrity had reached him; moreover, in no way disinclined to forego the opportunity of meeting ex-President ——, whose political star seemed to glimmer forth again in the ascendant.

It is almost superfluous to mention, that the dinner was all that could be expected, for whatever Mr. Heath's other qualities may have been, good taste he unquestionably possessed, and in the important matter of dinner-giving he was behind no one. And when it is considered how important a part that art has displayed in diplomacy, it could not be denied that his aspirations to shine in that career were not by any means presumptuous. An opinion, it is safe to say, that would have been heartily indorsed by all who were fortunate enough to partake of the memorable repast. Perhaps a little less starched ceremony on the part of the host would not have been amiss; still, that was more than compensated by the quality of the *menu*. As usual on such extraordinary occasions, an eminent *chef* from the metropolis directed the culinary operations, and many bottles of old South Side Madeira and choice Hermitage, that had lain for years in dusty racks, were brought to light, and decanted for the delectation of appreciative palates; such a palate, for instance, as a Chief Justice of great legal acumen and good digestion, or a portly ex-Federal dignitary possesses, or even that of a dainty young High-Church ecclesiastic full of zeal and sentiment, like Spencer Abbott. What a fine dinner it was, to be sure! Rather formal and cold, it is true, in the drawing-rooms as the host was receiving his guests. Mrs. Applegate was flushed and fidgety amid such illustrious visitors, and Mr. Mumbie was ill at ease in his capacious white waistcoat, tight gloves, and freshly dyed whiskers. Such grand company impressed him immensely, and for fear of lapsus linguæ, he restricted himself to monosyllabic replies. The Chief Justice, being hungry, was somewhat surly until dinner was announced, when he ponderously and feebly toddled into the dining-room in advance of the other guests, and regardless of Mr. Heath's intention to have him lead Mrs. Applegate in. This duty therefore devolved on the ex-Federal dignitary, who did it with much courtly grace. How well the host presided, and how elegant he appeared! His stately white neck-tie and glossy gray locks were arranged with a precision that was mathematical, and with his small elegant white hands he looked as if he were descended from a long line of partridge-fed ancestors. A worthy pendant, indeed, to the ex-Federal dignitary, whose proudest boast was that he had been complimented by a queen as the most elegant American gentleman she had ever seen. What a contrast the two presented to Judge Hull, with his fell of white hair streaming over his massive head and bent shoulders, his beetling sable brows shading a pair of cavernous eyes, and who always looked as if he were on the bench administering inexorable justice. He certainly did to the dinner, and it was with difficulty that he could be drawn out by the host, and made to enlighten the company with bits of prodigious wisdom. Finnegass, the editor of the *Sentinel*, who occupied a seat at the farther end of the table, and expected to gather material for a brilliant leader from the table-talk of the assembled sages, was greatly disappointed at the commonplace style of the conversation.

"Heath, this soup's not so bad," quoth the Judge during a short breathing spell; "I'll take another plateful. What do you call it? *Potage à la Reine*. Ha— queen-pottage, eh? Well-named, verily. A man might well sell his birthright for a mess of such, and not be a fool either."

"Touching the late proceedings in Congress, Judge," edged in Mr. Heath, "you cannot have failed to notice how the breach is gradually widening. There seems to be a disposition on the part of certain members to push matters to extremes, and bring about a rupture at any cost. Don't you think, that an expression of opinion—a decided expression on the part of the higher classes —the respectable and influential part of the community, would go far to—to —"

"This can be arranged and must be," replied the Judge, addressing his plate dogmatically. "The hot-heads of both parties must be made to listen to reason, and the conservative element of the country should at once take the reins. By the bye, this white Burgundy is the same I've tasted here before, is it not? Yquem, you said? A good wine—a very good wine. The field has been left entirely too much to the fanatics of the East and the fire-eaters of the South, and to stop the current of demagogism which threatens to overwhelm us, we need the best efforts of sound sagacious statesmen like our friend here."

The friend referred to by the Judge's fork was the ex-Federal dignitary, who bowed an acknowledgment of the flattering allusion, and with a little deprecatory wave of the hand replied, "No doubt—no doubt, Judge, you are quite right. All that is necessary is to bring the best men of the country together to concerted action, and the matter can be settled without any difficulty. But if we hold aloof—if the great legal lights, such gentlemen as yourself or our friend Mr. Heath; or the heads of finance, as represented by our friend on my left, Mr. Bawbee; or the masterminds of the manufacturing and industrial interests, such as our friend Mr. Mumbie; in short, if the intellect and wealth and respectability of the nation do not interfere, and continue to permit men like Sumner and Seward to persist in their incendiary leadership, we may—I say it without hesitation and with great regret—we may expect any catastrophe."

Mr. Mumbie, who had been listening with awe and attention to the words of the great men in whose presence he was, reddened with modest confusion on being designated as a master-mind. He had never taken exactly that view of himself, but on reflection, concluded it to be an eminently fit and proper one, and felt that the world had much to answer for in having so greatly underrated him hitherto. "I quite agree with you. I do indeed, sir. Your remarks are very correct, sir; very correct indeed, I assure you, sir," spoke he, feeling that he ought to say something to keep up his reputation of a master-mind.

Finnegass, the editor, emboldened by generous wine, ventured to remark: "In my article in last Monday's *Sentinel*, I alluded to this very subject, and put it in rather forcible terms to the—" But he was cut short by the Judge, who, being at leisure between courses, resumed his harangue: "The proper way to settle this trouble is very simple. It can be arranged with very little difficulty. I am quite confident of that, and speak advisedly. All that is necessary is a conference of the patriotic intellects from all sections North and South, East and West, to restore harmony to the councils of our country. Of course, forbearance is indispensable, and a spirit of conciliation should preside over all deliberations, and—this *paté* has the appearance of being very fine—very fine. I'll take some more of the truffles."

"I wrote an article which created—" again attempted Finnegass.

"Mr. Bawbee, a glass of wine with you, if you please," said the host, adroitly checking the editor, and nodding gracefully to the financier. Mr. Bawbee was a Western banker, of Scotch birth, who had made no end of pelf by starting banks and issuing paper money. He took the floor, figuratively speaking, and predicted the dismemberment of the Union. Mr. Bawbee being a shrewd, hard-headed Scot, had an opinion of his own. "It'll never do in the world, Judge. The matter has gone too far. Mark my words, gentlemen, you'll see the States divided into three confederacies, and that within two years. I know the sentiments and temper of the Western people, and if the South secedes, which it doubtless will, the West will sever their connection with the East. In my section they deem their interests more closely identified with those of the South, than with the manufacturing East, and will never permit the mouth of the Mississippi, their great natural highway, to pass into the control of a foreign people, hence it is not improbable that in certain eventualities they would join hands with the South; but I am inclined to believe, as I mentioned at first, that the upshot will be a division into three confederations, and perhaps, as the Pacific States grow in importance, into four."

"Tut—tut, Mr. Bawbee," interrupted Mr. Justice Hull, "all those minor differences and territorial jealousies can be reconciled. As I have before stated, a well-selected conference could settle the vexed question in a short time. Get the right men together, and I have, no doubt as to the result."

The Judge was inclined to be impatient of other people's opinions when they clashed with his own, and was always the Sir Oracle of his circle.

The Rev. Spencer Abbott, who was not greatly interested in the questions of state discussed by the other guests, diverted himself in dulcet small-talk with his fair neighbor, the daughter of the house. In spite of an evident desire to please, he was apparently unsuccessful, for Miss Edna showed signs of weariness by an occasional pouting of her delicate lips, and seemed much relieved when the cloth being drawn, enabled her and her aunt, who were the only ladies present, to retire to the drawing-room. Poor Abbott would gladly have joined them, for he was dreadfully bored by Finnegass, who, exalted by wine and in default of any other listener, attached himself to the clergyman, and treated him to choice extracts from stirring leaders, until it was only by steady sips of coffee and a supreme effort of will, that Abbott refrained from lapsing into slumber.

At length Rangle came to the rescue, and merriment prevailed; for that eminent senator, ignoring the weighty topics under discussion, proved a perfect cornucopia of jokes and funny anecdotes, and actually drew a smile from the grim old Judge.

By this time Mr. Mumbie had recovered his self-possession, and grown bold and garrulous. He ventured to occupy a vacant chair next to the ex-President (that had been set apart for John Heath who had not condescended to appear), and informed that dignitary that he (Mumbie) was a much older man than any one would take him for. As the ex-President, on being asked, failed to guess Mr. Mumbie's age, Mr. Mumbie imparted the information, triumphantly adding that Mrs. Mumbie was very much his junior, as he had married late in life. "Here's a knife," continued he, drawing forth the bone-handled jack-knife, "that I have carried steadily, sir, steadily for over fifty years. Now I don't think there are many such instances on record. My local attachments are very strong. It's a peculiarity in our family which—"

"Between ourselves, and what is said here will of course go no farther," said Mr. Heath, with a sharp glance at Mr. Mumbie, "had we not better take some preliminary steps at once, in regard to the matter we have been discussing? I think we are all of one opinion on the subject. With your permission, Judge, I would suggest that you and Senator Rangle should by all means go as delegates from this State. Our friend Mr. —— ought of course to represent New York. Then I have thought that perhaps Crittenden would be of all men the most proper to lead the delegation from his section. In fact, I have already written him on the subject, and will send for a copy of my letter and read it to you."

"Not now, Heath; I'll listen to it some other time," said Judge Hull.

"Very well, I merely wished to show that I have approached him in a cautious way, and in a manner that I do not doubt will meet with your approval. Now, how does the selection of delegates strike you? I mean, of course, as far as I have gone?"

"Well—well. I'll think of it—what liqueur is that?"

The Judge did think of it, and the conference was held, as we all know. The Judge, the ex-Federal dignitary, and Senator Rangle, were all there, and in company with other conservative gentlemen tried to stop the Niagara flood of progress with bulrushes. But the tide that was destined to sweep away the last relic of barbarism in our country, was rising fast, and the conservative brooms that were striving to stem it were flourished in vain.

Meanwhile Judge Hull took another *chasse-café* of cognac, to fortify himself against the night air, and looking at his watch, directed his carriage to be called, and rather unceremoniously departed. The Rev. Spencer Abbott slipped away to join the ladies in the drawing-room, while the other guests accompanied the host to the picture-gallery. After the ex-Federal dignitary, Senator Rangle, and Mr. Bawbee had retired to their respective bedchambers for the night, Mr. Heath remained closeted with Finnegass in the library, while the former concocted an article (the editor being incapacitated by the dinner from any intellectual effort for the time being), to appear in the next issue of the *Belton Sentinel*, and which he expected would create a marked sensation. This article, a lengthy and portentous leader, was prefaced by the following:

"We are gratified to announce that a movement of very great and general importance to the public, in relation to the present crisis of political affairs, is in progress; the particulars of which having been communicated to us in confidence, we do not feel at liberty to impart."

This statement having stimulated the reader's curiosity and attention to a proper degree, the writer, after a few paragraphs, relented from his stoical secrecy, and with generous confidence divulged the fact that he had been invited to be present—

"at an informal meeting of distinguished citizens, among whom were ex-President ——, Senator Rangle, Chief Justice Hull, Andrew Bawbee, Esq., the wealthy and influential Western banker, M. Mumbie, Esq., and several other gentlemen scarcely less eminent, held at the residence of our esteemed fellow-townsman, Hon. Rufus Heath, to deliberate and take into consideration the critical situation of our country. This assemblage, comprising, as it did, some of the greatest minds of the country, and men conspicuous for their ability in all the higher walks of life—the bench, the bar, the clergy, statecraft, finance, and the manufacturing interest being all represented—were enabled to bring to the consideration of the topic before them that mature reflection, and careful, dispassionate deliberation, which are the fruits only of rare sagacity and profound wisdom. Good faith forbids us to say more, and we have no desire to be premature, but we think we may venture to add, that it was decided to hold, at an early day, a grand National council, to sit at some central point, and to be composed of delegates from every section of the Union. We will not pursue the subject further at present, but we cannot refrain from observing that, the fact that these gentlemen, whose names are synonyms for all that is great, wise, and patriotic, should devote their energies to devise means to avert the storm that threatens the safety of the ship of state, is one of the most hopeful signs that an era of concord is at hand, when sectionalism, radicalism, and demagogism in every shape and form, will meet a merited doom, and be banished forever from the Legislative halls of a free, united, and prosperous people.

"It is but just to state that the idea and inception of this proposed National conference, which will doubtless mark an epoch in our country's history, is due to our fellow-citizen, Hon. Rufus Heath, whom the spontaneous and united voice of the people has designated as the next occupant of the gubernatorial chair of this State. When we see such evidences of enlightened patriotism, such an unselfish love of country on the part of a gentleman whose wealth and position are a sufficient guarantee that he is actuated by no desire for personal aggrandizement or ambitious motive, we do not wonder that his countrymen, without distinction of party, turn instinctively towards him as the proper leader and councillor in this hour of trial, when, if ever, sound statesmanship and disinterested devotion to the welfare of the whole country are needed. And while we know that it will be no easy matter to prevail upon Mr. Heath to run for the office, and that he would, with extreme reluctance, give up his retirement and important occupations, and could only be moved by a strong sense of duty to again enter the arena of public life, we feel that the people have the right to ask him, in this exigency, to so far sacrifice his personal interests and inclinations, and yield to their wishes, by accepting a post which he, of all others, is best fitted, to fill—that of GOVERNOR OF THE STATE OF NEW JERSEY."

This article had the good fortune to attract the notice of the metropolitan sheets, who commented on the purposes of the ex-Federal dignitary and his friends in various terms. The radical press poked facetiousness at the venerable statesmen; called them fossils; and compared them to the famous tailors of Tooley Street; but whose fault was it that the great Peace Congress resulted in unsuccess, and that the well-meant efforts of its members were fruitless? Whose, but that of those perverse spirits who would not recognize the fact that "Canaan was cursed," and that it was flying in the face of Providence and against Holy Writ, to meddle with his cursedness in any way?

VII.

Mr. Heath was very well satisfied with the result of his dinner-party. It had enabled him to appear in the light of a leading and prominent public man. He could in the future refer to the views he had propounded on that occasion, as the origin of the memorable "Peace Congress," whereby the demon of discord was banished forever from the councils of the nation, and the North and South were reconciled to remain perpetually locked in a fraternal embrace. Then the opportune time would follow when his great work, the "Federal Code," would be accepted by an admiring people as a complement to the Constitution, and an additional band to unite indissolubly the fasces of the Union. The prospect was brilliant and flattering, and dizzy eminences of fame bewildered him. But there was much to be done. It was the hour for action, and with fervent enthusiasm he set to work. He opened a correspondence with every prominent public man in the country, every prominent conservative man of course, on the necessity of casting aloof from old organizations and framing one better adapted to meet the exigencies of the period.

The crisis was imminent, and prompt measures to avert the peril were imperative. A movement had been inaugurated, of which ex-President ——— was at the head, which required the adhesion of every true lover of his country, etc., etc. This was about the burden of every despatch, and Mr. Frisbee, Mr. Heath's secretary, was almost distracted with the increased amount of writing and multiplicity of letters. Meanwhile Mr. Heath did not slacken in his efforts to obtain the candidature for Governor. He wrote numerous articles for the *Sentinel*, of like tenor to the one we have quoted, in advocacy of his claim to the nomination, and wherein, likewise, he showed no desire to emulate the violet. Senator Rangle, who had been much flattered by Mr. Heath's advances, was appealed to and promised his aid. John Peter, whose peculiar temperament was decidedly antipathetic to labors at the desk, was made serviceable in a different way. He was the go-between at primary elections and nominating convention, to fee agents and distribute largess. His chief mission, however, was to court popularity in Belton and the adjoining towns; for it will be remembered that the Hon. Rufus Heath, despite many munificent benefactions and public-spirited acts, was anything but a favorite with his neighbors. No amount of generosity on his part could countervail the effects of his ill-concealed airs of superiority, and patronizing suavity towards them, and wounded self-esteem never forgets nor forgives. Mr. Heath was unaware of the prevalence of this feeling against him, and his instructions to his son were intended simply to placate his open and avowed opponents. In particular was he anxious to conciliate George Gildersleeve. That individual, to be sure, was, as he expressed it, a "dyed-in-the-wool" Democrat, but Mr. Heath argued that at the forthcoming election old issues would be in a great measure abandoned, and he hoped, if not able to obtain Gildersleeve's support, to at least secure his neutrality. George, in truth, would have been a powerful auxiliary, for apart from the large number of men in his employment, who all liked him as a fair and liberal "boss," his bluff, hail-fellow ways won the hearts of the hard-handed everywhere; and he could control more votes than any other man in the county. No wonder, then, that John Peter suddenly became very deferential to him when he met him at Hank Bird's livery stable; no wonder that he solicited George's opinion on the merits of a new trotter, and even came down to the Archimedes Works for a social chat, where, meeting Mark, he actually shook hands with him, offered a cigar, and inquired in a pleasant way how he was "getting along." So astounded was Mark at these unexpected amenities, that he did not know how to take them; but his surprise over, he replied with equal friendliness, not being one to harbor resentment when a show of placation was made—especially when it came from Edna Heath's brother. So the two young men had a pleasant smoke together, recalled reminiscences of their school days; of old Pugwash, who kept the academy, and of the great conspiracy in which Jack was the ringleader, to thrash old Pugwash, when the boys signed a round-robin (an awful compact), with red ink in lieu of blood, that fluid—although the proper one to have used under the circumstances—not being readily procurable; and how old Pugwash, getting hold of the round-robin, turned the tables on the conspirators by flogging them one and all soundly. These and many similar incidents were talked over until all constraint wore off, and when they separated, Mark felt convinced that he had greatly misjudged Jack Heath, and was much pleased at the reconciliation. He told his sister-in-law that evening, when relating the circumstance of their meeting, that Jack was as good-hearted a fellow at bottom as ever lived, the only trouble with him being his inclination to drink.

"Dear, dear, what a pity!" said Mrs. Gildersleeve, whose sympathies were instantly aroused. "I've noticed signs of it for some time, and feel so sorry for him. He has grown so fleshy for a young man, and his face is always so flaming red. Such a beautiful complexion as he used to have, too, when a boy —and to think that it is all owing to this dreadful, dreadful habit of drinking! If he would only consent to join our Band of Hope. Don't you think, Mark, you might persuade him to join? or do you think it would be better to have Brother Close speak to him on the subject first?"

Mark shook his head dubiously at these suggestions, as if he mistrusted his ability or that of the entire Band of Hope, to say nothing of Brother Close, to induce Jack Heath to falter in his devotion to strong waters.

"I'm afraid it's inherited, sister Margaret," said he. "They say he had a grand-uncle who died from the effects of drink, and that his grandfather, old Mr. Obershaw, had a great propensity that way, and that the only thing that saved him was his stinginess. Much as he loved liquor, he loved money more, and seldom drank it except at somebody else's expense."

"Well, my child, let us not judge lest we be judged. Old Mr. Obershaw no doubt did a great many good deeds that we know nothing about, and as he is now in the hands of One who is all-wise and merciful, it does not become us to pass judgment on his memory. I don't see why it is that people are so censorious; I should think that after all the money that Mr. Obershaw spent in building that church and endowing it, that every sensible person would be convinced that he was a Christian, and I'm sure no one could find fault with the way in which the money he saved is being used, for there is not an institution, or a society, or object of any kind, that the Heaths don't give to."

"That may all be, sister Margaret, and it's very praiseworthy, no doubt. All I said, or meant to say, was that I didn't think Jack Heath was so much to blame for drinking, as he inherited the propensity from his grandfather, who they say had the reputation of being a hard drinker."

"Well, I suppose we shall all have to answer for ourselves," replied Mrs. Gildersleeve, reflectively. "And very likely it's his misfortune and not his fault."

The worthy lady's capacity for forgiveness and charity was unbounded; far more ready, too, to defend than to censure, and she doubtless would have had a good word for Satan himself, had his sable majesty been captured and arraigned for judgment.

VIII.

Month after month passed away, and Mark had not dared to repeat his visit at the Cliff. Gladly would he have done so, however, could he have found any plausible pretext. One important point, however, was gained. He had learned that Edna Heath was not the inaccessible princess he had imagined; and moreover, enjoyed the extreme gratification of knowing, or rather feeling, that she was aware of his existence—that she actually remembered, and even noticed him, when he met her at the church-porch on Sundays. These opportunities were almost the only ones he had of seeing her, but the smile and bow with which she recognized him were enough to fill his heart with pleasure during the intervening week. Occasionally when at work he would hear the well-known din of the Heath equipage dashing up Main Street in all the pomp of its domestics in drab liveries, and Dalmatian dogs, and his pulse would quicken, if through his window he caught a momentary glimpse of Edna among the occupants of the vehicle. He failed not to take his evening strolls towards the Cliff; to pass and repass the huge iron gates that seemed to bar him from his dearest hopes; and to linger about, indulging in all those absurd, preposterous fancies that addle the pates of all true lovers.

Summer came, and Edna went off with the Mumbies on a long tour through the White Mountains and Canada. During her absence, how desolate and dreary the world seemed to Mark! Belton became unbearable, and he wandered about its streets in a frame of mind compared to which Marius' feelings amid the ruins of Carthage were bliss. It was in one of these melancholy fits that he composed his elegiac stanzas, entitled *Love's Coronach*, and commencing with these lugubrious lines:

> Shadows from the pluméd pall,
> Enwrap my soul in woe,
> My life, my hope, my all
> Is gone! And every poignant throe
> etc., etc., etc.

But when she returned, the world seemed to recover its glory, life its spice, and he was happy in being near her, even if he did not see her. When autumn came, and the grove near the Falls and the maples along the river road were gorgeous with brilliant hues, Mark took long walks along the Passaic-side, chiefly to meet Miss Heath, who rode often on horseback, and went dashing along at a pace that the groom in attendance had difficulty in keeping up with. She always found time, however, to acknowledge Mark's salute, as he stood staring in respectful admiration at the lithe, graceful figure, so smart in dark riding habit, small white collar and blue silk cravat. He was selfish enough to wish at those times that her horse would bolt over the bank into the river, or do something that would give him a chance to rescue her life at the peril of his own, and so prove his devotion. Fortunately, perhaps, for the young lady, no such opportunity occurred, and our hero was obliged to content himself with less demonstrative worship and vent his passion in scribbling poetic numbers.

The shortened days and inclement weather of winter curtailed Mark's rambles, and his evenings were spent with his piano and books at home, or with his briar-wood pipe and chess at Dr. Wattletop's.

One evening as he sat down to tea in the little basement dining-room, his sister-in-law, with a significant smile, laid an elegant envelope by the side of his plate. "There, Mark," said she, "there is something that will please you, I've no doubt."

He opened the envelope with a little trepidation, and found it to contain, as he had half-suspected, an engraved request from Miss Heath, for the pleasure of his company at "The Cliff," on a certain evening.

"When it came this afternoon," said Mrs. Gildersleeve, "I was in such a flutter. Bridget was out to see her sick sister, and I was washing the dinner things when the bell rang. I just took time to dry my hands and ran to the door, for I expected as much as could be that it was one of the men from the Works that your brother said he would send to fix the grate, and I was so confused when I saw it was a stranger—the young man with a cockade on his hat that follows Miss Heath when she goes out horseback riding—I don't know whether you have ever noticed him or not?"

Mark said he thought he had; and his brother remarked that it was another of those English liveried flunkeys that that old aristocrat, Rufe Heath, had imported to demoralize our democratic institutions.

"George," said Mrs. Gildersleeve, reproachfully, "you shouldn't talk in that way, my dear. Mr. Heath does a great deal of good—a great deal; and as for the young man, I'm sure he was very respectful and well-behaved, indeed. I don't know, though, what he must have thought, for I must have looked very untidy, and I was so confused and flushed that I never once thought of asking him whether he would walk in and sit down, which wasn't a bit polite or hospitable on my part. I hope, Mark, you will accept this invitation, for you should certainly go out in society more than you do. I do wish you had been with us the other evening at Mrs. Sniffen's tea-party. I don't know when I have had such a delightful time. Bishop White was there, and the new minister who has been stationed lately at the Furnaces—the Rev. Mr.

Rousemup. His wife has a beautiful voice, and she sang 'Plunged in a Gulf of Dark Despair' so sweetly, that I'm sure there couldn't have been a dry eye present. I know you would have enjoyed it. But lately you have taken to staying in your room too much; you seem to have given up the Debating Society altogether and never go anywhere, except it is to Dr. Wattletop's, and I must confess that I don't half like it. The doctor, to be sure, is one of the kindest and best souls in the world, but he has such very queer notions. They even go so far as to say that he is a freethinker. Now I would be very sorry to believe that of any one; but he says such very strange things, if the reports are true, and Brother Close told me that Mrs. Slocum told him, that her nephew, James Cudlipp, said that when he lived at old Mrs. Bradbury's, and her brother died, he heard the doctor with his own ears say at the funeral, that when people became more civilized, they would burn the remains of the dead and preserve their ashes in marble urns, instead of burying them in the earth. Now, I do think such an idea as that is shocking and perfectly dreadful."

"Well, Maggie," put in her husband, as he buttered a fresh biscuit, "every man to his trade. Dr. Wattletop ain't no dominie, and don't pretend to be, but his head's level on physic, and he's no slouch of a sawbones, either. When he cut off Sammy Tooker's leg I timed him, and he had it all done clean in ten minutes and fourteen seconds by my stop-watch, and Sammy's brother said it was the best job of the kind he ever saw done; and he ought to know, being a butcher himself. Why, Pokemore, that you think is the greatest doctor in the world, I'll bet would have taken hours to do it, and made a botch of it after all. The only fault I have to find with Wattletop is, that he's such a pig-headed John Bull."

Mark ventured a few words in defence of his friend the doctor, and endeavored to allay the rising apprehensions of Mrs. Gildersleeve in regard to his imbibing any unwholesome opinions from the eccentric physician.

"Now, Mark," continued Mrs. Gildersleeve, "I do hope you will spruce up, and make yourself as agreeable as possible at Miss Heath's party. I'll say this for her, that there isn't a nicer, sweeter, or more charitable girl in all Belton than she is. Mrs. Sniffen says that she never calls upon her for any contribution for any object whatever, but what she gets all and more than she asks for; and I do believe she supplies every sick person and funeral in the town with hot-house grapes and flowers. Then she's so very lady-like too. Dear me, if I were a young man—well, I should think you'd feel very much pleased at this invitation, especially as you never took any pains to make yourself agreeable to the family. But then, to be sure, Edna Heath is kind to every one, and I do believe that every man, woman, and child in Belton loves her."

Mark felt as if he could not see the necessity for that, and, if it were so, as if the population of the town had audaciously conspired to infringe on his province.

His brother, as he rose from table, also proffered advice on the subject, "If you can hang up your hat in that house, Mark, you're made for life. She'll have more dollars than you can shake a stick at, or know what to do with. Never mind the old man; there's a good deal of nonsense in Rufe Heath's airs, and he's mild as milk if he finds you aint anyway awed. Keep a stiff upper lip —don't be cowed, and you're bound to win. Whatever you do, though, be independent—independent as a hog on ice, and they'll like you all the better for it. That's my advice. Time I was off to the Lodge."

Mrs. Gildersleeve did not entirely approve of her husband's way of putting it, and observed, "As to what your brother says, Mark, about Miss Heath's fortune, or her father's fortune, I know you never would be actuated by any motives in regard to that. Miss Heath, I'm sure, will be a treasure and prize to any man even if she never has a penny in the world."

"Very likely," said Mark, affecting indifference. "Miss Heath is certainly a very pleasant and refined young lady."

"Indeed, she is," said Mrs. Gildersleeve, emphatically, "and more than that, a very good young lady."

Mark's gratification at receiving the invitation was instantly dampened, when he reflected that he could not avail of it without exposing himself to unfavorable comparison in the eyes of one whom he was most desirous of pleasing. The old feeling of false shame, the morbid sensitiveness in regard to his lameness, revived; and he dreaded to challenge criticism in an assemblage where he longed to shine. Hence it was with a sharp pang of mortified vanity and disappointment that he set about writing a "regret," alleging as an excuse for not being able to accept Miss Heath's invitation, the conventional fib, a prior engagement. Twice he wrote such a missive, and each time tore it up when in the struggle between sense and self-love the former gained the ascendancy; but in the end that exaggerated self-importance which leads us to believe the rest of the world vastly interested in our haps and mishaps, our appearance and position—this infatuation triumphed, and the "regret" was despatched.

"Well, Mark," said Mrs. Gildersleeve on the appointed evening, "Miss Heath's party comes off to-night, don't it? From all I hear it's going to be a grand affair. They say there have been I don't know how many hundred invitations sent out, and some are coming even from New York."

"So much the better, then, for I don't think I shall be missed," said Mark with a forced smile.

Mrs. Gildersleeve dropped her work and looked at him in surprise. "Missed! You don't mean to say that you are not going?"

Mark looked rather confused. "I do mean to say so. I—I don't feel like it."

"Dear me, you're not sick, I hope?" inquired Mrs. Gildersleeve with a look of concern.

"No, sister, no—but I'm not in the humor to go."

"Why, really, I'm so surprised and sorry. I thought you would certainly take advantage of such an invitation, for I know you would enjoy it very much if you went. There is nothing ails you, is there, Mark?" said Mrs. Gildersleeve, repeating her inquiry.

"No, sister Margaret, no," replied Mark with a little impatience, and to escape his sister-in-law's inquisitive solicitude, he withdrew to his room. He took up his guitar and tried to thrum the *Jota Aragonesa*, but there was no melody there to soothe his troubled breast. He skimmed over a page or two of Burton's "Anatomy of Melancholy," that Dr. Wattletop had recommended him to read, but his feelings were too much in consonance with the subject treated of to be diverted by it, and he threw the book aside, filled his briar-wood pipe, and sought consolation in Killikinnick. Even that resource failed him, and the fire in the bowl died away unheeded. Then to shake off the tristful thoughts he paced his room, but the old wound inflicted by Edna's cruel commiseration seemed to bleed afresh, and the remembrance of that bitter pity unceasingly returned, until chagrin gave place to anger vented in fierce execrations on his halting foot, alternated with lamentations on his unfortunate condition. He believed he could have borne almost any other bodily infirmity better, and would gladly have given his right arm to walk as other men. What an effort it had cost him to deny himself the inestimable pleasure of beholding the object of his adoration in all the pride of her beauty! And yet, why had he done so? Although imperfect in a trivial degree, would he, after all, suffer much in comparison with others? Byron, the splendid Byron, was lame, and so was Walter Scott, and were they not the idols of society? Would her glance fall that evening on a handsomer face? He stopped before a mirror, that reflected eyes full of superb fire, and a brow as fine as any that ever adorned child of Hellas, and he smiled with gratified vanity, like a brainless coquette. But instantly ashamed of his weakness, he turned away, drew on his overcoat, and sought the streets to distract him from unwholesome reveries. Unwittingly his feet followed the accustomed path, and he was half way to the Cliff before he discovered his absence of mind. He would have retraced his steps and gone in another direction, but an irresistible impulse urged him on.

It was a fine frosty night in February. There was no moon, but the myriad of stars that studded the dark sky glinted like gems, and the atmosphere was bracing and exhilarating. Mr. Heath's residence presented a brilliant scene. The lamps on the gate-posts, those hanging in the porch, and the many illuminated windows shed rays that tinted to brilliance the snow covering the lawn and flecking the dark evergreens; while here and there a pendant icicle or the rime-covered bough of a tree coruscated like a crystal prism. Mark stood for some time in contemplation. He heard the sound of rippling music, the muffled patter of hoofs and creaking of wheels over the crisp snow as carriage after carriage deposited its burden at the porch. At length, as if drawn by some invisible magnet, he went stealthily up the avenue, slinking behind the evergreens, and endeavored to gain a position whence to look unobserved through the drawing-room windows. He felt like a spy, and started at every sound with fear of being discovered, but the temptation to see Edna was too powerful, and curiosity overcame his scruples. Climbing on the ledge of a conservatory, he could, by placing his feet on the chamfered stone-work of the building, reach the level of a large bay-window at one end of the drawing-room. An inside sash was partly open, so that he could both see and hear through the blinds and remain unperceived. He now witnessed a sight that soon banished his melancholy, for joy in its fellows has a contagious influence over youth difficult to resist, and he regretted the foolish resolve he had made to abstain from joining the party. They were nearly all young people; among them, however, many strangers to Belton. Mrs. Applegate, who matronized them, rustled about in a voluminous dress of moire-antique, and young Mrs. Heath sat in an easy-chair in one corner, resplendent with diamonds and languidly rattling a Spanish fan, while her lord stood leaning in a doorway looking sulky, bored, and uncomfortable as he fumbled away at a pair of tight gloves. The Rev. Spencer Abbott, in the neatest of clerical attire, was sauntering leisurely from group to group, with his hands behind his back and an air of mild benignity on his pallid countenance. Present, too, were Will Hull and his sister Constance, the Judge's grandchildren, and the Mumbies; Ada, Bob, and the younger brother, Decatur, a sprig from the Naval Academy, evidently under the effects of his gilt buttons and embroidered foul-anchors. Mark was not long in discovering Edna. Her fair face was heightened in color, and beaming with joy. His eyes followed her eagerly amid the couples that whirled swiftly by, and he caught glimpses of her satin-shod feet, arched like an Arab maid's. The music ceased, and the confused chatter of many voices arose. Close by him came a group of girls prattling together, and discussing their partners with the frankness of guileless maidenhood. Scraps of their conversation reached him. One of the girls was Constance Hull. Said she, "I do so like to dance with Alfred, he keeps such excellent time."

"But then he parts his hair in the middle, Constance, and I think that is so horrid. Did you notice his malachite sleeve-buttons and topaz studs? Wretched taste, isn't it? They say he is engaged too—dear me! I don't see how any one could marry a person with so little idea of what is becoming. Do tell me who that gentleman is that was dancing with Edna? I do think he is too handsome for anything."

"Why, don't you know? Why, it's Sarah Carver's cousin, Fred Spooner—isn't he splendid? He came all the way from Boston. He's quite smitten with Edna, and I know she admires him."

Mark's eavesdropping was sufficiently punished by this intelligence, but he was destined to suffer still further when he saw Edna dancing again with this admirer, who was a tall blooming fellow, all ease and grace. He felt a pang of jealousy when he saw them after the dance promenading together; Spooner chatting with animation and proud of his partner, while she looked at him evidently pleased and amused at his remarks. They came directly towards the window and took seats in the recess. Miss Hull and her companions had left the spot, and the young fellow probably desired to enjoy a *tête-à-tête*. He was pleading for a flower from Edna's nosegay. "I beg and beseech you to bestow upon me a bud from your beautiful bouquet."

"Dear me," said Edna, "what a quantity of B's!"

"Yes, quite a swarm, attracted by your excessive sweetness, of course," smirked Spooner, pleased at his effort at wit; while Mark, who had caught every word, thought it very silly, not to say impertinent.

Edna selected a rosebud, which she gave to her companion, who placed it in his button-hole. "I shall keep it forever, Miss Heath."

"Indeed, how long is your forever?"

"As long as memory holds a seat in this distracted brain, and longer. I'll take it home, and when it wilts I'll press it in my prayer-book."

"Where you are sure never to see it again," remarked Edna.

"Merciless Miss Heath!—Excessively warm, though, here, isn't it? Hadn't I better throw open the top blind?" and with that he pushed it open, causing

Mark to shrink aside to avoid discovery, "Warm as a dog-day, isn't it? Talking of dogs, are you fond of 'em, Miss Heath? I've got just the smallest black-and-tan—well, he don't weigh over twenty-three ounces, and if you would only accept him, I'd be so delighted. I think the world of him, and to know that he was constantly near you, would make me the happiest feller in existence. To be sure his ears aren't cropped yet. Do you like cropped black-and-tans? Or if you'd prefer a Spitz? I've got a real nice Spitz, but he's snappish. Spitzes are apt to be snappish, haven't you noticed? But then he's just as good a ratter as any black-and-tan you ever saw. When you come to Boston, if you and Sarah Carver will only come to Roxbury—"

By this time, the Rev. Spencer Abbott, who was on his third round of inspection, came up with a graceful droop to the couple: "Reposing after the fatigue of the dance, I presume, Miss Edna? What a beautiful bouquet! Really, Miss Edna, I think you have the most beautiful bouquet of any young lady present. Miss Mumbie has an elegant one, but the blending of hues is hardly so artistic in hers. Yours, ah—presents to the eye of the observer such a—such an exquisite juxtaposition of colors. How fragrant, too! Roses—heliotrope—Dame Nature's jewels. What a singularly beautiful conceit and myth that was of the ancients, that roses sprang from the blood of Venus. Dear me, there's quite a draught here. Ah! I see—a window down—aren't you afraid of catching cold? Lovely as a Lapland night—a majestic one, truly! How forcibly is one reminded of Milton's noble lines:

"'How glows the firmament with living sapphires
Hesperus that led—'"

Fortunately for Miss Heath, who feared the parson was about to favor her with a book or two of "Paradise Lost," Bob Mumbie came up to claim her for a redowa, and the Rev. Spencer Abbott sauntered off and betook himself to a critical examination, accompanied with poetical comments, of Mercedita Heath's fan. Mark noticed that Edna had left her handkerchief on the tripod near the window, and as Fred Spooner had darted away with Miss Mumbie and the coast was clear, a sudden and uncontrollable desire seized him to possess this handkerchief. Yielding to the impulse, and without further reflection, he raised the lower sash of the window, crouched under the tripod, snatched the coveted article, and frightened at his temerity, instantly withdrew. He hastened homeward, pressing the bit of cambric to his lips, and rhapsodizing as he went along like a demented Strephon. When he arrived home, he found his sister-in-law sitting up for him. She noticed that he looked somewhat flushed and disturbed, but as he seemed to avoid her scrutinizing eyes, she did not question him.

What a night of fever and torment he passed! The conflicting emotions that agitated him banished sleep. The delicate web he had filched lay under his burning cheek and throbbing temples; its subtle perfume intoxicated him, evoking ecstatic glamour and vivid visions of Edna's face radiant with joy and beauty. Then jealousy swept the chords of his sensitive nature, as he recalled the smiles bestowed on his presumed rival, and bitter curses on his defective foot followed, until, in the struggle between tumultuous passion and reason, his better sense triumphed, and tears bedewed his eyes—tears of vexation that he should be so childish, so vain, and envious. As he lay thus, his door was softly opened, and he heard the voice of his sister-in-law inquiring if he were indisposed?

"No, no, Sister Margaret, thank you. Please don't disturb yourself."

"I heard a noise, and feared you might be taken ill."

"No, thank you. Please leave me." His heart was stilled at this fresh evidence of tender solicitude on the part of one, who had been to him all that a mother could be. He contrasted her calm, cheerful ways and unselfishness with his egotism and discontent. Repentant, he prayed to be forgiven, and soon after fell asleep.

IX.

The next morning his jaded face told plainly of the mental struggle he had undergone. He took up Edna's handkerchief, pressed it to his lips reverentially, as if it had been a shred from the robe of a saint, and then reflected how he should return it to its owner without exciting suspicion or betraying his impertinent freak. "She's a seraph and I'm an idiot!" was his pithy conclusion, "An egregious and presumptuous idiot! If she knew all, what a laughing-stock I should be to her! I will not think of her again, but as one to worship. What am I, or what have I done to merit any favor from her? What could she ever possibly see in me? I must and shall try to forget her. No —I would be very ungrateful to do that. But I must only esteem, respect, and worship her at a distance; and if she prefers that tall, girlish, dancing-Jack, why—no, I have no right to think that. Well, I must return the handkerchief in some way, and then we shall be henceforth as strangers—not exactly strangers—but I will only think of her as an acquaintance."

He held to this resolution for at least a week, rigidly schooling his heart to submission; but alas, this resolve met the fate of its kind, for on the eighth day he accidentally saw the disturber of his peace, and away to the four winds of heaven went all humility and self-abnegation. And he met her of all places— in a workshop. Edna happened to be passing the Archimedes Works on her return from the stationer's, when the proprietor, who was looking out of the window of his counting-room, caught a glimpse of her, and going out accosted the young lady, much to her surprise, with a request to walk into his office a moment as he wanted to consult her. She good-naturedly complied, and went into the room, where the old book-keeper bustled about to dust a chair for her, and the junior clerks were rather distracted from their labors by the apparition of such a visitor.

"What I wanted was to ask your opinion of a new cart I've been getting, Miss Heath," said George Gildersleeve.

"A cart, Mr. Gildersleeve?" repeated Edna.

"Yes, a cart de visit."

"Oh, a photograph," said Edna.

"Yes. Mrs. Gildersleeve's sister, Mrs. Roberts, who lives in Trenton, hasn't got one of mine, and I promised to send her one; so I've been getting some struck off. Now here are the proofs of three different kinds. Snopple got 'em up; and as you're a young lady of taste, the thought struck me, as I saw you go by, that you'd be a capital judge and I want your opinion as to which is the best."

Edna, rather amused, scrutinized the pictures that represented George looking like a comely bulldog, and said that she thought they were all fair likenesses.

"But which is the best? This one's a new attitood for me. I never had one taken in that way before. Suppose you were picking one out for yourself, which would you choose?"

To please him, Edna gave the preference to one over the others.

"Well—I don't know but you're right," said George reflectively, as he admired the one selected. "I'll have a lot of these struck off, and when they're finished, I won't forget to send you one, unless you prefer one of these full faces."

Edna said no—that the first one mentioned would do, and thanked him. Noticing the horse-shoe over the fire-place, she inquired whether it were hung there to keep off witches, or for good-luck.

"Good-luck?—no, not exactly, although I shouldn't wonder if it had brought us good-luck. As for the witches, you see yourself it don't keep off the most dangerous kind—the young and beautiful ones," replied George, with an attempt to be gallant.

"Oh thank you, Mr. Gildersleeve; you're very flattering indeed," replied Edna with a smile.

"I wouldn't take five hundred dollars for that horse-shoe, Miss Heath," resumed George proudly.

"Indeed," said Edna.

"No, nor a thousand. That there shoe that you see there, came off Gineral George Washington's horse just afore he fought the great battle of Trenton. My grandfather shod him anew himself, and kept this old shoe. The forge was right here, and that chimney-stack was part of it. That's the story, Miss Heath; and at that time your great-grandfather, old Whitman Obershaw, ran a saw-mill just along by the head of the rapids, ten rods beyond the foot-bridge, and I've heard my father say often enough that the old man was a pretty hard case, and tight about half the time."

Edna, though nettled and confused for a moment at these free reflections on her maternal ancestor, could not refrain from smiling at the unconcerned way in which they were imparted.

"To think how you've grown lately, Miss Heath," continued the blunt iron-master; "why, it seems to me but last week that you and Ada Mumbie and

Judge Hull's granddaughter, were little bits of things, stopping, as you came from school with your arms full of books, to peep in at the foundry, half-scared, with your eyes as big as saucers. Well, time passes, and things change, and the Works are different now from what they was then. We've enlarged them considerable. Have you been through them lately? No—well, would you like to go? Without bragging a great deal, I don't think we can be beat much in our line in the world." George's world, by the bye, was bounded by New York and Trenton, and consisted chiefly of Belton.

Edna said she had been in Mr. Mumbie's paper-mill, and had been much interested, and thought she would like to see the Works, if convenient.

The establishment was a model one of its kind. In extent and completeness it had no superior, if a rival, in the country, and the owner took a justifiable pride in showing it. It covered several acres, and the buildings were fine ones of brick, with slate roofs, and some pretensions to architectural beauty. Gildersleeve led Edna first to a detached room well lighted, neat, and quiet as a boudoir, with a vine trailing over the glass roof. This was the engine-room, where tireless monsters of polished steel and brass, with gigantic fly-wheels and darting pistons, worked noiselessly and exactly as a chronometer, and enabled the proprietor to be consistently independent of the water-power if he chose.

Then they went to the foundry—a fearful place, where begrimed men, hideous in the glare of furnace flames, ran dragging pots of molten iron like Cyclops, while the ground trembled beneath the titanic blows of trip-hammers; next to the boiler-shop, where Edna was almost deafened; and to the machine-shop, a long room filled with whirling shafts, gearing, and lathes innumerable, where she was greatly amazed at the wonderful planes that sliced off glossy ribbons of steel, and the powerful shears and punches that cut the tough metal like pasteboard. Edna was much impressed by what she saw. She was struck with the many evidences around her of human skill and power. The admirable adaptation and complete control of superhuman forces seemed to her sublime, and she wondered that the presiding genius of such a marvellous palace of art could be the ordinary mortal beside her. Had Edna been an older judge of human nature, she would have discovered that George Gildersleeve was anything but an ordinary man. True, he was uneducated, rough, overweeningly vain, without tact; his fibre coarse and vigorous as a buffalo's, but his tenacity of will, love of order, vigilance, and business shrewdness were remarkable, and capable of conquering success in almost any department of life. His vigilance and love of order had not escaped Edna's notice, for as they went along, she remarked that his searching glances were directed everywhere, and she was amused to see him pick up a nail from the floor, and at another time reprimand an apprentice severely because a small bit of cotton waste had been left on the bright oil-cloth of the engine-room.

"Who suggested the name of your Works, Mr. Gildersleeve?" said Edna.

"Oh! that was Mark's notion. When we rebuilt them, I wanted to name them the George Washington Works, but I concluded that that would be too personal, so I let Mark have his own way, and he named them after Archy Medes. This Archy Medes was an engineer of ancient times, who discovered something in a bath-tub, I don't exactly remember what, but Mark can tell you if you want to know. There he is over there. See him, Miss Heath?"

They were in the finishing-shop at the time, and George pointed to the farther end, where Mark was, but with his back towards them so that Edna had not recognized the young man. He was standing with his coat off and a plan in his hand, giving directions to a group of workmen.

"He's setting up an improved lathe for driving wheels—a new idea of his own," explained George.

Edna stood watching Mark. He was very intently occupied moving hither and thither, now stooping and scrutinizing, then, with rolled-up sleeves, dexterously wielding hammer and chisel. His dark, delicate features reflected the keen concentrated play of the faculties, and revealed an expression of intellectual beauty that Edna had not before noticed. She thought she had never seen so handsome a young man. Mark unconsciously had made a more favorable impression in his homely guise than he ever could have done in a ball-room. At length he perceived her, and could not repress a look of confusion. Giving a few orders to the workmen, he drew on his coat and came forward to meet Edna with an embarrassed air.

"An unexpected pleasure, Miss Heath," he said, with a feeble attempt to be distant in accordance with the noble resolves he had recorded.

"The pleasure is with me, I'm certain, for I've been very much delighted and instructed. I know all about locomotives, and steam, and boilers, and I am indebted for it all to your brother, who was kind enough to invite me to see the Works, and explain everything. But I am very much afraid that I have interrupted you."

"A very pleasant interruption; for it's so seldom we are favored with the presence of ladies here, that we appreciate their visits correspondingly," replied Mark gallantly. Her pleasant, winning way had disarmed him completely, and he was at her mercy at once. Edna then bid the brothers good-by, remarking that she had tarried too long and must return home.

Of course Mark begged to be permitted to escort her, as evening was approaching, to which request she graciously assented. The most attractive trait, perhaps, in our heroine's character was her frankness of speech and manner proceeding from a nature singularly free from affectation. We say singularly, as it is well known that the best of our young ladies are not entirely exempt from little artificial airs and graces especially, if like the subject of these remarks, they occupy a position in society somewhat analogous to that of a duke's daughter among gentry. This artlessness was the more remarkable in the child of a family noted for its intense pride and pretensions. Edna was the exception; simple in her tastes, and ignoring the deference conceded to wealth to an extent that would have amazed her father, could he have spared enough attention from state affairs to study his daughter's character. Naturally, when a young lady of position remains unimpressed by people's purses, and is as courteous to the poor as to the rich, she cannot fail to become a favorite with all; and it is no wonder that the master of the Archimedes Works remarked to Gregg, the old book-keeper, after she was gone, that if he were a young man seeking a wife, she'd be just the girl he'd pick out, and that Gregg said she would be his choice too; nor that Knatchbull, the foreman, concurred, and added, that she was a "natty lass," to which George said, "That's so, and thorough-bred," and told Gregg to make a minute to remind him to send one of his "carts," a three-quarter face, to the young lady, as he had promised, and wouldn't disappoint her for the world.

Meanwhile Mark and Edna were walking on in silence towards the street that led to the latter's home; Mark, in his elation, scarcely knowing how to broach the conversation. Finally he recollected that it would be in order to thank Edna for the invitation she had sent him, and he did so, expressing his great regret at not having been able to avail himself of it, and his appreciation of the intended compliment.

"I think you would have enjoyed yourself," said Edna, "for I believe they all did. There were quite a number of charming young ladies present. Some of them, I think, you would have been pleased to meet."

"Name them, if you please?"

"Well—Miss Carver, from Boston, for one; pretty, accomplished—"

"And wealthy?"

"Pray, why do you ask such a question?"

"Is not that the supreme attraction?"

"What a sentiment for a poet! Do you know, Mr. Gildersleeve; that I never fail to read your verses in the *Sentinel*?"

"Do you, really? You are a true friend, indeed, Miss Heath, to sacrifice yourself to that extent. What an exertion it must be!"

"Indeed, I think some of them very nice. Mr. Abbott, who prides himself on his literary taste, endeavored to be very witty criticising some of your poetry, but Aunt Susan—that's Mrs. Applegate—Mercedita, and I defended you with our utmost ability, and we three decided that it was very nice indeed," said Edna earnestly.

Mark thought that "very nice indeed" was not exactly the verdict he craved, nor were Aunt Susan and Mercedita critics whose judgment would likely bias public opinion, and be considered final. Edna's good opinion was certainly worth having, however; and as for the Rev. Mr. Abbott's attempts at facetiousness, they were undoubtedly prompted by jealousy, and to say the least of it, were very unbecoming in one of his profession, and a disgrace to the cloth.

"Mr. Abbott, though, is a very fine reader," continued Edna, "but I must say I have not a very great opinion of his taste. Would you believe it, he is forever reciting 'Airy, fairy Lillian,' and says it's the finest thing Tennyson ever wrote? Now I think it's very flat, don't you?"

Mark agreed with her, and said it was very flat, very flat indeed. She certainly has taste, thought he, great critical acumen, but I wish she wouldn't call my verses nice.

"You must know," said Edna, who talked on unreservedly, "I'm a very romantic girl in spite of my matter-of-fact way, and read every bit of poetry I come across. In saying that I don't mean to disparage your productions, for as I said, I think some of them real nice and pretty. It may be that my opinion is not worth much, but one piece I read lately struck me as being full of beautiful ideas and similes. I mean those lines addressed to 'Eunomia,' the 'violet-engarlanded' person in 'purple cincture,' who, 'enthroned in the propylon of the temple of Fate, sweeps the lyre with skilful plectrum.' I believe that's the image, is it not?"

"I am afraid you are disposed to amuse yourself by ridiculing my poor efforts," said Mark, puzzled to know whether she were in earnest or not.

"Oh dear me, no. I haven't wit enough to be ironical, and am therefore always compelled to be downright and blunt. Do you know, too, that my ignorance is such that I had to look in the dictionary to find out what plectrum and propylon meant. Do, please, the next time you use such hard words, add explanatory notes at the foot, and oblige all such unlearned people as I."

She said this with a bantering smile that again perplexed Mark and set him reflecting. Now the shortest way to the Cliff was to turn off at Mill Street, which led to the foot-bridge over the falls; but when they came to the corner of that street, instead of turning off Edna kept on, taking the longer way home, and thus prolonging the walk, from which circumstance Mark augured favorably. At least, thought he, she is not tired of my company as yet. Their promenade took them across the public square, a pretentious little triangle of grass-plats inclosed by posts and chains. At one end of this park fronted a fine large old mansion, whose low eaves, broad heavily-panelled door, and ponderous brass knocker denoted work of the last century. It was the homestead of the Hull family, and on the door-jambs were still visible hacks made by the sabres of Knyphausen's Hessians. Mark and his companion had just passed the house when the old Judge came out on the porch to look at the thermometer hanging by the side of his door. How could he fail to notice the youthful couple? Old as he was, and long past the age of frivolity, they interested him, and he stood contemplating the pair until they were out of his sight. As he turned to reënter the house he gave a sigh of regret. How barren seemed all his fame and honors! He would have bartered them all for the return of one hour of the sweet hallucinations of youth so irrevocably passed away. Meanwhile our young people continued their discussion on poetry in general, and Mark's productions in particular, until the young man, assuming a serious expression, said, "You were speaking about the lines to Eunomia. As regards the spirit or intention in which they are composed, I must certainly be credited at least with sincerity. Every line, every thought is an exponent of the author's feelings. They may be awkward, inelegant, or halting, but the words are nevertheless the earnest utterances of the heart."

All this was said fervently, and Edna replied: "I haven't any doubt of it at all. You poets all have some ideal lady-love, I believe, gifted with every possible quality; some ethereal paragon whom you never permit to touch the earth; consequently, I presume you are very much dissatisfied with young ladies as you find them."

"Permit me to say you are much mistaken. My verses were addressed to no imaginary being. Eunomia lives and breathes."

"Indeed! why, now that you have so excited my curiosity, I am afraid I shall not rest satisfied until I learn who this interesting damsel is—this purple-cinctured Eunomia."

"I can gratify you in that respect very readily, if you wish it."

"Well—but—I wouldn't for the world be indiscreet. If it's perfectly permissible. Otherwise, let me remain in ignorance, please." She said this hesitatingly, as if perhaps she had gone too far; or was it Mark's admiring gaze that embarrassed her? For the young man seemed to be oblivious of all but the being beside him, and who could blame him? for Edna, animated by the walk and conversation, looked more beautiful than ever. She wore a round hat wreathed about with a blue veil which contrasted charmingly with her fair complexion, and the satin sheen of her lustrous blonde hair. Mark watched the blithe face, and endeavored to analyze, and impress its beauty indelibly on his memory. What charmed him most was the virginal grace of lips and chin, the pure cheek, and the exquisite contour of the slender white throat. So absorbed was he in his admiration, that the promenade seemed to him incredibly short, in spite of the circuit they had made, for the entrance to Mr. Heath's residence was now near at hand. It was time to part. "I am hesitating," said he, "whether to reveal—if you will not think me presumptuous—after all, no one is better entitled to know the name of the one addressed as 'Eunomia,' than you."

"No one better entitled to know than I?" repeated Edna, as a sudden enlightenment suffused her face with a blush.

"No one; for Eunomia is but another name for Edna. Forgive me, if in seeking for inspiration from your beauty and goodness, I have been too bold in my admiration; but Edna," he added, taking her hand and gazing at her with appealing ardor, "I have loved you so long and earnestly!"

She lowered her eyes at this declaration, but her hand lingered in his. There was nobody near; he pressed her hand gently to his lips, when she quickly withdrew it, and with a bow, disappeared through the gateway. Mark stood for a moment as if amazed at his audacity, and then, joyful and happy, walked away as if treading on air, bewitched by the delightful anticipations of newly implanted hope. Sweet anticipation! How full art thou of brilliant illusions and blissful glamour! And yet, without thee, what an insupportable burden would life become! Precious Jack-o'-lantern, that transports the lover, nerves the warrior, cheers the student, and inspires poet and painter!

X.

"Bet you hundred to eighty—hundred dollars to eighty—eighty—old man's 'lected!" were Jack Heath's exclamations, as he stood rather unsteadily in the bar-room of the Obershaw House, thumping his fist on the counter. It was the night before election day, and of course the bar-room of the Obershaw House, the headquarters of Mr. Heath's party, was thronged with politicians and loungers, drinking, smoking, and discussing the chances of the candidates for office; for we should state that the Hon. Rufus Heath had succeeded in his efforts to obtain the nomination for the governorship, as the numerous posters on the dead walls of Belton, headed "CONSERVATIVE UNION NOMINATIONS," staringly announced.

Jack Heath had been for a week on what he called a "tare," and had but just "brought up" at the hotel. He was still a little "sprung," as the bar-tender qualified it, but had an eye to business nevertheless, as he seemed anxious to secure bets on his father's election. "A hundred to eighty—bet any man hundred to eighty old man's 'lected. Come, I'll make it hundred to fifty— fifty, who'll take that?"

"I will—just for a flyer," responded a short red-whiskered man, who kept a livery stable in the town; "I'll take it."

"Put up the ducats, Hank—put 'em up! Here, Bangs, old fel, hold stakes, will you? All right—hundred to fifty more! Who's next man?"

"Here you are," said another individual. "Going to vote for the old man too, but I'll take your offer for the fun o' the thing."

Jack fumbled away at his pocket-book, drawing out the bank-notes and laying them in Bangs the landlord's hand with drunken solemnity and slowness. He found no lack of takers, and soon stripped himself of money to back his father's chances. Then a little contention arose about the count, and Jack indulged in a good deal of abuse and swearing. However, the party being in good humor, coaxed him, and vowed he was the best fellow alive; so Jack, mollified, ordered a basket of champagne to be opened, and "Here's to our next Governor, Rufus Heath!" was drunk with three times three and a "tiger." Then Jack, a little more inebriated, withdrew to play billiards, at which game he was an adept, and in spite of his condition he made some excellent caroms, better than many sober players could achieve; but he also missed some easy shots, and his anger rising at that, he dashed his cue savagely at the table, ripping up the green cloth so that Bangs had it down on the bill against him in no time. Then Jack ordered more wine, telling Bangs to charge it to the old man's account for "'lection spenshes," and again the company were called upon to toast the future Governor of the "Jersey Blues," which they did vociferously.

Now Jack, pulling out his watch, stared at it stupidly for some time, until a dim notion coming to him that he was too tipsy to discriminate between the hands, he requested somebody to tell him the time. "Pas' twelve, eh? Time I was home—mus' go home early—got work to do to-morrow morning—old man's 'lection day."

"Better stay here to-night, Mr. Heath," said the hotel-keeper, who was familiar with Jack's habits. "We'll take good care of you. I've got a nice room all ready and comfortable for you, and you'll be fresh and fine for to-morrow's work."

"All right, Tommy Bangs, old fel. Let's have night-caps all round 'fore we turns in, eh? Whiskey-skins, Bangsey. Stiff, and not too sweet. Charge old man 'lection spenshes."

The whiskey-skins being disposed of, Mr. Bangs and his bar-tender led Jack tenderly up the stairs, and put him away comfortably to bed.

About the time he awoke the next morning the election was in full blast. The population were entirely given over to the business, and Belton was emblazoned with multi-colored placards, calling upon the citizens to "awake," to "arouse," and above all to "rally." Wagons decorated with long muslin strips bearing the name of a prominent candidate, and some watchword of uncertain application, such as "No monopoly," "Working-men's Rights," and the like, were driven about gathering voters, who were stimulated to exercise the right of suffrage in the right direction by the stirring notes of a fish-horn, blown by an active partisan alongside of the driver.

The polls were surrounded by a motley crowd of fellow-citizens, who beset the wayfarer with importunities to vote for this or that candidate; and as each wagon drove up and deposited its load of voters the new-comers were received with hurrahs and friendly hustlings. The master of the Archimedes Works was conspicuous and ubiquitous, shouldering his burly frame through the thickest crowds, jeering his opponents, joking with his friends, and airing his wallet on the slightest provocation. Jack Heath, owing to his exertions on the previous evening, did not make his appearance on the scene of action until mid-day, but his presence infused new vigor in the contest. A crowd of henchmen were at his heels, and the bar of the Obershaw House dispensed strong waters and tobacco, galore and gratuitous, to all the supporters of the "Heath ticket" who chose to partake. And as many so chose, the bar-tender and his assistants had their hands full, you may depend, for the thirst of people who appease it at another's expense is sufficient to appall the stoutest stomach.

As the day waned, the fellow-citizens merry with potations deep disported themselves with antics gay. Individuals were bonneted; ballots, those executors of the freeman's will, were scattered to the winds; and the ticket-distributors who were unlucky enough to be caught in their boxes found themselves suddenly in a topsy-turvy position, heels in the air, and kicking wildly to extricate themselves, to the intense enjoyment of the hilarious and playful electors. At sunset the polls closed, and the citizens who had rallied so nobly repaired to their homes, with the exception of some zealous politicians who remained to learn the result of the voting. The bar-rooms were still tumultuous with the wrangling of excited partisans, and Jack Heath lorded it at the Obershaw House, but he soon succumbed to the fatigues of the day, and was kindly put to bed by considerate Mr. Bangs at an early hour.

The Hon. Rufus Heath remained at home during the eventful day. He had no doubt as to the result of the election, and felt certain that he would carry it. Candidates always feel so. The amazing self-conceit that induces every ticket-holder in a lottery to expect a prize would permit no other supposition than one of success. Still, being a cautious man, he was anxious to have his belief corroborated. Meanwhile so confident was he of the issue, that he employed himself in preparing a draught of his inaugural address, and revolving in his mind a proper disposition of his affairs preparatory to a removal of his home to the capital of the State. He anticipated, too, no little gratification in teaching his opponent a lesson, for he deemed it no less than a piece of impertinence that an obscure village lawyer, who had acquired some cheap fame by vulgar appeals as a stump speaker, should presume to cross swords with him in a contest for position. At length night came, and towards ten o'clock a messenger brought various returns that had been announced, almost all indicating majorities in his favor. He went to bed, but found it difficult to court slumber with such a stake still weighing in the balance. The next morning he became rather uneasy as the minutes passed and no friend came to congratulate him on the result. Mumbie, he certainly expected would have been on hand betimes. The newspaper, too, did not arrive at the usual hour, delayed probably to give the latest results of the canvassing. At length it came, and he saw at a glance from the returns of certain decisive counties that he was defeated.

The editor endeavored to depreciate the importance of these indications by stating that the final result was still in doubt; that later news might alter the complexion of things, etc. But Mr. Heath was not to be deluded by such assertions, and was convinced that he and his party had lost. As the first check in a career of uninterrupted prosperity, it proved a bitter disappointment; so bitter, that he lost his temper—an unusual occurrence for him—swore at James for some trivial offence, snarled at Mrs. Applegate, and snubbed poor Mumbie, who had come rather blunderingly to sympathize with him. To one unaccustomed to obstacles and reverses they come with double severity, and Mr. Heath took his defeat deeply to heart. Friends, to be sure, proffered condolences, advising him to try again; that in the next attempt he would certainly be successful, etc., etc.; but a sense of discouragement had taken possession of him which no sympathy or counsel could remove. Probably the bitterest pill to swallow was the discovery that his own county and town had given a large majority against him. He was much surprised at this, being utterly unconscious of his personal unpopularity. Small comfort he got too from George Gildersleeve, who never spared a beaten adversary, and gripping the patrician's hand when he met him a few days after, bade him be of good cheer in such words as these: "Sorry for you, Heath, but it couldn't be helped. I could have told you how it would be. Too much of the old Democratic leaven about here. This county cooked your mutton, and I carry it in my breeches pocket. Liked to have helped you—you're an old friend; but you can't expect us to desert our life-long principles, scratch our ticket, and go for outsiders when the woolly-heads are getting so rampant. There is no safety in these times but sticking to the old ship. But I wouldn't be down in the mouth about it. If you'll only come round to our side of the house, I'll engage to send a good-looking man of about your size to Trenton or Washington. You ought to be there; you've got the brains, and have forgotten more than half those fellers ever knew; but you ain't the right stripe, that's the trouble, and you're on the wrong track."

Mr. Heath endeavored to take this advice good-humoredly, and attempted a smile at the blunt sallies; but the smile was a forced one, or a "yellow laugh," as the French express it.

XI.

It was long past midnight, and between the small hours that usher in the light of a new day, when the stillness of the mansion on the cliff was broken by a piercing shriek. It was an appalling cry of distress that awoke the slumberers and froze the timid ones to their couches with fear. Mr. Heath sprang from his bed, and ran precipitately to his daughter-in-law's apartment, whence the cry proceeded. Poor Mercedita met him at the door in her night-dress, and in answer to his inquiries pointed in speechless horror at the floor of her dressing-room, where lay stiff and stark the body of her husband!

Jack Heath had come home the previous night for the first time since his fortnight's debauch. He was in a shocking condition, with filthy clothes, and a bad bruise over one eye, resulting, doubtless, from a fall. His wife, incensed at his conduct, refused to speak or notice him; and Jack, still tipsily stupid, threw himself on a lounge in the dressing-room to sleep. During the night he awoke; tormented by the "horrors," and thirsting for some stimulating liquid, he seized a crystal flask of cologne that lay on the toilet-table, and drank it to appease the infernal craving that possessed him. The congested condition of his brain, super-excited by this fiery draught, induced apoplexy, and the stroke was fatal. His wife, asleep in the adjoining room, awoke soon after, and not hearing his usual heavy breathing, was much surprised. She imagined he must have left the room, and after waiting awhile, arose from her bed, went into the dressing-room, where there was a dim light burning, and found that he had fallen from the lounge and lay on the floor. She shook him without effect; raised his arm—it fell rigidly. She tried to arouse him, called him loudly, but the dull ear heard not, for the sleep that bound him knew no waking; and then, as the truth flashed on her, with a shriek she summoned the household. They led her away, agitated, probably, more by terror than grief, but Mr. Heath remained gazing at the corpse of his only son. What a spectacle to meet a father's eye was this inert bulk, repulsive with the stigmas of dissipation fresh upon it! In the middle ages the heir of the house fell in battle, killed perhaps by the shot of an arquebuse or the blow of a partisan; or he met his death in some midnight encounter, and was brought home with a broken rapier and doublet dripping with blood—there is romance in that. But now he falls a victim to the bottle, and furnishes but a vulgar theme. Nevertheless the drama is none the less real. Mr. Heath's contemplation was sad, but full of worldly reasoning. The curse of unearned wealth, he mused, has fallen on my son. Had he been the child of a bricklayer or born to labor, he would have been alive now; or had not the blood of the Obershaws with its coarse appetites, predominated, he might have been an honor to me. Unmoved remained Mr.

Heath as he philosophized thus, until the sight of his daughter's emotion, as she covered her dead brother's face with tears and kisses, stirred the parent within him, and his eyes clouded and cold features relaxed.

Another funeral, another solemn procession to the tolling of the bell of St. Jude's, and the body of John Peter Heath was laid beside that of his grandsire in the family vault, in the yard of the little church.

XII.

Six months passed away.

The young widow had left Belton, which had never possessed any charms for her, to visit her maternal relatives in the island of Cuba. It was doubtless a relief, as she had never known any happiness during her wedded life. Her departure increased the sense of loneliness that pervaded her former home, for it now seemed enveloped in an atmosphere of gloom. Mr. Heath was rigid in all the observances of mourning. The entrance gates to his grounds, which were formerly always kept hospitably wide open, were now as constantly closed, and the domestics wore black. As for Mr. Heath, he had lapsed into a singular state of taciturnity, and sought seclusion. It was evident that he no longer possessed the energetic and elastic spirit of his younger days. Then disappointment would have spurred him to increased exertion, but now the repeated blows dealt at him by destiny and the approach of old age, though hardly perceptible in his still erect and vigorous frame, were telling on the springs of action.

There are periods in a man's existence when he pauses to review his life. It is true such periods rarely occur to the slaves of vice, or to those under the dominion of a ruling passion, and perhaps never to the robust individual of limited ideas to whom the mere act of existing is a pleasure; but they come repeatedly to the free intellect, perhaps at the very instant of realization of some long toiled-for or expected success, or at the moment of disappointment, to ask it what it is living for, and whither it tends? Such questions never enter the head of men like old John Peter Obershaw, nor disturb the tough self-satisfaction of those like George Gildersleeve; but the texture of Mr. Heath's mind, when at rest, was impressionable, and its subtle energy liable to relax and weaken. We have related how he succumbed to despondency on his succession to the immense wealth of his father-in-law, and although this feeling was soon shaken off and banished in the pursuit of ambitious projects, it now returned as the blight on his ambition, and death of his only son pressed the iron through a heart enamelled by worldliness. As time wore on, his sorrow, instead of diminishing, seemed to increase, and an expression of deep chagrin settled permanently on his countenance. He apparently lost all interest in his great work, the "Federal Code," and the secretary who had assisted him in its preparation was dismissed. He seldom left the house now, spending his time chiefly in the library engaged in meditation, or in the occasional perusal of a chapter of Jeremy Taylor or some other standard theological work. He even seemed to shun his family, and ceased to manifest interest in his daughter. Edna, quick to discern this change in her father's habits, attributed it solely to the death of her brother, and dreading the effects of prolonged grief, strove with the assistance of her aunt to divert his mind; but to little purpose. Each time that they tried to interest him in household matters, or to enliven him, they met with a rebuff. Even Mr. Abbott, who endeavored to bring balm and consolation, found his counsel unacceptable, and the worthy young minister did not repeat the attempt. In short, the man of even temper, the polished gentleman, was becoming irascible, and it was a relief to the family to learn one morning that Mr. Heath, to improve his health and divert his mind, or for some other unexplained reason, had determined to set off on a journey.

Edna, too, had certain perturbations of mind and heart to contend with—ideas and reflections that would obtrude upon her, and that, although temporarily banished during the period of mourning, reappeared with greater frequency when her sorrow became assuaged. These thoughts dated from the time of her meeting with Mark Gildersleeve, when he avowed she inspired his poetic flights. In her simple estimation, his verses were productions of merit and beauty; and there was something extremely pleasing in the thought of having long been the object of the hidden admiration and laudation of a young man gifted with such talent, and splendid eyes. Fred Spooner, to be sure, was taller and had red cheeks, but then Fred's knowledge, although a Harvard undergraduate, did not seem to transcend dogs. He could entertain her only with the exploits of his bull-terrier Spot among the rats, or discuss the beauties of his diminutive black-and-tan Spark; while Mark knew ever so many things, could quote Tennyson or Browning as readily as Mr. Abbott, could work a steam-engine, and sang superbly; while all Fred Spooner could do in that way was to roar, sadly out of tune, the touching lay of "The Lone Fish-ball," or "Shool." Perhaps Mark might become, in time, as celebrated as Dante or Petrarch, and she would be immortalized like Beatrice and Laura. Edna could not help dwelling on the flattering idea, until it took root in her gentle heart. In short, Miss Heath was fast drifting into love, and not a little surprised to find how constantly her thoughts would revert to the young engineer, in spite of her exertions to employ them otherwise. Perhaps, these exertions were not very strenuous, for the girl was of an unsophisticated nature, and not disposed to be rebellious; hence she yielded to her inclinations more readily than the circumspect daughter of a rigid precept-inculcating mamma.

At this time the gigantic conspiracy of the Secessionists culminated, and the demon of Civil War, that Mr. Heath and his conservative coadjutors had vainly attempted to exorcise, bristled his angry crest. One morning the portentous news came that the first hostile shot had been fired by the South. Instantly, the faithful in all parts of the North sprang to arms to avenge the insult offered to the glorious old standard of the nation. Peaceful Belton partook of the patriotic ardor, and manifested its loyalty by a profuse display of bunting. Party differences were forgotten, and Republicans and Democrats, Free-soilers and Conservatives, native and foreign-born citizens, all joined in protesting their devotion to the Union, and their determination to defend it to the last. George Gildersleeve, who, moved by his antipathy to the abolitionists, had been inclined to excuse the threats of the Southerners, now turned against them, and came out wonderfully strong for the Union, accompanying his loyal protestations with frequent allusions to the immortal Washington, and the patriotic services of his grandsire in the horse-shoeing line; in testimony whereof the Archimedes Works flaunted a starry banner of magnificent dimensions. A mass-meeting of the citizens to take measures towards the suppression of the rebellion was at once held in the public square. This square was the pnyx or forum of the Beltonians. In the centre a Phrygian cap was borne skyward by a tall liberty-pole, whose base was defended by a rusty old carronade, which was popularly supposed to have done wonders in freedom's cause during the trying days of Seventy-six, and was venerated accordingly; the probability being that it had never inflicted other damage than scorching some of the amateur artillerists, who every Fourth of July put the superannuated piece to use in firing salutes. At the meeting, though, it formed an appropriate buttress to the temporary stand erected for the orators, and gave a stern dignity to the occasion. In the absence of Judge Hull and Mr. Heath, who were both away from home, George Gildersleeve was called upon to preside; but fluent as honest George was in a caucus or sidewalk harangue, he lost his tongue on the rostrum, where he prefigured too closely his boasted porcine model of independence, and hence was forced to decline the proffered honor. Mr. Mumbie was then pitched upon as a proper figure-head, but he also declined, having the fear of Mrs. Mumbie, whose sympathies were with the South, before his eyes. At length a chairman was found in Mr. Poplin, the owner of the silk-mill, and the meeting proceeded with spirit. Stirring addresses were made—a deal of enthusiasm evoked, and a string of resolutions passed unanimously. The practical result was the decision to organize without delay a "Home Guard," and George was appointed captain of the first company. Vague apprehensions were afloat among the staid denizens that Beauregard and the South Carolinians might invade Belton, and the patersfamilias of the town had made up their minds not to be caught unprepared, but to be ready to strike doughtily for their altars and firesides at a moment's notice. So in less than twenty-four hours, fifty-three good and true men were enrolled in this formidable legion, and committees appointed to procure arms and uniforms. Considerable agitation was manifested over the selection of the latter. By virtue of his calling, Mr. Muldoon, a tailor, was chairman of the committee on uniforms, and moved probably by personal predilections, reported on "grane" as the most appropriate color; from which Snopple, the minority, dissented, and recommended, with an eye to the picturesque, the old Continental blue and buff, with a cavalier hat. But this recommendation was not acted upon, the suggested costume being voted unsuitable for "hard service," and as the Guards intended adopting the rifle as their weapon, Mr. Muldoon's "grane" carried the day, with red seams and yellow facings, however, in deference to the aesthetic feelings of the wily Snopple, who foresaw an increase of patronage growing out of this investiture. Among the junior members of the community, the warlike spirit rose equally high, but took a different direction. Of them all, none was more deeply stirred by the electric current of patriotism than Mark. From the outbreak of the conflict, his blood tingled to join in the fray. He flung aside all other occupations, and threw his whole soul into the popular cause. Let us confess, though, that he was not purely unselfish in his eagerness, for he foresaw a new avenue to fame, and one where the goal was more accessible to a determined mind than in the path he was pursuing. As a poet, mediocrity at the utmost was all, he was forced to admit, that he could ever hope for. But in war, what was there beyond the reach of a stout heart and true blade? He felt brave enough to cast his life in the scale if need be, and stake it for renown. Glory is a tempting bait for hot-heads and enthusiastic natures, and its sway over Mark was irresistible. Beyond glory, too, there was a sweeter, dearer reward that he might win. A guerdon fit to nerve even a craven to prowess.

"By cock and pie and mousefoot! my lad, but this is serious," quoth Dr. Wattletop, when Mark imparted his intention of turning soldier. "Fired by bellicose ardor, we burn to seize the anlace and cry havoc, eh? Nonsense," was the commentary that followed. "Believe me, my boy, stick to your innocent amusements. Permute the syllables of our noble tongue into new and strange rhythmical combinations as much as you please, but seek not the bubble reputation by checking musket-balls in their mad career. Stick to the shop, Mark, to itrochoidal paths and spheric sectors. 'Honor, indeed, who hath it? He that died o' Wednesday.' Stick to the shop, I tell you. You're a promising engineer, and there's glory enough to be acquired as such, and better still, money."

"Very true, doctor," answered Mark with a smile. "That *is* an inducement. You know how devoted I am to its acquisition."

"More's the pity, my lad, more's the pity. The sceptre that rules the world in this century is a golden one. However, I was young myself once—long, long ago, I'm sorry to say—and can appreciate your sublime disdain of opulence. But what has started you off on this new path, may I ask?"

"The duty I owe my country—patriotism," exclaimed Mark rather proudly.

"Patriotism—umph! The last refuge of a scoundrel, as Dr. Johnson said. Have you no worthier motive? Forgive me, my boy, I don't intend any personal application—it's a quotation that occurred to me. But patriotism has an exceedingly bad reputation, permit me to say, and is responsible for more crimes than liberty and religion combined. *Dulce et decorum est,* and so forth, 'Fidelity to one's country right or wrong,' may be fine ringing mottoes; but after all, the incentive is vain and selfish. Patriotism is the parent of national prejudice, and prejudices of all kinds are the greatest foes to justice. In the year A.D. 18,000, when 'man to man the warl o'er shall brithers be for a' that,' patriotism will be looked upon as a species of fetichism. Patriotism! I dislike it almost as much as I do generosity. Still, if you must kill, kill for some other cause. Here you Yankees are breathing fire and slaughter because a portion of your countrymen choose to follow the example of their forefathers. They are rebels and traitors and what not, because they follow in the footsteps of the men of '76, as you call them. The great question which underlies it all is apparently set aside and overlooked. The rallying cry is not the extinction of slavery; not freedom to fellow-beings from an undeserved servitude; not justice; but the Union—whatever that may be—and patriotism forsooth! the slogan that has marshalled unnumbered hosts to the perpetration of so many wrongs, and which is only, if I may so define it, disguised selfishness, as loyalty is after all but refined snobbishness."

Now the doctor, although hating slavery, had a lurking sympathy for the South. To his mind, they were abstractly in the right; it was sheer inconsistency for a union of states the outgrowth of secession to prevent those among themselves who desired it from taking a similar action. Mark, it is true, while he had lately become to a certain extent a proselyte to the teachings of the abolitionists, and admitted the wrong of slavery, and the necessity of wiping out that blot from the national escutcheon, made it subordinate to his great desire to preserve the Union and save from destruction "the greatest and freest country on earth, to which he had the honor to belong."

"Is it the greatest and freest because you belong to it?" inquired the doctor with a sly smile. "I notice that our great men are the greater for being our countrymen, and that our country is also the greater because it is our country.

We love the person or thing that sheds glory or honor in any way upon us, more because it does so, than because it is glorious or honorable in itself. For instance the walls of Shakespeare's home are written over with the names of visitors. Now, why is this? What leads Snooks and Noakes to scribble their names on the door-jambs of the shrine at Stratford-upon-Avon? Is it to honor Shakespeare or themselves? Perhaps they cannot quote two lines of his works, perhaps have never even read them. It arises purely from that ignoble desire to gratify in some way the measureless vanity of man. Snooks and Noakes care nothing for Shakespeare, but the world recognizes him as a celebrity, and they by connecting themselves, in however remote a degree, with celebrity, fancy they thereby acquire an atom of it."

"I don't see how any of this applies to me," said Mark, seemingly a little hurt at the doctor's remarks. "I'm sure I am not actuated by any such small and contemptible motives. Don't misunderstand me," he continued with rising enthusiasm; "I intend devoting myself to the cause of the Union, solely because I believe it to be the right one, and to carry justice with it."

"Ah! well—I like that way of putting it better," said the doctor. "You know, Mark, how I have always endeavored to imbue you with the belief, that to be just is the only rule of life, and that I should be sorry to see you swerve from that in any way."

"But I do believe that the cause of the Union is the just one, and that of the Secessionists the unjust one. I also believe that ours involves the cause of freedom throughout the universe. Our country, doctor, is the beacon of light and hope to the oppressed of all nations."

"So I've heard," said the doctor dryly, "and that millions yet unborn—and so forth. Well—well, my zealous young friend, bent on it, I see—God be with you. I hope it will all turn out right. But Mark, how—how are you going? Will not your—your—" He hesitated, fearing he had trenched on delicate ground, for he reflected that the young man's lameness might interfere with his project.

"Of course," said Mark, guessing the remainder of the question, "I prefer joining the cavalry."

"Well, a wilful lad must have his way, I presume, as well as a wilful woman. So boot and saddle, my boy, and may Southern steel and lead spare you to return to us, is the earnest wish of your old friend, Basil Wattletop. But whom shall I have to play chess with? Have you thought of that?"

"Ah! doctor, it's a grander game I shall engage in this time, but only as a pawn."

"Why a pawn?"

"Perhaps I shouldn't say that, for I'm striving for something better. You know I'm not altogether astray on horseback, and can ride, I believe, better than I can walk, which perhaps is not saying much; and old Copp, our night-watchman, who was sergeant-major during the Mexican war, and considered one of the best swordsmen in his corps, is teaching me sabre exercise, and if I only pass a fair examination at Trenton, I shall get a commission as lieutenant, I hope."

"No fear but you'll make the effort. So it goes: spondee, dactyl and anapest avaunt, and our nose now is continually in Jomini, or Cavalry Tactics, I'll warrant. That's our game now, my unappreciated genius, is it?"

Mark smiled at his old friend's banter, for the inconstant had indeed given the Muses the cold shoulder, to pay his devoirs to fierce Bellona. He even left uncompleted a stirring ode suited to the hour, entitled THE FASCES, destined to illuminate the columns of the *Belton Sentinel*, and which might have established his reputation as a second Korner. And wonderful was the zeal with which he set about qualifying himself for his new vocation. At break of day he was off scouring the roads on some mettlesome steed to acquire a perfect seat, and the evenings he spent practising sword-cuts and "moulinets" with old Copp, or poring over some volume on the art of war (which, to say the truth, proved of but little practical value to him), till long past midnight. Thanks to his perseverance, he soon had a smattering of the rudiments of the profession of arms sufficient to enable him to pass an examination. This and a little of his brother's political influence, secured him a lieutenantcy in the volunteer cavalry.

George Gildersleeve, however, was not at all pleased at the prospect of parting with Mark, or rather with Mark's services, for he foresaw a vast increase of business for him growing out of the requirements of the War Department, and needed a valuable coadjutor now more than ever. He even went so far as to offer Mark a partnership in the Works if he would give up his intention of joining the army and remain at work, which the young man, however, peremptorily refused. George, knowing the bent of his brother's character, saw the uselessness of further efforts to dissuade him from his purpose, and complained to Dr. Wattletop about the matter in strong terms, laying the chief blame upon his old enemies, the anathematized abolitionists, or "woolley-heads," as he ordinarily designated them. "He always has some dam whim or other in his head," said George, alluding to Mark. "Now it's nigger on the brain, and I believe he thinks more of freeing the darks than of saving the Union. So I'd rather he'd stay at home. It's all very well to go if he was wanted. I'm ready to go myself at a moment's notice if I'm needed—

when the country calls I'm there, you can bet your life; and I'll shoulder a fire-iron as quick as any to help give the seceshers a warming, and for the matter o' that, the pusillanimous woolley-heads as well. They both deserve it. But this boy's no call to go. He's a deuced sight more useful here, but you might as well talk to a post. My wife's done all she could and so have I, but it's no use. Now, major, I wish you would see what you can do. You've about as much influence over him as any one. Dammit, I'd furnish a dozen substitutes rather than have him leave. He's the best draughtsman I know of, and worth any three men in my shops. Work's crowding on us, and I can't spare him—that's the fact. If it hadn't been for the black republicans we wouldn't have had this here parra—parracidal war, and everything would have gone along lovely."

Dr. Wattletop had been to the "Shades" that afternoon, and made the following dignified reply, as he settled his chin in his swaddling cravat and shouldered his walking-stick like a drill-master: "In days gone by, Mr. Gildersleeve, in days gone by, Sir, had you Yankees remained loyal and steadfast (with a tighter grasp of his stick), I say, loyal and steadfast, as it was your bounden duty, to your sovereign King George of glorious memory, you would now have formed part of the mightiest and grandest empire on which the sun ever shone, and enjoying and sharing in true, sound, conservative, and constitutional freedom. There would have been no strife or fratricidal war in regard to slavery, for slavery cannot exist on British soil; but you chose to rebel against righteous authority, and now, the monster you have conjured threatens to devour you. Sorry for you, very sorry; but permit me to say frankly that you deserve it all. You certainly deserve it all, and have brought it on yourselves;" and the doctor shook his head very decidedly, as if, while he could not entirely forgive the American nation, he might be willing to temper his judgment with mercy.

The master of the Archimedes Works was at a loss, for a moment, how to reply to this unexpected philippic; but finally drove his adversary off by asserting, rather vehemently, that the American people intended settling their family difficulties in their own way, and if John Bull attempted to interfere he would get a repetition of the warming Old Hickory gave him at New Orleans.

"Or at Bladensburg, mayhap," added the doctor, as he walked away, convinced that his parting shot was an extinguisher, and chuckling as he muttered "*Hoc habet! hoc habet!*"

XIII.

The regiment to which Mark had been assigned recruited chiefly in Belton from among the artisans, and sons of the neighboring farmers, and it was not long before the complement was made up. As time was precious at this juncture the regiment was directed to proceed without delay to Washington, to join the corps forming under Kearney.

A parting surprise had been prepared for Mark by the men at the Works, who had contributed to purchase a handsome sword, which was presented to the young lieutenant a few days previous to his departure. Work was suspended two hours before the usual time, and Knatchbull, foreman of the machine-shop, and the oldest man at the Works, was deputed to make the presentation speech. He was an Englishman, but heart and soul with the country of his adoption. Unfortunately, to American ears, his eloquence was marred somewhat by a strong Northumbrian burr. Nevertheless, it was not ineffective, and Mark, who was totally unprepared for such a manifestation, had his feelings so touched by this exhibition of friendship for him by his late associates, that he was unable to make a coherent reply. He thanked them with a full heart, and one and all, big and little, shook hands with him; then shouted themselves hoarse, until George Gildersleeve, who had become reconciled to Mark's leaving, and even promised him the finest charger money could buy, delivered his sentiments in the following pithy address:

"Mark Gildersleeve! remember the man whose horse wore that old shoe over there (pointing to the fire-place in the counting-room), and remember your grandfather who shod him just afore the great battle of Trenton, and stand by the old flag, now and forever! That's all. Now boys we've had enough chin-music; step upstairs and wet your whistles."

And up they all went into the loft, where the consumption of punch, champagne, and sandwiches was wreathed about with the flowers of patriotic song, and till long towards midnight the vale of Belton resounded with the choric melodies of the "Star-Spangled Banner," and "Rally round the Flag," whose stentorious strains were borne across the Passaic to reverberate and die amid the distant Preakness hills.

The eve of departure was at hand. Mark had not had any interview or communication with Miss Heath since her brother's death. He had seen her several times, either at church or while she was riding, and exchanged salutations, but had not attempted to visit her. But now, he could forego it no longer. Clad in a bran-new uniform, that displayed his square shoulders and sinewy waist to advantage, he went with palpitating heart to the Cliff to take leave of Edna. He hoped to be fortunate enough to see her alone. He had not long to wait in the vast drawing-room, when light footsteps announced the young lady. She looked slender in her black dress, and rather pale, but a light blush mantled her features as she received him with a cordial smile. He colored in response, and their looks spoke volumes to each other.

"I—I trust," said Mark, "the audacity of my avowal at our last meeting, Edna, has already been forgiven, but I hope the avowal itself is not forgotten?"

"You seem determined to remind me of it at all events," replied Edna, parrying the question, and withdrawing her hand from his, as she motioned him to a chair. She took a seat opposite to him on a sofa, composing the folds of her dress in a nonchalant way, as if she feared having betrayed too much gratification in her greeting. There was an awkward pause for a moment. Then Mark, exchanging his seat for one beside Edna, and arming himself with persuasive audacity, took up her words. "Remind you, Edna? Oh! could I but impress you with a faint idea of how intensely I adore you—how completely you control my wishes, ambition, aspirations—my heart! Did you know how entirely the remembrance of you is interwoven with every thought of my life, you would not wonder at my cherishing jealously every kind glance and every smile as a priceless boon."

Edna attempted to frame some coy reply, but the artless girl was unable to carry on the coquettish play of a sued maiden against the resistless ardor of such an impetuous wooer. She could only remain silent, with lowered glance and burning cheek, while her daring suitor continued, "I may be exceedingly presumptuous in aspiring to you, Edna. I have nothing to offer, and I know you deserve all that earth can give, but all I ask now, is to be permitted to hope, and meanwhile to worship, for no divinity is too exalted to spurn the humblest devotee; but I need your consent and encouragement; without that, the task I have undertaken will be purposeless, and all honor I might win prove barren. I have come to bid you farewell."

"Farewell," echoed Edna, raising her eyes to his.

"Yes," said Mark, "to-morrow morning I leave for Virginia, and I've come to bid you farewell, and beg some token—some favor, Edna, which I know you will not refuse me; and if it should be my fate never to return—"

"Oh, don't say that," exclaimed Edna in tones that betrayed her anxiety.

"I trust I shall return, Edna, and in a position to make me more worthy of the interest you manifest in me. Dearest, the sweet confession I read in your eyes —in your tell-tale blushes, nerves me for every danger," etc., etc.

Mark was getting along famously in the time-honored way, when, at this tender stage of affairs, who should make her unwelcome appearance but Aunt Applegate, fortunately a myopic matron, who underwent an introduction to Mark, without seemingly noticing the confused looks of the sentimental pair. A voluble dame luckily was Mrs. Applegate, who had known Mark's mother and several of his dead and gone relatives, and instantly resurrected many incidents and reminiscences connected with the existence of those personages, thereby giving Edna time to assume a properly demure countenance. Our budding warrior and lover, while feigning an hypocritical interest in the conversation of the intruding lady, would, we fear, have seen her led off to the rack or stake with glee and gratitude. In happy unconsciousness of the kind feelings towards her, Mrs. Applegate continued, touching upon the prevailing topic: "So you are going to the war, Mr. Gildersleeve? Isn't it dreadful? Dear me, I don't know how it will all end. Edna told me you had joined the cavalry, and I think you are very sensible in doing so, for you have a great advantage over the foot-soldiers, and if worst comes to the worst, and matters become serious, you can, in case of danger, always get away from it much faster. Edna said—I believe you read it in the paper, didn't you, dear? Yes. So I thought—that you were a lieutenant. Now I should think that was doing very well for so short a time. Mrs. Mumbie is so worried about Decatur. He is at the Naval School, you know, and she is afraid he may have to go and fight. She's a Southerner, and all her sympathies are with the South," etc., etc.

Mrs. Applegate continued in this strain for some time, duly impressing on Mark the necessity of keeping his feet dry upon all occasions, and avoiding damp ground as a couch. She offered furthermore to present him with a quart bottle of picra, a remedial agent of great virtue and nastiness. "I prepared it myself, and am never without it, and wouldn't be for anything. Mr. Applegate used to say, 'Now, Susan, if you'd only advertise it, you'd make your fortune.' It's the very best thing in the world to ward off chills and fever; and now I think of it, Mr. Gildersleeve, if you could introduce it in the army, and induce the soldiers to take it occasionally instead of their vile whiskey and brandy, what a blessing it would be! I'm sure for my part nothing would give me greater pleasure than to furnish the recipe. Now, if you'll bear this in mind, and write me, I'll send it to you at any time."

Mark promised to do so; he would have promised anything, even to taking a daily dose of picra for a month, if Mrs. Applegate would only have allowed him a few minutes' longer *tête-à-tête* with his sweetheart, but it was not to be, and he was about to take his leave when Mrs. Applegate requested him to stay to tea, an invitation which he gladly accepted. The meal was rather a stiff and ceremonious affair, but Mark was supremely happy as he sat next to Edna. Mr. Heath, who had returned from his journey apparently not much improved in health, was rather mystified at the young officer's presence, and stared somewhat at his shoulder-straps. Mark noticed that the patrician had lost much of his old rigid pride, and looked fatigued and care-worn. He appeared to take but little interest in the momentous events of the day, and his one or two listless questions betrayed a remarkable ignorance of what was going on around him in relation to the war.

After tea they withdrew to the parlors, with the exception of Mr. Heath, who retired to his room. Mrs. Applegate, complimenting Mark on his voice, requested him to favor her with "Angels ever bright and fair;" which the young fellow did, you may rest assured, to the very best of his ability, as he sang to Edna's accompaniment. Then other visitors came. First, the Rev. Spencer Abbott, somewhat amazed, and perhaps a little displeased at Mark's presence, but too well bred to show it; next, Bob Mumbie and his sister Ada, to whom Mark underwent an introduction—an embarrassing ceremony where all the parties have known each other from childhood, but tacitly agreed as they grew up to be as strangers. However, the ice was soon broken. The young rector was pleasant enough and had a batch of entirely new conundrums to offer. Bob Mumbie, though rather doltish, was a good-natured, amusing fellow, while Miss Ada chose to make herself unusually agreeable, succumbing, perhaps, to the potent fascination of the lieutenant's blue coat and gilt buttons. She was a rather pretty girl, with a clear brunette complexion; but strongly marked brows knit over brilliant black eyes, and disdainful lips, gave her an imperious expression. She attacked a sonata of Beethoven, but it was evidently beyond the capacity of her unpractised fingers, and it was a relief when her brother offered to treat the company to "The Old Folks at Home." Bob Mumbie's forte was Ethiopian minstrelsy, and he sang the simple lays of the plantation with all the pathos of a professional. Led on by the general applause, Bob followed it up with "Old Uncle Snow," then "Sally Come up," and concluded with a "Walk round," after the manner of the celebrated Mr. Bryant, to the intense amusement of Mrs. Applegate, whose capacious form shook with laughter, and of Edna, who enjoyed it scarcely less. All this was horridly unæsthetic, and Mark, the prig, only rewarded the performance with a condescending smile. Perhaps, was he jealous that his efforts had not met with equal success, or that Edna had requested a repetition of "Uncle Snow"? For all that, and in spite of it, he enjoyed himself, and passed a delightful evening; one that he often recalled as he smoked his corn-cob pipe and ruminated before the lonely bivouac-fires during the tedious Peninsular campaign.

Mark was grievously disappointed though, when about taking his leave that evening, to find Mrs. Applegate accompanying her niece to the door to press on his acceptance a large bottle of picra. He was fain to content himself with exchanging a lingering pressure of the hands and an eloquent look with Edna. She found means, however, to give him a small folded paper which of course contained, to his supreme delight, a tress of her bonny blond hair. Any one witnessing his behavior as he went home that night, stopping every moment to cover the precious keepsake with kisses, and then as he crossed the bridge to the town, to fling a bottle rather impatiently into the river, might reasonably have entertained doubts as to his sanity.

And the sweet enchantress who had cast this spell? She was rather startled when stopping at her father's room to bid him good-night, he abruptly asked her what that young man had called for? Fortunately he did not notice her deep color as she answered that he had merely come to bid them good-by, and Aunt Susan had asked him to stay to tea.

"Ah! yes—going to the war, I see. Well, good-night, darling," was all Mr. Heath remarked, and Edna was much relieved when she discovered her father's curiosity extended no farther. But what a long serious meditation she had after retiring to her room! How often she stopped and reflected as she braided her hair for the night! She was now fairly in love. This last step of Mark's had achieved her conquest. What young lady with any kind of a heart could resist the fascination of a gallant who was both a poet and soldier? And not only that, but who had the finest black eyes and chiselled features conceivable? Even Ada Mumbie, who had never condescended to notice him before, was now forced to admit that he looked "splendid" in his uniform. Edna had read of Sidney, and fancied Mark must be just such another individual as that model knight. As for Fred Spooner, who wrote her such school-boy scrawls from Harvard, what was there chivalrous about him? But Mark could only be compared to one of those delightful mailed beaux of old who went ambling about the world smiting every one who didn't instantly acknowledge that their own particular lady-love was vastly superior to all other ladyloves in existence; and she hadn't any doubt but that Mark was ready to enter the lists at a moment's notice for such a purpose; and we may add that we do not think she was much mistaken in her belief either. So she decided in her mind that as soon as she was nineteen, and Mark became a general, which would doubtless be contemporaneous events, they would be married. Then a sad expression shadowed her face, as the thought crossed her mind that perhaps he might fall in battle. When she knelt at her bedside in her vestal robe, an appeal for the protection and safe return of the young lieutenant was not omitted, we will venture to say.

The sun came out bright and encouragingly the next morning, when a clear bugle-call roused the recruiting camp on the outskirts of Belton. The men were under order to leave for Washington by an early train. It was a memorable day for the town, and the citizens assembled to see the gallant lads off. The cavalry-men were dismounted, lightly equipped with blankets and haversacks, while their officers carried their sabres with all the pride of veterans. They defiled through the principal streets on their way to the railway-station, accompanied by the "Home Guard," and preceded by the Belton brass-band ringing out "John Brown's march," while the people cheered lustily. There was Mark with his cap bearing its insignia of crossed sabres set jauntily on one side of his head, marching proudly along, unmindful for the moment of his halting gait, which was more apparent than usual, as he kept step with the even ranks. As his eyes wandered towards the throng on the sidewalks, he caught sight of the figure of a young girl closely wrapped in a dark shawl. It was Edna; and as she stealthily waved her handkerchief he colored to the temples, bowed an acknowledgment, and so they parted.

More leave-takings at the depot. Poor Mrs. Gildersleeve sobbing like a child, until her handkerchief was soaked in tears, and her husband, the bold captain of the "Home Guards," feeling probably almost as bad, but affecting an exaggerated bluffness, and proffering the rather un-military advice to Mark to "stand no nonsense and look out for number one." Then Dr. Wattletop had his good word of cheer and encouragement for young Rupert, as he called him; and the Rev. Mr. Sniffen said his kind say; and lastly, old Copp gave him a parting grip, whose intense heartiness nearly brought tears into his eyes.

All this solicitude shown in his behalf, and regret expressed at his departure by his friends caused Mark to feel as if he didn't deserve it at all, and was rather an ungrateful wretch in going away. "What shall I do to merit all this?" was his reflection as the train sped on that bore him off. "I must not disappoint them, and I shall not. No, I'll not enter Belton again if the war lasts until I can wear spread-eagles on my shoulder-straps, unless I am brought in on a stretcher," vowed he, thinking probably that in either event the expectations of his friends would be met and his condition a source of satisfaction to them.

Time passed on with Edna, measured only by the intervals between the receipt of letters from Mark. These missives were of course frequent and fervid, and responded to in as nearly similar a strain as maidenly reserve would permit. There was nothing particularly novel or striking in Edna's letters, but Mark esteemed them as compositions of wonderful merit. He believed he saw in her well-balanced sentences, and neat, flowing penmanship a reflex of her natty ways and symmetric character. These precious notes he always carried about him, and they were read and re-read until he knew their contents by heart. Edna, on her part, made as absorbing a study of her lover's correspondence.

Mark was with the Army of the Potomac in its memorable campaign in the Peninsula. Promotion was rapid among the volunteers, and he was soon advanced to a captaincy. By this time he had been in several engagements, and behaved with credit. Naturally, at his first experience of actual warfare, he was uncertain of himself, and dreaded lest his heart should fail him. The gravity of the commanders at the approach of battle; the sullen boom of distant cannon drawing nearer and nearer—the preliminary pause inspires the novice with dread and awe; but the first flutter of fear over, the sharp crack of rifles and smell of powder soon kindles the blood of a true soldier, and Mark found himself in his element, oblivious of danger, and dashing with the foremost into the fight.

He was chary of imparting his own exploits, but Edna heard of them occasionally through the public prints, which she diligently scanned every day for news from the ——th New Jersey Cavalry. Once she had a fearful fright, for she found Captain Mark Gildersleeve's name among the wounded. But, to her relief, a letter from him came soon after, which informed her that the injury he had received was but slight, and that he expected to be in the saddle again in a few days. The truth was, that our hero's career had come within an ace of an untimely close. While out on a reconnaissance, his troop had fallen in with a portion of Jeb Stuart's horse, and Mark, who had often longed for an opportunity for a hand-to-hand combat with some of the noted Southern troopers, drew his sabre and rode with reckless impetuosity into the midst of the enemy. He was about to single out an adversary, as if to engage in a joust, when he was instantly surrounded and a stroke dealt at him which only the stoutness of his leathern cap-visor prevented from terminating his existence. As it was, the gash he received was a serious one; but fortunately his companions had arrived in time to rescue him from further peril, and disperse the rebels. The wound soon healed, but it left a scar which, though it rather impaired his good looks, he deemed a favor for this reason: since he had been in the army he was often subjected to the query, suggested by his lameness, of where and how he had been wounded; the embarrassment of an explanation and the recollections revived by it, were such as to cause him to accept with gratitude the ugly seam that now disfigured him, but would thenceforth probably divert the attention of inquisitive persons from his other physical defect.

Mark wrote to Edna in a pleasant, jesting way concerning the embellishment his countenance had undergone. He promised to send her a likeness of his improved appearance at the first opportunity, and alluded to the wound he had received from the rebel trooper as a mere pin scratch in comparison with the one inflicted by her on his heart, with much more to the same purpose, and signed himself "Le Balafré."

Edna was pleased to find that he took it all in such good part, and replied beseeching him not to expose himself so rashly—she was certain he was rash and reckless, and for her sake to be cautious and prudent, ending with the hope that the war would soon end, and enable him to return home.

Beside her solicitude for Mark, the girl's thoughts were greatly occupied with her father's changed health and habits. Despite his cold, undemonstrative temperament, Mr. Heath was strongly attached to his child. If his manifestations of affection had been few and far between, on the other hand he had never chidden her, and she had been indulged in every way, and her lightest wishes gratified. The daughter more than reciprocated the love so charily bestowed, and her impressionable nature seemed to reflect her father's changeful moods. Now her intuition told her that he suffered. He had not been the same man since the death of his son. At times he shook off his despondency, and appeared to regain some of his former energy; but the effort was but momentary. His business matters were now entirely conducted by others, and he even grew neglectful of his personal appearance—a symptom that struck Edna with alarm. One morning when he breakfasted with the family in his dressing-gown and with an unshaven face, Edna, after he had left the table, remarked to her aunt on the great alteration in her father's habits: "I never knew him to do such a thing before. Yesterday afternoon I saw him go into the picture-gallery, and I went in very soon after. He was staring fixedly at that picture of the Sistine Madonna, and did not notice my coming in. When I went and spoke to him he started with such a pained expression that it made me feel dreadful."

"My dear child," said Mrs. Applegate in a reassuring tone, "you must bear in mind that your father is getting old. You can't expect him always to remain smart and active. Years will tell on all of us. Besides, everybody has something the matter with them; if it isn't one thing it's another. Now Mr. Applegate used to say that gout or rheumatism was more certain if not so desirable as riches, and I know that years before he died—"

"But, aunt," interrupted Edna, "father is not so very old. I do not think his condition is natural. I feel sure he suffers very much; I know it. Whenever I talk to him he don't seem to be aware of what I am saying. I often write letters to him as I used to, on some subject that I think will interest him, but he lays them aside without opening them. I can always tell whenever anything ails him; and besides, his last trip did not do him a bit of good. He broods so constantly over Jack's death, and seems so very miserable, that it makes me feel dreadful to see him; and then, if I ask him if he feels ill, he seems so annoyed, that I dare not question him further. I am afraid that unless something is done his health will be seriously affected. Do send a note to Dr. Wattletop to come and see him."

"As you please, dear; but you know how strongly your father objects to having anything to do with doctors, and how angry he may be if he finds out we have taken such a step without consulting him. So we must expect a scolding."

"Never mind, aunt; I'll take all the blame on my shoulders," replied Edna. "I certainly feel it is our duty to ask some physician's advice. Suppose you ask Dr. Wattletop to call; you might say you wished to consult him in case an excuse is needed. Then you could explain the matter to the doctor without alarming or annoying father in the least. Wouldn't that do?"

"Well, my dear, perhaps it might. At all events, I'll send the doctor a note, and ask him what we had better do. There can be no harm in that."

Dr. Wattletop came as requested under pretext of prescribing for Mrs. Applegate. He remained to dine, and was seated opposite Mr. Heath, who replied to the customary inquiries respecting his health with a curt and nervous, "Thank you, never better, never better." But he was so uneasy beneath the physician's big interrogative eyes so constantly directed toward him, that he feigned some excuse, and left the table before the end of the meal.

The physician was struck with the marked alteration in Mr. Heath's aspect. That energetic, refined aristocrat, had suddenly become a listless, peevish old man. His keen ice-gray eyes were dull, and the muscles of his once smooth, marble-like face were now flaccid, and covered with a growing unkempt beard. Slovenliness had replaced tidiness, and every part and action of the man denoted a great change in his physical and mental condition.

Dr. Wattletop was perplexed. He questioned Mrs. Applegate and Edna, but could elicit nothing to assist him in finding a clue to the cause of this sudden and extraordinary transformation in an individual the least likely to be affected by care or illness. "A man of brazen constitution—heart idem—brain idem," cogitated the doctor, "on whom emotions and troubles would gnaw in vain, who was apparently not deeply moved by the loss of his son, now shows unmistakable signs of mental distress—for mental it is." Basil Wattletop, M.D., albeit an experienced leech, was nonplussed, and muttering something to the ladies about "splenetic affection," "torpid liver," and the like, took his leave, to await further developments.

A few days later the doctor was surprised to receive a message from Mr. Heath, asking him to call at his earliest convenience, on business not of a professional character.

The doctor took the first opportunity to comply with the request, and on arriving at the Cliff was shown into the library, where Mr. Heath received his visitor, and motioned him to a chair, with something of his old courtliness of manner. The physician noticed that his host exhibited an improved appearance, and in particular that his toilet had been carefully attended to.

"When I wrote you that note, doctor," said Mr. Heath with a weak smile, "I did not expect so soon to have the pleasure of a visit from you. I believe I was careful to state that what I wanted to see you about was not of a professional nature."

"Precisely," said the doctor, nodding his head in acquiescence.

"Hence I trust it has not interfered with any of your engagements?"

"Not at all," replied the doctor.

It seemed as if Mr. Heath were reluctant to approach the object for which he had summoned Dr. Wattletop, for he remained a few moments in silence with his fingers to his forehead in meditation, while the other watched him curiously. At length he abruptly said, "You are a freethinker, I am told, doctor?"

The physician, somewhat taken aback by this unexpected question, replied: "Well, it depends altogether upon your definition of the term. If you mean by freethinker, one who exercises his reason in an independent way, I certainly am."

"Do you, for instance, doctor, believe in eternal punishment?"

"No, certainly not," said the doctor, very decidedly.

"It's a fearful thought," ejaculated rather than spoke Mr. Heath, as a shudder seemed to pass over his frame.

"Fearful? It's wicked, abominable, impious. To suppose that a beneficent God would condemn a weak mortal to a doom cruel beyond conception, would punish in a way that even imperfect man would not, under any provocation, is simply monstrous. Fortunately there are but few who really believe in such a doctrine, and those who do, are, I find, perfectly satisfied that they will escape, even if the rest of the world is sent to perdition."

"Doctor," said Mr. Heath, "you will be very much surprised when I tell you that although I have been a communicant of the Episcopal Church for twenty years, and have conformed strictly to its forms and observances, I have no settled religious belief."

"Not a bit surprised, Mr. Heath, not a bit. In fact, I believe that fully three-quarters of the attendants at Church are in the same condition. Indeed, when I think of the indifference with which the most solemn and important truths are received, the mechanical piety of so-called devotees, and the facility with which they are swayed by trivial weaknesses, foibles, and vanities, I believe I am understating the proportion of practical unbelievers to the earnest and consistent professors. I have found this as my experience of men, that while all dread falling below what we may call the average of morality, the mass are indifferent about rising above it. In other words, while no one desires to be worse than his neighbor, no one cares about being any better. This accounts for the force of example, and the frequency of the tu-quoque style of argument. It is true there are exceptions, earnest men and women full of enthusiastic zeal, but if anything, these exceptions prove the rule."

"Mr. Abbott explains this indifference and the present low state of morality to a want of spirituality in the Church," remarked Mr. Heath.

"Want of fiddlesticks," replied the doctor. "Want of consistency is the trouble. Example—example is the great teacher, and in fact the only teacher. If you and I are inconsistent or unjust, we infect the rest and the contagion spreads, and no doctrinal exposition can countervail."

"Permit me, doctor, to offer you some refreshment," said Mr. Heath, rising to ring the bell, perhaps to change the topic of conversation, which now diverged into commonplaces.

Presently a domestic returned bearing a liqueur case.

"Will you please help yourself, doctor. Here is some Sherry—or if you prefer it, Monongahela."

While the doctor was dealing himself a liberal allowance of the whiskey, Mr. Heath resumed his seat and his meditative expression. Finally he drew himself closer to the doctor's chair, as if to beseech his attention, and said, "You and I, doctor, have arrived at that stage of existence when the illusions of youth have vanished—when all the feverish ambitions and vanities have lost their sway over us, and when we can look calmly at the approach of death. I will confess to you, doctor, that until lately I have not realized the insufficiency of this life; never until the loss of my son. As I stood beside his grave I recalled the words of Burke under similar circumstances: 'What shadows we are and what shadows we pursue!' This sense of disgust—of intense *ennui* of existence is dreadful—unbearable…. What is coming? Where can I get light as to the future? Where lean for assistance?"

This apostrophe was interjected, and as if called forth by the speaker's sorrow.

A pause, and he resumed:

"Doctor, as one of my own age, and as a man in whose intellect, judgment, and heart I have the fullest confidence, I desire to make you my father-confessor. I crave sympathy and counsel. Perhaps I should apologize for burthening you with my trials and sorrows, but pity me—pity me!" He laid his hand on the physician's knee with such an appealing look, that the latter was touched. "Whom else can I consult with—whom turn to? I am at sea yawing like a rudderless ship."

The doctor, who had been not a little surprised at the tenor of his host's conversation, expressed his condolence, and proffered his assistance in any way that it might be found serviceable. Mr. Heath looked for a moment as if he were about to confide something—then checked himself, and rising leaned on the mantle-piece in a pensive attitude. Dr. Wattletop took this for an indication that the conference was at an end, but the Monongahela being excellent, he lingered to refill his glass. Meanwhile Mr. Heath again sat down and addressed him:

"You say, doctor, that you do not believe in eternal punishment, because, as I understand you, it is irreconcilable with reason."

"Because it is irreconcilable with the attributes of the Almighty. Again, where is the sense or harmony, or even necessity of it? I can understand temporary punishment, but not everlasting punishment; that would resolve itself simply into revenge, a feeling that the Creator is incapable of harboring. No, sir, I believe there is a punishment for sin, but not an everlasting one. I believe in the harmony of Nature, and that its laws are inexorable. They cannot be infringed without suffering. I do not believe in the forgiveness of sins."

"Do not believe in the forgiveness of sins! Have you no faith, doctor?"

"Faith, Mr. Heath, is in the first place a matter of cerebral organization, and secondly of accident. Had you and I been born with crania of a certain conformation, of either Jewish, Mohammedan, or Calvinistic parents, we would have remained in the faith we were born in, whether Jewish, Mohammedan, or Calvinistic, to the end of our days. Had John Knox, for instance, been born a Hindoo, in Benares, he would have become the fiercest fakir of them all. The mass of mankind dislike the trouble of thinking, and follow the paths traced out for them in infancy. Take your friend Mumbie, as an illustration. Here is a man of average respectability, who goes to church because it is the correct thing. What are his views, think you, on the hypostatic union? It is immaterial to him whether the minister preaches from the Zendavesta or the Koran; a certain number of hours have to be spent listening to him, and then he jogs along day after day, in the same grooves, satisfied if he keeps up to the average of respectability. Faith, Mr. Heath, as connected with dogmas and formulas, is of little consequence, in my estimation. Who do you think is the better man,—the one who believes in consubstantiation, or the one who believes in transubstantiation? My good mother, who was a pious woman, brought me up in the tenets of the Established Church—hence youthful predilections and associations attach me to that fold. At one time the perusal of Paley's Natural Theology, the Bridgewater treatises, and works of that character, shook my faith, and left me a sceptic. Such works, although intended to strengthen faith, serve but to stimulate inquiry. Possessing an analytic mind, the subtle problems of Nature had a wonderful fascination for me, and in trying to solve them, I became for a time a proselyte to the unsatisfactory theories of materialistic philosophy, until, fortunately, I found in the teachings of Descartes a solid foundation for belief. No logic can successfully assail the faith that springs from intuition. Now, like Kant, I never cease to wonder at the starry heavens, but far more at the intuitive knowledge of God and the Moral Law."

"The Moral Law," echoed Mr. Heath, abstractedly. After a few moments he returned, "Does not charity cover a multitude of sins?"

"It's a convenient mantle, surely. As I said before, I do not believe sins are ever forgiven, but bring their own punishment inevitably. Here in this world they certainly do, for all sages agree on this: that happiness is only attainable through the practice of virtue, and if this be so, the converse must necessarily be true, and those who do not practise it must be unhappy. As the physical health is governed by certain hygienic laws whose infraction inevitably produces disease, so is the spiritual health governed by the moral law, whose infraction also as certainly brings suffering. To be good is to be spiritually healthy—wickedness is deformity or disease of the soul."

"Then you are not a believer in total depravity?"

"No. The thing that reconciles us to ourselves and our fellow-beings, is the knowledge that the evil we commit proceeds more from unwisdom than from depravity. Man is far more of a fool than knave."

"I must ask your indulgence, doctor, and pardon for the liberty I have taken in thus catechising you; but as I said, I am emboldened to do so by the great esteem in which I hold you, and respect I entertain for your opinions and judgment. One more question: If this idea of duty, this Moral Law, as you term it, is from God, why is it not the same in all men? A savage can slay treacherously and sleep peacefully afterwards. Is not the moral law the creation of intellect?"

"No, intellect merely unfolds and develops it. The sway of the moral law is in proportion to the quality of the soul and the degree of reason. Its power is diminished in beings of limited reason or imperfect souls; hence, in a savage or a troglodyte it is naturally less than in an enlightened man—and still less in a horse, with its deficient reason and incipient soul," explained the doctor.

Mr. Heath again rose from his seat, paced across the room, and for the first time helped himself to a glass of spirits; then turning to the doctor, expressed, with forced lightness, his thanks for the instructive exposition he had been favored with. At this intimation the doctor took his departure, muttering to himself as he descended the staircase, "Very odd—I wonder what the deuce he wanted to see me for? Wished me to be his father-confessor. Egad! I think he assumed that *rôle* himself. If he had but asked me to feel his pulse or look at his tongue, I might have clapped a fee down against him. As it is, I have had all my trouble for nothing. That whiskey, though, was excellent— excellent."

Edna had been waiting below to see the doctor, and as he was about opening the street-door to leave, she approached with a look of concern: "Don't you think, doctor, that father is better—don't you see an improvement in him?"

"Yes," replied Dr. Wattletop, cautiously, as he drew on his gloves; "Yes—I think, I—he looks better—rather better."

"Oh thank you, doctor; I'm ever so much obliged to you," replied Edna, joyfully.

"Still, it will be just as well, in case you notice any change in him or new peculiarity, to advise me of it. Good-by."

XV.

Mr. Heath again sent for Dr. Wattletop. This time the interview was of a more practical character. He desired to lay before the physician certain plans in regard to the erection of a free hospital for the county. The need of such an institution had long made itself felt, and Mr. Heath had determined to build one and endow it liberally. Dr. Wattletop approved of the project, and proffered his advice and assistance. Besides the hospital, Mr. Heath announced his purpose to erect, also at his sole expense, a home for orphan and friendless children.

The doctor listened patiently, and acquiesced as Mr. Heath communicated his ideas, until turning abruptly from the discussion of the plan, he said, "Does it not strike you as a sad commentary on the condition of society, that such institutions should be made necessary?"

"How so?" inquired Mr. Heath.

"Of course I am aware of what will be said about charity, benevolence, generosity, and the like, but for my part I detest them. Man seems to have a horror of being just, and will adopt any makeshift instead. Now—"

"You surprise me, doctor," interrupted Mr. Heath, testily; "from your qualities of head and heart I expected different counsel, and encouragement from you."

"My qualities of head and heart," said the doctor, "have only taught me this: that there is but one virtue—justice; and that the other so-called virtues are but pinchbeck ones. From man's neglect and aversion to its practice spring all wretchedness and misery. I don't propose, though, to be Quixotic in my propaganda, and while the infant mind to-day is being trained in prejudice, self-glorification, conceit, and falsehoods of all kinds, my puny efforts in advocacy of a different education would avail naught. Therefore, my dear sir, now that I have entered my protest, my best efforts to aid you in carrying out your plans are at your service, and you may command me. Only let me say this, to hide nothing from you, that while what you propose doing is munificent, and as the world goes, worthy of all praise—springing as it must from kind impulses—in my judgment it is all valueless as an exemplar, or educator, in comparison with the performance of a simple act of justice."

Mr. Heath seemed to be very much displeased at the doctor's frank exposition of his opinions, and said, as he gathered up his papers, "I am afraid, Dr. Wattletop, that you and I diverge too widely in our ideas on the subject we have been discussing, and as concord is indispensable in carrying out successfully the objects I have in view, I think, upon the whole, I shall not be able to avail myself of your valuable services."

"As you please, Mr. Heath, as you please, sir," replied the doctor, rising and taking his leave; not, however, without a certain disappointment, as the recollection of the choice Monongahela he had tasted on the previous visit floated to his palate.

"That man," soliloquized the doctor, on his way home, as he reflected on his interview with Mr. Heath, "that man has something on his mind. Soul-sickness of some kind. What crime must he have committed, to force him to atone by such prodigal dispensations? What is the medicine for his cure, I wonder? Shall it be Sublapsarianism or Supralapsarianism, or an electuary compounded of Pædobaptism and Sabellianism? Methinks yon stalwart son of Holy Mother Church, Father Maguire, would be most successful in this case. The heroic surgery of the disciples of Loyola is often efficacious in such maladies. Strange that that honest, consistent, unselfish, truest soldier of the Cross should be the automaton of an order whose cardinal doctrine is 'passive obedience,' whose aim is to destroy free thought and enlightenment, and remand the world to the middle ages."

These latter reflections of the doctor were drawn forth by the appearance of the parish priest, who was passing by at the time. His reverence was a good-humored, blue-eyed Celt, with whom the doctor had occasional polemical encounters, and sorely tried with his latitudinarianism.

Mr. Heath next convoked the clergymen of the various denominations in Belton, and invited their co-operation in carrying out his philanthropic projects. They readily acceded to his wishes, and expressed their entire concurrence in his plans. Of course these praiseworthy acts of Mr. Heath met with general commendation, and as they involved the expenditure of very large sums of money, elicited many encomiums on his munificence and beneficence. In fact, he was giving evidence in every way of what the Rev. Mr. Sniffen called a "change of heart." There was an unmistakable earnestness now in his attendance at worship, and a lowering of his crest that denoted an attempt to walk in the paths of humility. There was also a perceptible amelioration in his health, arising probably from the diversion of thought called forth by his benevolent schemes. Edna noticed these gratifying changes in her father's physical condition with joy, and he seemed to appreciate her filial attention and solicitude by increased affection for her. His sole pleasure now was in her society, and as warmer days came he enjoyed long drives in company with her. Edna had a pair of fleet ponies which she drove like an experienced whip, and her basket-phaeton was often seen on golden afternoons scouring along the banks of the beautiful Passaic, or through the wooded hills of Pompton, with her father languidly reclining beside her, and a dapper groom in the rumble.

One evening, as they were returning home from a drive, and were within a few rods of the gateway, a man who had been lying on the sward by the road-side staggered to his feet, and motioned as if he wished to speak to them. He was a rough fellow, a tramp, and evidently intoxicated. Edna, somewhat alarmed, would have whipped up the ponies, but the man stood in front of them gesticulating, and for fear of hurting him, she drew in the reins and stopped. The groom, leaping from his seat, was about to deal harshly with the interloper, when at a sign from his master he desisted. The fellow, with an unsteady gait, approached Mr. Heath, and held out his hand, saying: "I told 'em, old man, I told 'em wanted to see you. That chap at the gate over there wouldn't let me in. Told 'im you was my friend—best friend ever had in the world—ain't that so, old man? How you been, old top—all right, eh?"

The under-gardener, who acted as lodge-keeper, here advanced, and explained that the man had made several attempts to force himself in the grounds, saying that he was acquainted with Mr. Heath, and wished to see him on business.

"Sho I did—sho I did—'portant business, I said, 'portant business, old man," repeated the fellow.

At the apparition of this stranger, Mr. Heath's features became livid—his lingers grasped the side of the phaeton nervously, and for a moment he seemed unable to utter a word. Edna fortunately was too much occupied in watching the intruder and cause of all the trouble, to heed her father's agitation, while he with a strong effort collected himself.

"Wouldn't b'lieve me—told 'em you was my friend—best friend, eh, old man? That's so, that's so," repeated the man with drunken persistency, while Mr. Heath alighting, bade Edna rather peremptorily to drive on, and with a hasty gesture waved the gardener away.

The stranger was a red-bearded man of powerful build, within about ten years of Mr. Heath's age. His aspect was coarse and vulgar, and his garments worn and filthy. Judging from the tattooing on the backs of his hands, and his red, rugose neck, he was probably a seafarer. Mr. Heath led him, not without some trouble, up to the house and into the library, where they remained closeted together all the evening. Meals were brought up to them, and the household saw no more of the man, for he apparently disappeared before the next morning.

Although Edna was not a little surprised at this occurrence, and at her father's bearing towards the stranger, she made no allusion to him, and Mr. Heath anticipated any remarks from his sister by saying that the man was an unfortunate being with a family dependent upon him for support, whom he had several times assisted, and who presumed to return. "I doubt whether it is really a charity to help such people," added Mr. Heath, with affected carelessness. "Still one cannot resist these appeals, especially when an innocent family of small children is likely to suffer, for a slave to drink seldom reforms."

"Has he a large family?" asked Mrs. Applegate.

"Yes, yes, I believe so," replied Mr. Heath, manifesting annoyance at being questioned. "I know nothing at all about him but what he says."

This closed the conversation on that subject, but Mr. Heath's weak nerves were so shaken by the incident, that for several days after he remained at home, and refused any longer to accompany his daughter in her walks or rides. A fortnight or so later, Mrs. Applegate, who was reading the newspaper, incidentally remarked:

"I see that they have caught that Peterson, the pirate."

Mr. Heath, who was reclining in an easy-chair, started as if a bolt had struck him. "What! Who?" he exclaimed.

"Dear me, Rufus, how you startled me! I merely said that that dreadful murderer that they called Peterson, the pirate, and who escaped from jail, has been caught. You must remember the time there was about it. It was a little after John's death. I remember there was a story going around that his name was not Peterson, but Klove, and that he formerly lived in Belton. Old Mrs. Cosgrove told me then that she remembered him very well, and that his mother was a washerwoman. She said, too, that he was a thief when a boy, and ran away to sea after robbing his master."

"Mrs. Cosgrove is a silly gossip, Susan," said Mr. Heath, impatiently. "The boy was not a thief."

"Indeed—why, Rufus, I heard from—"

"Never mind; it's of no consequence, and we will not argue the matter," interrupted Mr. Heath. "Let me look at the paper a moment."

In order to render this colloquy more intelligible, it will be necessary to state that about eight or nine months previously the public mind was intensely agitated and shocked by the details of a murder of a very atrocious character. The crime had been committed by a sailor who had shipped for a short voyage on a small coaster. When at sea he had slain the captain, mate, and cook, and then running the craft near shore, had scuttled her, leaving in the yawl with a small sum of money belonging to the captain, to obtain which had been the sole motive of the triple murder. Landing on the sea-coast a few miles below Sandy Hook, the murderer had been captured by some fishermen, who had watched his suspicious movements. The smack, instead of sinking, was found adrift, with the proofs of the horrid deed still fresh and visible. The guilt seemed, therefore, plainly fixed on the accused, and there was but little doubt that the trial would result in his conviction. Still the evidence against him was but circumstantial, and his counsel, a man of ability, made strenuous and persistent efforts to clear him. In the progress of the case, it came out that the prisoner was an old and hardened desperado, who had been incarcerated many times in various countries for misdemeanors of every degree. It was furthermore discovered that he had given to the court an assumed name, and that his true one was Klove, and native place Belton. This revelation, naturally enough, created some excitement among the older inhabitants of that town, who still remembered Klove as a boy of fourteen, who had been forced to leave the place in consequence of an accusation of theft. This charge, although not proven at the time, was now resurrected, and brought up to his prejudice as an illustration of how youthful depravity would lead eventually to the gravest and blackest crimes. Mr. Heath, who was a clerk at the time Klove was living in Belton, and had a distinct recollection of him, was naturally much interested in the progress of his trial, and read and re-read the reports of it as they appeared in the newspapers, with an absorbing interest. In singular contrast was his dislike to having the subject mentioned or talked about in his family. Mrs. Applegate, who had a predilection for the horrible, was full of the murder, and discussed it at every meal, much to her brother's annoyance. As the trial drew near its close, Mr. Heath took a short trip, being absent about a week. While he was away, the trial, which was held at Freehold, came to an end; and, in spite of the skilful efforts to exculpate him, the prisoner was convicted. The case was too clear to admit of the slightest doubt, and the jury found him guilty of murder. His lawyer tried strenuously to obtain a new trial, but without avail, and he was remanded for sentence.

The very next night Klove broke jail—a bar of the window of his cell had been wrenched out, and watch-spring saws and files were found lying about, conveying the impression that he had received assistance. A turnkey was suspected of complicity and dismissed, although the proof was hardly sufficient to implicate him. It was this escaped pirate—this murderer whose recapture, after having eluded the officers of justice for several months, when announced by Mrs. Applegate to her brother, produced such a shock to the latter's feelings. The fellow, it appeared, instead of fleeing to some distant land, had repaired to his former low haunts in New York, and spent his time in idleness and carousing, for he was apparently well supplied with money. While in liquor and in an unguarded moment, he had betrayed himself by some compromising remark, which, coming to the knowledge of the police, caused him to be speedily secured, and on a requisition from the Governor of New Jersey, conveyed back to his quarters in the county jail at Freehold. He was now placed in double irons, and kept so strictly guarded day and night as to preclude the possibility of a second evasion.

Soon after Klove's recapture, Mr. Heath again started on a mysterious journey. During his absence the news came that strong efforts were being made by some influential person to obtain a pardon for Klove from the Governor. To account for these singular manifestations in behalf of so great a criminal, it was rumored and popularly believed that Klove was not Klove, but the losel son of a venerable bishop of the Episcopal Church, distinguished alike for piety and learning, who was naturally anxious to save his offspring from the disgraceful, though well-merited, death of a felon. Nothing transpired, however, to sustain this report, which was simply a figment of the imagination, due, doubtless, to the popular love for the marvellous. Meanwhile Klove had been sentenced to death, and lay in prison awaiting his doom.

A fortnight or so elapsed before Mr. Heath returned. Edna saw at a glance that there was a change for the worse in her father's condition. He was evidently laboring under a recurrence of one of his melancholic spells, with aggravated symptoms. His form had wasted, and his countenance become haggard. In short, he plainly exhibited the signs of one borne down by a great weight of grief. To his daughter's affectionate inquiries, he replied only in monosyllables, and repaired immediately to his apartments. Edna consulted with her aunt, and Dr. Wattletop was again summoned; but Mr. Heath peremptorily refused to see him or any other physician, and the two ladies were left a prey to their apprehensions.

Mr. Heath's condition excited the doctor's professional curiosity. It was an abstruse physiological problem, and spurred his zeal. By dint of patient investigation, and consultation with the family, he discovered the great interest Mr. Heath took in the pirate Klove. He questioned the groom and gardener in relation to the stranger who had been harbored by Mr. Heath, and by comparing their descriptions with others, came to the conclusion that the mysterious visitor and Klove were one and the same man. To satisfy himself clearly on that point and obtain a further clue to this singular affair, he proceeded to Freehold. Here he was not only confirmed in his conclusions, but learned, furthermore, that a gentleman, a stranger, answering closely to a description of Mr. Heath, had been noticed in attendance at the trial, and in frequent consultation with the prisoner's lawyer.

There was no longer any doubt in the doctor's mind of the existence of some connection or intimacy between the pirate and the patrician, which the mere fact of the former's having once lived in Belton would scarcely account for. He was inclined to suspect a secret tie of kinship, had it not been clearly established at the trial that Klove was born in Germany, and brought to the United States in childhood by his parents. Still cudgelling his brains for a plausible theory to account for Mr. Heath's singular proceedings, he was at length forced to refer them to some phase of hypochondria.

Mrs. Applegate was decidedly of the opinion, now, that her brother was going out of his mind. She had often heard of such cases, she informed Dr. Wattletop. Mr. Applegate had a friend who was taken so, though, to be sure, his trouble arose from the Millerite excitement, and fear of the world's coming to an end. "Of course Rufus has no dread of that kind or anything of the sort, but I do think and believe that it all grows out of his son's death, and nothing else."

"Do you really think that he is so much affected by his son's death?" asked the doctor, with an incredulous expression.

"I don't think he has been the same man since. To be sure he didn't take on so much at first, and didn't seem to realize it fully; but I believe he feels it more and more, and it is that that has made him so different from what he used to be. Poor Edna! dear me, she worries so about her father, and I'm very much afraid she'll fall sick if this continues. Her room is near his, and she says she hears him pacing the floor at all hours of the night."

"Insomnia, eh?"

"And he talks to himself so often; and then again, if you speak to him, or question him, he looks at you so vacantly without replying."

Precursory sign of cerebral disease, thought the doctor.

"It's dreadful—dreadful!" continued Mrs. Applegate. "I can't help but think sometimes that Rufus is losing his senses, and yet such a thing as insanity was never known in our family."

Dr. Wattletop had arrived at a somewhat similar conclusion. He believed Mr. Heath's disease was taking the form of monomania, brought about by the combined effects of disappointment and grief on an overwrought brain. In such a condition the distracted mind was not only readily affected by any striking or impressive event, but apt to identify itself therewith in some bizarre manner.

"It is very important in Mr. Heath's present state, Mrs. Applegate, that we should keep his mind as free as possible from any agitation. No exciting news should reach him. If it were possible to keep the newspapers from him, it would be well; but I presume that is out of the question. However, be careful and vigilant. I think he needs rest and tranquillity more than anything else now. If he would only consent to see me, and if I could only interrogate him a little, I might form a more intelligent opinion of his condition. At the last interview I had with him, we had an interchange of opinions on subjects connected with certain plans of his, and I don't think he was pleased with my comments on them; so I don't know how far my attendance on him would be acceptable now."

"He won't hear of any physician's being spoken to about him. I have tried my utmost, and Edna has pleaded; but he's as obstinate as can be, and won't listen to us," said Mrs. Applegate.

"Sorry. As it is, I am to a certain extent groping in the dark, and under the circumstances, as you can readily understand, it is very difficult to prescribe a course of treatment with any degree of confidence. I don't know what else I can say or recommend just now. As I said, prevent as far as possible any vexatious, exciting, or annoying news from reaching him. Note every symptom, and advise me."

Such commonplace advice was doubtless all that the physician could offer, as Mr. Heath stubbornly refused to see him or any other medical man, and indeed, had given himself up to such complete isolation, as to deny audience even to his business agent, and to the architect in charge of the construction of the Hospital and the Home, so that the building of those institutions was now perforce suspended. He even began to evince an aversion to the society of his family, and to avoid meeting them, took his meals by himself in his own apartments.

XVI.

One Friday Klove was hanged.

The public prints of the following day were filled with details of the occurrence, and Mrs. Applegate, mindful of the doctor's injunctions, strove to keep her brother from reading them. A futile effort, though, for Mr. Heath, on finding that the newspapers were not brought to him at the usual time, rang the bell violently, and rated the servant soundly for the omission.

The magnifico was in his chamber, and looked as aged as a man of eighty. His hair and beard had turned white, his eyes were cavernous and feverishly bright. Roused momentarily by the incident just mentioned, he returned to his seat in an arm-chair near the fire, where, wrapped in a dressing-gown, he had probably passed the night, as his couch was undisturbed. He soon relapsed into a gloomy meditation, holding in his hands the folded newspaper, which he apparently hesitated and dreaded to read. Suddenly, with an effort, his fingers spread the sheet open, and he scanned the columns rapidly until his eyes rested on the account of Klove's execution. To an unusually long description of the horrible affair was appended what purported to be the confession of the malefactor, made to the clergyman in attendance, and reported verbatim. It ran thus:

CONFESSION OF KLOVE, THE PIRATE.

When I was a boy I lived in Belton, in this State. My mother was a widow, for my father died the year after we came to this country from Germany. There were two of us children, me and a girl. My mother did washing for a living, and I worked for a man named Cook, who was very hard to get along with, and to him I lay all my troubles. I suppose I must forgive everybody now, as I hope to be forgiven myself, but it's mighty hard to let up on him. Now I ain't a-going to say that I didn't kill the men aboard the smack, and that I am unjustly sentenced to die; but I say this, and I believe, as I hope for mercy hereafter, that if it hadn't been for the unjust way in which I was treated when I was a boy, by that man, I wouldn't be here now. The way of it all was this: One day Cook sent me with some money to pay a bill at the store. I didn't know how much there was, but when the store-keeper counted it he said it ran short ten dollars. When I went back to Cook and told him, he got angry, and said he had given me the right sum, and I must have stolen the difference. Now he had a grudge against me, and I believe he never gave me the money, but wanted to get me into trouble. I knew I couldn't have lost it, and the shop-keeper counted it before my eyes, and he couldn't have taken it. Howsomever, Cook swore I stole the money, and they locked me up. They didn't keep me long, though, for they couldn't bring any proof, and was obliged to let me off. But I couldn't stay in Belton after that, for no one would employ me, and they all shunned me for a thief. So I left the place and went to New York, but as I was a stranger there, and didn't know any one, I couldn't find work. Then I shipped for a three years' cruise, for I thought by that time all would be forgot, and I could go back home. As bad luck would have it, my shipmates found out that I had been locked up for thieving, and when one of the crew had his chest broken open, and some things missing, they laid it to me. I was innocent, but they wouldn't believe it, and the character I had got went against me, and I wasn't spared a bit. The captain abused me, the mate rope's-ended me, and the men kicked me and called me jail-bird, until I was more miserable than a dog. My whole feelings were changed. I got bitter and revengeful, and if it hadn't been that I couldn't get away I would have knived some of my shipmates. When the vessel touched at the Sandwich Islands, I ran away and knocked about with the beach-combers, a wicked set of outcasts, until I became bad as any of them. I lived among the Islands several years. I shipped again, ran down to Valparaiso, and made several voyages up and down the coast. One day I got into a drunken row in a pulqueria, and stabbed a Chilian. This caused me to be sent to work in the mines as a convict. I got away from there after staying three years and shipped in a French ship to Bordeaux, and from there I got to New York. I hadn't been in the States for ten years, and all that time I hadn't heard anything from my folks. I had become so reckless as to have no wish to see any of them. When in New York I went one night to a dance-house in Cherry Street, and there among the women I found my sister. We didn't know each other at first, but I discovered her by a queer scar on her neck, which she got from a burn when a child. After questioning her, I found out that my mother took on so about me that she left Belton soon after I did, and went to New York. There she fell sick, and died in want, and there was my sister a degraded creature. What little good was left in me was turned by this sight into bad, and I swore to be even with a world that had been so unjust to me and mine. The old feeling of vengeance rose up in my breast—the devil got hold of me, and I thought of Cook. That night I started off to find him, and went to Belton. I hung around there till I found out he was dead and gone some years. If he had been living I would have killed him, sure. All that's wrong, I know, but I couldn't help it. Then I felt just like waging war on all the world. I went to California, and kept a drinking shop on what they called the Barbary coast, where I used to rob miners. Finally I shot one that showed fight, and the Vigilance Committee drove me off, and I came back to the States and went to New Orleans, staid awhile, and came north. I knocked around New York for a time, and finally shipped on the smack, where I committed the deed that's brought me here. The world has got the best of me at last, and it was very wrong and sinful for me to kill the men, and it is right that I should suffer for it and be hung; I ain't a-going to deny that; but I know this and repeat it, that if I had been treated right when a boy, if I hadn't been accused of stealing when I was innocent, I wouldn't be here now, and my sister wouldn't have been ruined. We might have been as happy and as good as any, so let Almighty God judge. Before I go I want to say this: that in the trial I was fairly treated, and I want to publicly thank all those people who were so kind to me. One gentleman has been very good to me, did all he could to help me, and I can't be too grateful to him. He happened just to have remembered me when I was a boy and lived in Belton, and to this kind and benevolent man, I say, may God bless him and reward him.

Rufus Heath read those lines with dilated eyes and shortened breath, like one undergoing the rack. When he had finished, he let the paper drop and uttered a deep groan. His head sank back on his chair, and he pressed his hands over his temples and brow as if to smother distracting thoughts. He remained thus for some time, until a light hand was placed on his shoulder, when he started as if it had been a blow.

The intruder was Edna, who, having knocked at the door and receiving no reply, had entered the room with some anxiety. "Father, dear father, how you frighten me! What ails you? Are you in pain?" exclaimed she, alarmed at his wild aspect. "Do tell me, please tell me, what is the matter?"

"Matter—matter," repeated Mr. Heath abstractedly, as he rose and walked towards the window. "No—no—nothing, child, nothing. Why do you—Ring the bell for James and leave me—leave me, I tell you. I have business to occupy me." He was rattling his fingers nervously on the window-panes as he spoke, and looking vacantly out. His daughter strove to draw him aside, and looking in his face asked anxiously if she might be permitted to send for a physician. "I'm sure there's something the matter with you—you look so very, very strange. Do please, father, may I?"

"No, no, no! Leave me, Edna, and do as I bid you." She obeyed, and Mr. Heath made a struggle to regain his self-possession. When the servant came, he directed him to bring a decanter of brandy. As soon as it was brought, with a trembling hand he poured out a tumblerful and gulped it down. It seemed to affect him no more than so much water, and pacing the room, he forced a laugh as he soliloquized: "Idiot, idiot, and threefold fool! What is it to me that this vagabond and ruffian has met his deserts? Nothing, surely nothing. Then why should I worry about it? Why should I be tormented and maddened by it? Those who murder must expect to be hung. A man is responsible only for his own crimes—the crimes he himself commits, and surely none other, none other. What a monstrous, cruel, wicked doctrine it would be that would hold men to account for the remote and indirect consequences of trivial and commonplace acts. Skilful lawyers cheat justice every day; thousands and thousands of villains have been rescued from the clutches of the law by their paid advocates, and set loose on society, to again plunder and kill. As well hold these advocates responsible for the crimes subsequently committed by their clients, as to tax me with—pshaw! it's too absurd to deserve a moment's thought. What a simpleton I am to quake like a puny child because a low ruffian meets his merited fate! How ridiculous—absurd—preposterous! No, no; I am getting old and childish—old and childish," he continued to croon, until interrupted by the entrance of a servant with luncheon, who was quickly bidden to withdraw.

The luncheon remained untouched.

Again in the arm-chair, and staring with a look of despair at the fire; again torturing thoughts seethe in his brain. The pirate Klove was hung yesterday for murder. What a blood-stained desperado he was, and what a life he had led! Where was his soul now? Who would exchange places with him to gain the whole world? And all this had arisen, he said, from the dishonesty of some one who had caused him to be unjustly accused of stealing a small sum of money. What a flimsy and shameless apology! What an atrocious attempt to shift the responsibility of hellish deeds to other shoulders; to drag some innocent person to everlasting perdition with him! Suppose Cook, his employer, had really given him the money, and had no intention of wrongfully accusing him—what then? Perhaps the money was lost, and if so, if any one had found it they would naturally have kept it. Of course, anybody would do that. It's a very common thing for persons to do. It is an everyday occurrence. No one but a fool would act otherwise. Ten dollars is but a trifle, and to attribute to the loss of a sum so paltry such terrible, awful consequences, is simply ridiculous. But the boy should not have been allowed to rest under the imputation of having stolen it. He should have been saved from arrest. They discharged him—yes, they discharged him. He was not long imprisoned. True, but he should have been cleared from suspicion at any cost—any cost! His innocence proclaimed in thunder tones far and wide! To omit that was wrong, fearfully, bitterly wrong! Not doing so, forced him to leave home in disgrace; made him an outcast, killed his mother, drove his sister to shame. Horror!... And he thanked the kind gentleman who had been so good to him, and with his dying breath, bade God bless and reward him! "O Christ, help—

116

help me!"

These last words escaped from Mr. Heath in a lacerating cry. He pressed his hands to his face as if to shut out some horrifying sight, and remained so until he gradually fell into a dreamy stupor. The excited mind ceased to work, and became numb. Luminous images floated before his mental vision, and kaleidoscopic interminglings of uncouth objects and faces.

Then the wearied and distracted brain lapsed into a feverish slumber—a slumber alive with fearful visions. He dreamt he was in a prison-cell. It was night, and the grated door swung open to admit the jailer and hangman. They pinioned him, and led him out to the scaffold. At the foot of the gallows lay a coffin, containing the corpse of Klove, with horribly distorted features. The hangman was about pulling a cap over his face, when Mr. Heath awoke with trembling limbs, and a cold sweat starting from every pore.

It was evening, for he had lain in that stupor and sleep for hours. Again he resorted to the brandy to dissipate the lingering impressions of the frightful nightmare, and then rang the bell. The servant appeared, and desired to know what his master wanted. Nothing—nothing. Yes, to have light in the library— he would read. Did Mr. Heath wish to have dinner brought up to him? No, no; leave me—leave me. The man lit the gas in the library, replenished the grate, and left.

The library was the room adjoining Mr. Heath's, and thither he went. He took a volume from a shelf, and returned to his apartment; then resumed his seat and lethargic stare at the fire. The book fell unheeded from his grasp.

Hours passed, and again the coarse, distorted, purple features of Klove appeared—once the countenance of a timid boy, who stood falsely accused and cowering before a stern magistrate; thence driven by a storm of hisses, and flying from home, followed by a widowed mother and child-sister. And the brand THIEF clings to the hapless lad, and enmeshes him in a web of misfortune; now reckless with despair, he plunges into vice and crime, until the law forces him to yield up his spotted soul on the gallows!

And how fared the real thief?

He, sly and sharp, in sudden glee at his trover, bought with it a lottery ticket that drew a prize. This windfall, shrewdly invested, brought him a fortune, then an heiress; and thus he waxed in wealth and station, until he became one whose possessions bred envy, and whose position commanded respect; while the innocent and wrongly accused boy became an outcast, a criminal—an assassin! Driven to perdition by the wealthy and respectable citizen!

"It's a dream—a dream. The foolish dream of an enfeebled man, whose reason and judgment are failing and wandering; who is frightened at shadows conjured by his imagination. My mind wanders. Why will those dreadful thoughts return? That sinking terror!"

"I must leave this room—this place—for the air is full of jibing imps!... I must go, for all this luxury mocks me. Away from this roof—from these ponderous walls, that are loaded with iniquity, or they will fall and crush me.... In some quiet, retired spot I may live in happiness and peace...."

Mr. Heath left his room, and with stealthy steps descended the stairs. It was late; the house was silent; all had retired for the night save he. With nimble fingers he opened the hall-door noiselessly, and went out on the lawn. He was bareheaded, and in his dressing-gown and slippers. The night was dark, gloomy, and rainy. The cold drops falling on his unprotected head seemed to soothe and refresh him.

"So, so—this is better," he exclaimed, with a sigh of relief. "How dreadful was all that pomp and glitter! How fortunate I am to have escaped from those torturing, horrible riches! That wealth was consuming me like licking flames —that load of ill-gotten money crushing my poor brain—my poor brain. Now I am free, free! and will seek a home where poverty, and peace, and happiness abide."

With almost preternatural adroitness he picked his way, in spite of the obscurity, over his grounds and out at a postern gate to the open road. He walked along rapidly, and seemed intent on reaching the town. He changed his apparent intention, however, for he retraced his steps and turned abruptly into a by-path that led along the river-side. On he went towards the cliff, proceeding as unerringly as if in broad daylight, and without the slightest hesitation, guided, perhaps, by some instinct similar to the marvellous second-sight of the somnambulist. The least deviation might have brought him to the edge of the precipice. At length he reached the foot-bridge. It was a frail structure of wood spanning the chasm, with its ends resting on the lofty basaltic walls. Mr. Heath was about to cross this bridge, but stopped midway and gazed in the direction of the town only to be distinguished by the faint glimmer of a few lights. He seemed absorbed in reflection, and stood there in that wild, rainy night, unmindful of the cold and wet, and motionless amid the continual thunder of the falling waters, visible through the blackness in swiftly agitated scrolls of snowy foam. But his thoughts were elsewhere; back to the time when he was a young man beginning life, and had seen the boy Klove standing on that bridge with his little sister by him! The two children were staring in open-eyed awe at the appalling depth below them, and the boy held the girl tightly by the hand in precaution. It seemed but yesterday. He, Heath, then a clerk, was taking some papers to Mr. Obershaw, when he passed those two innocent children on the bridge. Better for them—far better, had he flung them both into the raging torrent below! Again he met the boy at old Van Slyke's store. There was a dispute about a missing bank-note, and the lad was in dismay at the loss. He, Heath, had seen the note fall on the floor, and put his foot on it. He could distinctly recall the feeling of gratification with which he slyly secured it, and the singular superstitious prompting that induced him to buy a lottery ticket with it. That bank-note had borne him luck, and proved the corner-stone of his opulence and grandeur; and its loss had entailed the destruction of two souls! What fearful, fatal results from so light a theft! How deeply had the boy fallen—a malefactor, a deeply-dyed murderer, and his sister—that helpless child! O Christ! that awful conscience-throe! Why had he not sent them both to eternity then? Better for them and for him. Mercy, mercy! that terrible lead-like load is coming again, and pressing —pressing so fearfully on the throbbing brain. Help—O God!... Easier now —and hark! A voice seems calling to him. No, it's but the sighing wind. Oh for rest, and forgetfulness, and peace! Rest and oblivion. Take all—all! and give me that. Cannot wealth buy it? It is there, though—down there! How quietly those black boulders sleep amid that boiling foam. One leap and I am free!

With a frantic toss of his arms Rufus Heath flung himself off the bridge. A form vanished into the dark abyss, and all was over. Sullenly and persistently, as before, the Passaic plunged over the steep, bearing in its rapid tide the magnifico of Belton, like a drifting log.

———————————————————

Early the next morning, as some artisans were going to their work and walking along the riversde, their attention was attracted by a partly submerged object near the bank. It was the body of Rufus Heath, kept to the surface by the swirl of an eddy. With the assistance of a boat, the corpse was drawn ashore, and kept there until the coroner could be summoned. Like wild-fire the news spread through Belton, and crowds hurried to see the drowned body of its chief citizen.

And then through the circle of gaping, curious spectators came a cry of anguish that separated them like the thrust of a sword; and they hustled aside as the daughter hastened with faltering steps to her dead father. With clasped hands, knit brows, and brimming eyes the poor child knelt to embrace the wet and bruised head. Her low quivering sobs awed them all, until George Gildersleeve, tenderly unclasping her clinging arms, raised her fainting form, and bore her away.

XVII.

The huge battlemented villa on the cliff was a gloomy enough residence since the death of its owner. The remaining occupants, oppressed by their bereavement, moved about the silent rooms like shadows. Mrs. Applegate was of the opinion that a change of scene was absolutely necessary to dissipate Edna's excessive grief, and that a continued stay in their present habitation might tend to impair her health. Edna, however, seemed reluctant to leave her home, and it was only at the urgent solicitation of the Mumbies that she did so. Mr. Mumbie was one of the executors of Mr. Heath's will, and was also appointed Edna's guardian. Mr. Mumbie felt the loss of his old friend Rufus Heath deeply. His first impulse was to put his whole family in mourning, but on second thoughts he confined himself to delivering a eulogy on the character of the deceased to every one he met, prefacing it by the sage remark, solemnly delivered, that it was a very sudden death. As this was a proposition that did not admit of much controversy, the listener generally coincided. "Ah! sir, such is life," continued Mr. Mumbie, addressing Dr. Wattletop, who added, "And death."

"Very true—and death," repeated Mr. Mumbie, pausing to reflect, as if this side of the axiom had never struck him before, "and death, as you very justly remark. Ah! sir, at a moment like the present, how hollow everything looks! What's money at a time like this? How transitory and vain are our pursuits—everything, in fact!"

"Paper-mills, for instance," observed the doctor.

"Yes, sir, every worldly matter; and the reflection will force itself upon us, that in the midst of life we are in death, and there's no use kicking against it. Now Mr. Heath was a very peculiar man; I knew him thoroughly. We had been much together from boyhood, and we were always like brothers—if anything, rather more intimate and affectionate than brothers. We began life together; to be sure, I had a little the start of him, but then our tastes and sympathies were exactly alike to a shade. Mr. Heath, sir (impressively), was a very remarkable man—very remarkable man, indeed. He was not only a scholar, and a Christian, but a gentleman as well. He was also, if I may be allowed the expression, a high-toned man—very high-toned indeed, sir. He was a man of wonderful abilities, wide scope (with a circular flourish to exemplify the scope), and great grasp (clenching his large fist)—great grasp of intellect. I will state to you, and I trust you will see the importance of not repeating it—I will state to you in confidence, that I was consulted in regard to a plan on foot—a plan in which our most eminent men were engaged: I am not at liberty to divulge names, but it is sufficient to say that they were our most super-eminent men; consulted, sir, in regard to a plan that would eventually have set Mr. Heath on the very pinnacle of greatness—the very pinnacle."

"Rather an uncomfortable seat, I should fancy," commented the doctor.

Mr. Mumbie stared with a puzzled expression at the physician. He never could understand him, and took refuge in repeating the eulogy in succession to Blanks the stationer, and to Snopple the photographer. Mr. Snopple acquiesced fully in Mr. Mumbie's estimate of Mr. Heath's character and virtues, and stated that any one could see with half an eye, by merely looking at a portrait of the defunct gentleman, that he was no ordinary mortal, but had a very instructive and superior physiognomy; and that, by the bye, reminded him that he had in his studio a very fine negative representing Mr. Heath in three-quarter face and characteristic pose, from which copies could be struck off, which he would agree to furnish colored, if preferred, in the highest style of art, for twenty dollars each, frame included; and which would be an ornament to any parlor, and one that no family in Belton should be without.

Mr. Mumbie said he would see about it. Mr. Mumbie had no time to think of anything just then. He was overwhelmed with the responsibilities thrust upon him.

"The fiduciary obligations imposed on me by the death of my friend Mr. Heath, are very great—very great indeed, and onerous (with a sigh). Still it is a duty I must perform; a sacred trust and burden I must accept. We must all bow to the decrees of Providence;" and Mr. Mumbie, to console himself, cast up mentally the fees the executorship was likely to bring him, which completed and perfected his reconcilement to the decrees of Providence.

To do him justice, he was a faithful guardian and trustee; and as for his wife, she outdid herself in motherly solicitude for the young heiress, whom she immediately took under her protecting wing.

Edna, Mrs. Mumbie insisted, must come and live with her. She must be removed at once from the painful associations connected with her old home, as Mrs. Applegate had very wisely advised, and her guardian's family was the place for her. Edna complied, and the Mumbies treated her like a favorite child. The best room in the house was allotted to her, and nothing was considered too good for dear Edna. So the stately dwelling of the late Mr. Heath was abandoned, and given over to the care of the gardener, as Mrs. Applegate, who had been handsomely provided for in her brother's will, departed to take up her residence in Philadelphia with an aged relative.

Mrs. Mumbie had ulterior views in regard to Edna. The desirableness of securing that young lady as a helpmeet for her son Bob, had not escaped the attention of this sagacious and good mother, and she decided to bring it about. Let us add, too, that whatever Mrs. Mumbie determined to do she generally accomplished, as her husband had discovered at the outset of his connubial life. Mr. Mumbie had a very high opinion of his spouse's ability, and no little dread of her temper. She came of one of the very first of the celebrated first-families of Virginia, the Skinners, and was connected, moreover, on her mother's side with the Yallabushas of Mississippi. Everybody had heard of her father, Colonel Roger Skinner, of Pokomoke, one of the first poker-players of his day, whose true Southern hospitality and peach-brandy were the themes of universal commendation. Mumbie met the fascinating Miss Sallie Skinner first at Saratoga, where he at once succumbed to the potent bewitchment of her raven hair and brilliant eyes. He ventured, after many misgivings, to propose, and was accepted, much to his surprise and delight, as he had hardly dared to hope that such a divinity would link herself with an ordinary mortal. Other people, who had heard the vivacious belle ridicule poor Mumbie's large ears and amorphous feet, marvelled too; but the truth was she had accepted him in a fit of spite at some recreant lover's desertion. Of course the marriage was considered a *mésalliance* in the aristocratic circles of Pokomoke, and the bride's relatives for a while treated the paper-maker rather contemptuously, but as poker and peach-brandy had seriously impaired the substance of the Skinner family, they gradually became reconciled to the match, and condescended to accept largess from the wealthy manufacturer. Mr. Mumbie had a heart corresponding in size to his ears and feet, and proved a perfect dove and treasure of a husband. Malicious tongues said he dared not be otherwise, for the first and only time he attempted to cross his wife, she simply flung herself on the carpet, and beat a tattoo with her heels, screeching terribly the while, until Mumbie, frightened and subjected, promised anything and everything to avoid a repetition of the scene. This, to be sure, was in the early period of their union. Now Mr. Mumbie, through long servitude, was so thoroughly broken to harness and under control, and Mrs. Mumbie had gained such undisputed and serene ascendancy, that stratagems were unnecessary, and she ruled through superior force of character.

This was the energetic and ingenious lady who determined to direct the destiny of her husband's ward, and relieve her from the trouble and difficulty of selecting a husband. To gain her ends, she surrounded Edna with every attention, and was more than a mother to her in fact, pending the time when she would be one in law. The young heiress began to find herself installed as a being of immense importance, and was much surprised at the vast amount of consideration shown to her by her elders. She was shrewd enough to suspect that much of it was due to her wealth, and despised it accordingly; for there was too much good sense in the girl, and her character was too frank and independent to yield readily to the pernicious influence of parasitism.

The correspondence which had been kept up with regularity between Edna and her soldier-lover was interrupted by the death of her father, Mark's intuitive delicacy forbidding him for a time from intruding on the grief of a mourning daughter, further than in sending a formal letter of condolence. It must be admitted, too, that Edna in her grief had but few thoughts to bestow on the suitor who was serving another mistress in the swamps of the Chickahominy. At length, to make amends for her negligence, she wrote him a long epistle, the superscription of which happened to meet Miss Ada Mumbie's eye. Notwithstanding the intimacy existing between the two young ladies, and contrary to the usual custom in such cases, Miss Heath had never confided her tender regard for Mark Gildersleeve to her friend Miss Mumbie. The latter, anxious to know if any such feeling existed, taxed Edna with it, and affected pique at her want of confidence. That young lady at once, with a blush, admitted the soft impeachment. Ada Mumbie was an outspoken young lady, and took after her mamma in respect to having an opinion of her own. She raised her eyebrows very significantly at Edna's confession, saying: "Why—Ed-na Heath, the i-dea! I declare, I am surprised beyond anything. I never would have thought it. He may be a very industrious, excellent young man, but *so* very much your inferior in every way. Why, he's not even a person you could flirt with, much less correspond. His brother is an exceedingly common man—exceedingly so. Why, what can you be thinking of?"

Edna, nettled at this, bridled up and answered, "I don't know what you mean by so much my inferior. He's far cleverer than I am, or you either, Ada. He's very refined and polite and gentlemanly, I'm sure; and just as good as gold."

"Mercy on us, Edna! I declare I didn't know you were so very much interested in him, or I wouldn't have ventured to say a word. To be sure, my acquaintance with the gentleman is so very slight that I am hardly competent to judge of him. I expressed myself as I did solely out of friendship for you. You know very well that the position you occupy in society, and your large fortune—"

"Ada, you might have spared me that last remark," interrupted Edna in a vexed tone. "I hear so much about my fortune—my wealth, that I detest the very mention of it. Oblige me, please, by never again alluding to it in my presence."

"Well, dear, don't let us quarrel over it. I'm sorry, and promise you I'll never say another word about it: there now;" said Miss Mumbie, and Edna kissed her friend in token of amity and restored concord. The friend intended to be a valuable auxiliary to her mamma in bringing about, in time, a match between her brother Bob and the young heiress; but she found she had made a misstep. Thus far, though attentive and agreeable in his clumsy way, Bob did not seem to make any appreciable progress in his suit. When his sister imparted the discovery she had made, to wit: that he had a rival, and one that Edna seemed to evince considerable partiality for, he redoubled his efforts to please. Unfortunately, Bob was not a being calculated to captivate the fair. His physical graces were few, and his mental less, and he only served to amuse Miss Heath until he succeeded in boring her. She, rightfully ascribing this increase of homage on the part of the enamored Bob to her ingenuous declaration to his sister, rather regretted it, especially as she feared having perhaps shown too much warmth in her defence of Mark Gildersleeve. Thenceforth by a tacit understanding, the subject was not again referred to between the two girls.

Mrs. Mumbie, on learning of the danger to her son's prospects, determined to nip it in the bud. "I am really astonished," said she to her husband, "that so well-bred a girl could have allowed her thoughts to stray away so unguardedly. A machinist, dear me, how low! Working with a hammer—all over oil, and grease, and smoke. It's positively amazing what crazy notions girls will get in their heads. I suppose, though, it's all owing to his turning soldier. Of course, it's nothing but a mere girlish fancy, but it might grow unless checked. Change of scene and a new train of ideas will soon dissipate the foolish whim. A tour abroad is just the very thing—the very thing. Mr. Mumbie, we must go to Europe."

"But, my dear, it's impossible to go now. I can't leave—"

"Mr. Mumbie, we must go to Europe," was repeated with emphasis, "and the sooner the better. Speak to Edna on the subject at once—she needs the voyage. Ada needs it—so does Bob. It's time they saw something of the world, and it will improve their minds vastly."

Mr. Mumbie did as he was bid. Edna was delighted at the idea of a trip to Europe, and readily assented to her guardian's proposal. At the same time he deemed it well to improve the opportunity, in view of what he had learnt respecting his ward's inclinations, by imparting some information which might tend to give her a better estimate of her worth and position in the world than she seemed to possess.

"Edna, I believe I have never spoken a word to you about business matters. I thought it would be as well to get everything into shape before I said anything. Of course it is something that you don't know much about, and yet I suppose I ought to ascertain if you've any wishes in regard to the management of the estate, and so forth. If so, I am ready to take them into consideration," said Mr. Mumbie.

"I have one wish, sir," said Edna.

"Well, what is it?"

"I should like to have father's intentions carried out in regard to building the Home and the Hospital, exactly as if he were alive," said Edna earnestly.

"But, my child, that would cost a great deal of money, a very great deal, and —"

"I don't care if it takes all the estate; I presume there is enough to do it," said Edna decidedly.

"Of course there's enough and more than enough, but I should not be justified or permitted to use any funds in that way. So there's no use in saying anything more about it now. When you come of age, why then, we can talk it over again if you're of the same mind. Now, Edna," continued Mr. Mumbie, taking up a roll of paper, "I've got something to show you that will interest you. I have prepared and completed, after a great deal of labor, an inventory of your late lamented father's estate. The estimates are, if anything, in many cases below the real values. Here is the schedule—and what do you think it all foots up? What do you think it all amounts to in dollars and cents?"

"I don't know," replied Edna. "A great deal, I've no doubt."

"But guess—try and guess," insisted Mr. Mumbie with an air of triumph.

"Please don't ask me; I'd rather not," said Edna seriously.

"Rather not!" repeated Mr. Mumbie with astonishment; "why, bless me, why not? Don't you want to know how much you are worth?"

"No—no—" said Edna quickly, and shaking her head.

"Why—why not?"

"Because—because—" said Edna, her eyes suddenly moistening, and sensitive mouth quivering.

Mr. Mumbie looked perplexed. "Why, Edna, it is clearly your duty that you should gain some knowledge of the way in which the vast fortune you have inherited is invested. You must begin to learn something about it, and about taking care of it. It is very seldom that so young a person is so fortunate as to have such riches left them, and—"

Edna burst into tears. "Oh, please, sir, don't say anything to me about it now. I suppose it's very wrong in me, but they all talk to me so about my wealth, that it makes me feel wretched. They appear to envy me—and to think I ought to be so happy in being rich, until it seems as if they thought I had profited by my poor—poor father's death. I wish I were poor and had nothing."

This is very extraordinary indeed, thought Mr. Mumbie, who imagined he had prepared a pleasant surprise for his ward. "Well, well, Edna, dry your eyes, my child. We won't talk business if you don't like it. Mrs. Mumbie says she thinks the trip to Europe will do you good, and I've no doubt it will. So get ready and we'll all be off as soon as possible."

In less than a fortnight after this conversation, Edna, and the Mumbie family with the exception of the youngest member, were at sea on their way to Liverpool. Before leaving, Edna wrote a letter to Mark, bidding him an affectionate farewell; promising that her absence would be but a short one, and reiterating her oft-expressed wish that the war would soon end and enable him to return home safe and famous. By the time this epistle reached its destination the one it was addressed to was a captive in the hands of the enemy. An expedition had been planned to make a dash into the capital of the Confederacy and rescue the prisoners confined on Belle Isle. Mark Gildersleeve took part in this hazardous undertaking, which through lack of support failed, and he with a few others as rashly venturesome, were surrounded and captured; not, however, until after a gallant struggle in which several were killed and a number wounded. Among the latter Mark, who received on that occasion a carbine bullet in his bridle-arm, which he repaid by lodging the contents of his revolver into two of his assailants. Another shot, however, disabled his horse, and he was made prisoner. He suffered severely from his wound, owing to a want of proper medical attendance; but fortunately the ball, which had taken an erratic course, was easily extracted, and his vigorous constitution did the rest. He spent some five weary months in Castle Thunder and was then exchanged. On his return to his regiment he found the letter from Edna, announcing her departure for Europe, awaiting him. He had written to her several times during his captivity, without receiving any reply; now her silence was explained. His letters had probably not been forwarded properly, or if forwarded had not reached her. He had had an almost irresistible inclination to revisit Belton, but now that it was bereft of its chief attraction the desire vanished, and he returned to his duty, with an increased determination to carve his way to distinction at whatever cost.

Meanwhile Miss Heath and her friends had arrived in Europe. It was her first visit there, and she found so much that was novel and pleasing that her mind was constantly occupied and diverted. Some time was spent travelling through England and Scotland; then they proceeded on the usual tour through the Continent, making a lengthened stay in Paris. The following summer was passed in Switzerland and at the German watering-places. In the former country they met some pleasant English people, and among them a party of Cambridge students. One of the Cantabs was very attentive to the young ladies, and Edna declared he was the most entertaining and agreeable young gentleman she had ever met. He was handsome withal, judging from a description of him given in a letter of Edna's to her friend Constance Hull, in which she said: "His complexion is just lilies and roses—in fact it exactly matches the blush-rose in his button-hole; and his large, limpid irids are of forget-me-not blue—suggestive hue! Everything's 'awful jolly' with him, and he makes the nicest beverages with sherry and claret, and sliced cucumbers, called 'claret-cup,' or something of that sort, but at any rate, it's perfectly delicious; and he's just as full of fun as he can be, and always ready for some frolic or other." Such delightful walks and excursions as they enjoyed together, and how sorry they all were to part with him. Even Mrs. Mumbie seemed to regret the separation, perhaps because he was the nephew of a lord, and had paid some attention to Ada, who certainly was smitten with him. As for Edna, she was suspiciously quiet for a few days after his departure, and we fear that during that time her thoughts seldom reverted to her absent suitor, the striving Union volunteer. But his image arose again to reproach her, as she reflected that she had not written a line to him in a very long while. To be sure he had not replied to her last epistle; in fact, she had written three or four without receiving any response, and had half made up her mind not to write again until she had received an acknowledgment of her letters. Perhaps, thought she, they may not have reached him. Still he might write to me at all events. Poor fellow! who knows, he may be sick, or wounded, or in prison. Dear me, I've been so distracted with all I've seen and heard, that I'm afraid I don't think as often of him as I ought to. I'll sit down at once and write him a good, kind, long letter to make amends. And she did so, but it met a fate similar to the previous ones, bearing the same superscription, that she had sent, and found its way, we regret to say, into the hands of Mrs. Madison Mumbie, who consigned the tender lines to congenial flames, after having cynically perused them. While in Paris, Edna, in recognition of the kindness shown her by her guardian's family, had presented the mother and the daughter with expensive *parures* of diamonds. The one selected for Mrs. Mumbie was in particular composed of the finest and most costly stones. Mrs. Mumbie was profuse and almost abject in her acknowledgments and thanks to dear Edna. Could that generous young heart have known that this velvety woman had been treacherously intercepting her correspondence—rifling the depositaries of her secret thoughts, she would have shrunk from her as from a reptile. But to youthful innocence baseness such as this exists not.

The next winter was spent in Italy, chiefly in Rome. Edna's enthusiasm for the glorious old city knew no bounds. Between sight-seeing and shopping she had not an idle moment. The quantities of silken sashes and jewels of coral and mosaic she bought for presents, and the money she spent and flung away to lazzaroni, would have driven her grandfather Obershaw as wild as Shylock was at Jessica's extravagance. She created a great sensation among the artists. The sculptors wanted to model her lips and chin, and the painters raved about her hair and complexion; altogether, between the studios, the ruins, the Carnival, and what not, she was having, as she expressed it in her correspondence with Miss Hull, "a splendid time." There was a long postscript to that letter to this effect:

P.S. You remember I mentioned in my last, that we had engaged a new courier in Paris, a handsome Italian named Luigi, who was so very refined and *distingué*-looking, and such an excellent linguist. Well the secret is out! He is a Count, and his name is Borgia, Count Gasparone Alessandro Borgia, a scion of the illustrious family of that name—just think of it! He betrayed himself to Ada in an unguarded moment. He was stripped of his patrimony by confiscation, and adopted his present vocation the better to elude the malignity of his enemies, who are continually seeking to persecute him. Who those enemies are, I do not clearly understand. Sometimes he says they are the Jesuits, and at other times he accuses Mazzini and the red-republicans. He hints also at hereditary foes of his house, the Orsini and Sforzi. Evidently he shrinks with intuitive delicacy from speaking of himself and his misfortunes, and feels his position keenly. Ada caught him in tears once or twice mourning the decadence of his house. He assured her, on his word of honor, that all the stories that were in circulation respecting the poisoning propensities of his family are malicious falsehoods, and is very indignant at the outrageous way in which the dramatists have treated his distinguished ancestress—and I don't wonder at his anger. I think he says she was his great-great-grand-aunt; but I won't be certain. Since we have learned his title and rank, we have all felt a delicacy in treating him as a courier. Mr. Mumbie almost insisted on his taking his meals with us, but he firmly, and dignifiedly refused, which I think was very honorable in him, don't you? I flatter myself not a little on my sagacity and knowledge of people that I felt certain the moment I saw him that he was no ordinary person. The seal of high birth is unmistakably set on his noble brow and statuesque features; and then, O Constance, such eyes! such flashing, melting orbs!…

The Fosters leave for home next week. I intrusted them with a present for you which they kindly consented to deliver. It's a turquoise set, and I hope it will suit you. I'm sure it will be becoming. I did intend to surprise you with it myself, but it's so uncertain when we shall return that I thought I would avail of the opportunity to send it at once. Please accept the set with the best love of

Ever yours,
EDNA.

XVIII.

It is not our purpose to follow Mark closely in his career during the war. Suffice it to say, that after his exchange he had rejoined his corps, and taken part in the memorable battle of Gettysburg, where the legions of the South, flushed with victory, were checked in their advance on Northern soil, and driven back by the Union soldiers. With steady courage he perseveringly sought laurels. His gallant bearing on several occasions attracted the notice of his superior officers, and his noteworthy conduct in leading an attack on the forces of General Imboden on the Cashtown road, whereby a large number of rebels were cut off and captured, won him the grade of major. The young fellow, as we mentioned, started in life with an unusual stock of vanity, fortunately counter-balanced by a chivalrous spirit and scorn of the mean. Much of this vanity had been eliminated, probably on the homoeopathic principle of like curing Life, for his profession was one decidedly calculated to foster that weakness. He was sensible enough, however, to avoid the arrogance engendered by the possession of authority of which he saw so many examples, and better still to preserve his soul from that callousness and ferocity which are the worst fruits of horrid war. He felt the insidious approaches of the baleful influences, but resisted. Bearing in mind, also, his old friend's injunction to beware of the sway of prejudice over reason, he strove to be just and unbiassed. There was some of the old paladin spirit in Mark. He recognized among the enemy many who were as earnest and sincere in their cause as he was in his; perhaps he was frequently led to think that the advantage in that respect was on their side, as he saw with inexpressible disgust the host of mercenaries whose sole thought was how to turn their country's misfortunes to profit, and, worse than all, lukewarm, disobedient generals, sacrificing their soldiers' lives to gratify some pique or partisan feeling. His blood boiled, too, at the unmentioned cruelties practised on the unfortunate race who had been the innocent cause of the fratricidal strife. This sympathy very nearly led him into serious trouble on one occasion. Among the regiments in the Army of the Potomac were several recruited from the dregs of the large cities of the North. Many of these men were without respect for their flag, and capable of any deed, or ready for any adventure that promised plunder or diversion. It was a common practice with them to shoot at any negro they found astray, in the vicinity of their camp. Mark, while away by himself one day in Virginia, came across a party of these fellows on some marauding expedition. Presently one of them espied a negro standing at the door of his cabin, near the edge of a wood, and without more ado, raised his musket and shot him dead. So enraged was Mark at this wanton murder, that, unable to contain himself, he drew his revolver and sent a bullet into the assassin. He fell, seriously wounded. His companions were about to retaliate, but intimidated by the major's bearing, and somewhat by his rank, hesitated, and concluded to report him at headquarters. The matter resulted in a court-martial, but Mark was acquitted with a reprimand.

War either makes or mars a man. The soul is drawn so completely out of the commonplace grooves of ordinary life, so far from the shrinking influences of wealth-seeking, and into an arena where emotions and passions contend so fiercely for mastery, that it comes out of the ordeal either sensibly debased or refined. Fortunately for Mark, it had purified his character; had given him a broader view of the aim and scope of life, enabling his will to crush out all vain hopes and envious desires, and find his pleasure in the performance of his duty and the approbation of his conscience. In short, he had become a true man. To how many, however, did the campaign prove a curse—how many contracted indolence, and habits that unfitted them for the avocations of peace, or exchanged their rectitude and purity of heart for vicious tastes that embittered their future lives.

Time passed. Mark became attached to General H——'s staff, and spent many months before Petersburg. It was there he performed an exploit which has remained legendary in the annals of the war. During a night attack on one of our batteries, the rebels had succeeded in spiking a siege-gun which commanded their position, while it protected our working parties of sappers. As soon as the piece was rendered useless, the enemy's sharp-shooters, swarming in rifle-pits close to our lines, seriously impeded further progress on our part. Vexed at this interruption, the commander called for volunteers to unspike the gun; but as this involved getting on the breech, and becoming a target for the foe while the work lasted, no one seemed willing to undertake it. In this dilemma, Mark, being known as a skilled machinist, was consulted; and after an examination, he reported in favor of the practicability of the job, while admitting the extreme peril attending it. Perhaps any intention of executing it would have been abandoned, had not a comment, made by one of the men to another, to the effect that it was easy for officers to set tasks for privates which they were not willing to do themselves, been accidentally overheard by Mark, which stung him immediately into offering to accomplish the hazardous feat. Armed with several well-tempered bits and a brace, he went forth at nightfall on his perilous errand. Straddling the breech of the monstrous cannon, and crouching as low as possible, with the brace against his chest, he plied the drill vigorously. Scarcely had he begun to work, when he was perceived by the vigilant rebel marksmen, who immediately opened fire. He could see the long rifle-pit, not a hundred yards distant, ablaze with the flash of fifty rifles, and feel the wind of their bullets as they whistled past him. Fortunately, favored somewhat by the obscurity, but far more by good luck, he remained unscathed, save by a skin-grazing touch. In fifteen minutes (it seemed to him an hour) the vent was clear; a primer and lanyard were then passed up to him, and these affixed, he slipped off the cannon as quick as possible. Seeing him drop, the rebels imagined they had shot him, and sent up a yell of exultation, which was suddenly checked as a discharge of grape from the liberated gun scattered death among them. Mark was not destined to escape entirely uninjured, for in his haste to get off the gun, and anxiety to avoid any danger from its recoil, he fell heavily, and was picked up with a dislocated shoulder. This accident, however, entailed but a short confinement, and he was soon able to be on duty again. Needless to add, that Mark received full meed of praise for his daring achievement, which furthermore earned him the grade of colonel.

In this his hour of triumph and full flush of gratified vanity, one thought was constant and uppermost. How would Edna receive the news of his renown? If she felt but one momentary responsive throb of pride, he was repaid, and repaid a hundred-fold, for all he had risked and undergone. But would she hear of him? Where was she? Although he had written her several letters he had received none from her, since the one announcing her departure for Europe. Her silence was unaccountable. So long a time had elapsed that he began to despond. "Well, well," thought he, "it's inexplicable, and useless to indulge in conjectures. I'll not do her the injustice to believe that it is intentional neglect on her part. We'll see what it all means when she returns. Meanwhile I must console myself by re-reading her old epistles."

He occasionally received a communication from his sister-in-law, who kept him advised of all the Belton gossip—births, deaths, marriages, and so forth. At length one came, conveying the welcome intelligence that the Mumbies and their fair charge had returned home. Mrs. Gildersleeve stated that she had seen Miss Heath, and that she was looking remarkably well, but exceedingly grand and dignified; adding, "You would hardly know your old sweetheart, now, Mark. She holds her head as high as a queen, and goes sweeping through the streets as if the earth were not good enough for her to tread on. I do not think, I am sorry to say, that travelling has improved her a bit." This was uncommonly severe criticism to come from the worthy lady, and amazed Mark; but perhaps her opinion was somewhat colored by the fact that Miss Heath had, unintentionally or otherwise, neglected to return Mrs. Gildersleeve's bow; an omission certainly sufficient to bias the judgment of the least prejudiced woman who respects herself.

There was a lull in the conflict. The shock of arms and bruit of war gave place to the patient, silent work of the engineer. Inch by inch, the Union army advanced its lines of investment, and slowly the constricting circle was closing. Dull monotony succeeded, broken only by the occasional bursting of a shell over the trenches, or the crack of a sharp-shooter's rifle and ping of bullet, startling some too venturesome spectator. Apart from this, all was inaction or weary routine. Deeming it a favorable time to apply for leave of absence, and longing to see Edna, Mark sought and obtained a furlough, and was speedily on his way north.

It would be difficult to describe the Colonel's feelings as he approached his home. The anticipated delight of meeting his friends, relatives, and above all, Edna, was mingled with a vague sense of apprehension—a premonition of some disappointment that he could not shake off. He had been away full three years. It seemed to him at least ten; and he dreaded to be confronted by unpleasant changes. Belton, at least, was still the same, and in its usual quiet mood. Contrary to the expectations of many of its inhabitants it had not as yet been invaded by the Rebels; still, as untiring vigilance was the price of liberty and safety the "Home Guard" kept up its organization and weekly drills, under the patriotic supervision of Captain George Gildersleeve. The first thing that attracted Mark's attention, as he passed up Main Street, was a full-length colored photograph in Snopple's show-case, of his brother, in all his panoply, figuring conspicuously in company with portraits of Generals Grant and Sherman.

Mark had hardly been in the town five minutes, before the fact was known from one end of it to the other; and Dr. Wattletop devoted himself to informing everybody he met, that Mark Gildersleeve had returned from the "wars, bearing his blushing honors thick upon him."

Of course the fatted calf was figuratively killed by Mrs. Gildersleeve, and the doctor took tea at her table that evening, and a joyful meal it was. The colonel noticed a marked change in his old friend. Age was shrinking his once rotund form, and his countenance wore the expression of one seeking rest after a strife with life. His disputative spirit was apparently quenched, as he evinced no disposition to take up several thorny assertions on the part of the doughty captain of the "Home Guards," who monopolized the conversation. This martinet criticised very severely the dilatory and bungling way in which the war was carried on, and set forth a plan of operations of his own, which, he was ready to back with any amount of money, would, if carried out by the commander-in-chief, bring the rebels to terms in the short space of time limited to three shakes of a sheep's tail. No one had a stronger belief in himself than George Gildersleeve. It was a faith, too, that increased with his years and prosperity, and perhaps had contributed not a little to the latter.

As for the young colonel, he was singularly taciturn. Perhaps a little disappointed in finding that his lady-love had left the town, albeit it did not mitigate in any great degree the pleasure he felt in being once more in his old home. Certainly his appetite was not affected; and the quantity of clover-honey, of preserves, both quince and crab-apple, of stewed oysters, of Sally Lunn, and waffles he consumed, were sufficient to give an able-bodied ostrich a gastric derangement.

After the meal they sat in the little parlor. Mark opened his long-neglected piano and tried a few bars of a favorite *Nocture*; but his stiff fingers made poor work of it. It was pleasanter to sit beside his second mother. There were a few more silver threads in her smooth hair, but her serene, loving face seemed to him as young as ever. Presently the Reverend Samuel and Mrs. Sniffen dropped in, for whom the colonel had to fight his battles o'er again.

"And how about that exploit of yours, unspiking the cannon? We've all heard of it, colonel," said the minister. "Mrs. Bradbury's son, who was there at the time, wrote a full account of it home, but we want to listen to it from your lips."

"Yes, yes, Hotspur, out with it," added the doctor. The red shone through Mark's gypsy cheek, as he gave a confused and stammering recital of the incident; and he felt decidedly relieved, when he had concluded, at his brother's blunt remark that he deserved to have been shot for his pains, as no one but a fool or a crazy man would have attempted such a job.

"Mercy, George, don't say that!" said Mrs. Gildersleeve, who had been listening, pale and with a shudder, to Mark's narrative.

"George is right," replied Mark; "it was nothing but a foolhardy freak, done on the spur of the moment; and I would not have attempted it if I had taken time to reflect."

The colonel was rather anxious to slur the feat; for, on analyzing the motives that impelled him to its performance, he was obliged to confess that it was pricked vanity and the desire to win Edna's admiration, rather than any stern sense of duty or devotion to his flag.

"You never wrote me a word of all this, Mark," said his sister-in-law, reproachfully. "However, perhaps it is just as well;" and addressing Mr. Sniffen, who was about taking his departure, she asked him if he would, before leaving, kindly lead in prayer, so that they might all return thanks for the safe return and preservation of Mark from so many dangers. "You will join us, will you not, doctor?"

"Most certainly, my dear lady," was the reply; and the old materialist, who had sought with a scalpel for the soul in a cadaver, the stoic, the Pythagorean, knelt and united in sincere devotion to the Father of all, whom we worship, each after his own little system, way, or fashion.

After the departure of the guests, the circle around the grate-fire was still further narrowed, and Mrs. Gildersleeve opened her budget of news. She first inquired of Mark if he did not think the doctor had greatly changed? "Very much," replied Mark.

"Poor man," continued Mrs. Gildersleeve, "I feel so sorry and anxious about him. He has lost a great deal of his practice—almost all the paying part of it. He has still a host of patients, but they are mostly among the poor, from whom he gets little or no pay. I believe if he had all the money due him he would be rich; but he never tries to collect anything. About six months ago his dog died—that large black one, that was always with him; and he cried like a child, said he had lost his best friend, and wrote a very singular obituary, that was published in the paper. After that he took to drinking very freely; and one day while under the influence he struck with his cane a teamster who was beating a horse; and the man had him arrested, and if it hadn't been for your brother, the doctor would have been put in jail."

"I think he served the teamster right," remarked her husband, "only he didn't give him half enough."

"Very likely; but the doctor made such a ridiculous speech about it in court. Spoke about animals having reason and souls, and that some men were inferior animals to the brutes; and accused the clergy of cowardice in shirking the question of the connection and duty of man to his fellow-animals, and a lot more of such stuff. To be sure he was under great excitement. Mr. Sniffen thinks the doctor got those perverted notions from living so long in India among the heathen. Since that time the doctor has not been the same man. He never touches a drop of anything, and he is always grave. He has failed, too, very much. Poor man! I feel so distressed about him, and was so rejoiced to see him join with us this evening in prayer. It is certainly very hard for a man of his years, for he must be eighty, to be left without any one, away from relatives. I should so like to help him if I knew how to approach him without offending him. He is such a very peculiar person."

"It is his own fault," said George. "I offered to run him for coroner, or put him in as county physician, if he'd get naturalized and become a citizen; but the pig-headed old duffer got as indignant as if I'd insulted him; talked about his sovereign and her Gracious Majesty, until I shut him up. So he's no one to blame but himself. Ten o'clock, eh? I'm off to bed. I suppose you and Maggie will talk here for three hours yet;" and George retired with a stretch and a

136

yawn.

When they were alone, Mrs. Gildersleeve touched on the topic nearest to her brother-in-law's heart. It was done in the light of an apology. She said: "In one of my letters, I am ashamed to say, I spoke censoriously and unjustly of Miss Heath, and I wish to take it all back; but it shows how particular we ought to be not to judge hastily. Miss Heath, I suppose you know, has come into her property, and her first thought and care is to carry out her father's intentions about building those charitable institutions. It will cost ever so much. I believe Mr. Mumbie tried to prevent or rather persuade her not to lay out so much money, but she wouldn't listen to it; and they say is even going to spend more; but that's just like Edna Heath."

How intensely the colonel's heart indorsed that opinion. "Where is she now?" he inquired.

"She's living in New York, with the Mumbies. You must certainly pay her a visit, and renew your old acquaintance. Mr. Mumbie sold out his paper-mill, and has retired from business."

An hour or more of such conversation and Mark withdrew, to find himself again in his little bedroom. Nothing was disturbed. There was his bookcase with its narrow desk, where he had passed so many hours in brain-racking devotions to the immortal Nine; and as he glanced over the turgid lines of some uncompleted poem in the portfolio, his smile justified the belief that time brought its own severe criticism to poetasters. There lay in their accustomed places his guitar and zithern, and over his bed-head hung, as of yore, the engraving of Carlo Dolce's *Mater Dolorosa*, whose exquisite mouth and chin were but counterparts of Edna's. It was so natural to lie in the bed where he had slept since childhood; and he seemed to breathe such an atmosphere of peace and quietude, that the tremendous events he had passed through during three years, seemed like a hiatus in his life, or a dream. Did the war exist? Here, all was tranquillity undisturbed by alarms; but away on the banks of the Appomattox, his brethren in arms slept in suspense; the vigilant picket watched the wily foe; the bursting shell tore the limbs of some sleeping soldier, and starving conscripts, in butternut rags, were flying from the rebel trenches to hospitable imprisonment within the Union lines. Such thoughts filled Mark's mind as he tossed uneasily on his downy couch and soft fringed pillow, until, to court slumber, he was obliged to wrap himself in a blanket, and seek repose on the hard floor.

The next morning, in his impatience to see Edna, he would have started at once for the metropolis, but there were his old associates at the Works, who could not be neglected. He went there, and shook hands with them all, from Knatchbull to the youngest apprentice. How they all crowded around and questioned him, and seemed to be as much interested in him as if he belonged to them, while his brother stood by with an approving look, as if the colonel were entirely the product of his care and training. Mark found the Works still further enlarged; for his brother's business had increased prodigiously, and George, while alluding to this, did not fail to remark to the colonel, with a spice of malice, that if he had remained at home and accepted the partnership, he would by this time have possessed a small fortune. "A clear hundred thousand were the profits last year—a clear hundred thousand. What do you think of that, old man?" But the old man, as he affectionately called him, did not seem to think much about it, for he merely replied, "Glad to hear of it for your sake," and seemed as indifferent as ever to such favors. George then said, as a consolatory offset, "Whenever you want to come back, you're welcome. Your old place is waiting for you, and it will pay you better than soldiering in the end."

Then there was the visit to the Falls. No true Beltonian returning from a long absence ever failed to pay his devoirs at that shrine. It seemed as if the old legend of the Indians, that the Great Spirit abided there, had perpetuated itself, and found believers among their white successors. Mark passed an hour of the fine January fore-noon in pleasant contemplation near the cataract. It was an old friend. Its roar, its crags, its emerald waters were familiar to him from childhood, when he spent holidays around the pebbly shores seeking flint arrow-heads, or in older years when he resorted thither to derive inspiration and metaphorically court the nymphs and dryads. The torrent that sped on in sublime and unceasing monotone had measured his existence like a clepsydra.

Mark extended his walk to the cliff—to the villa that had seemed to him a very palace of enchantment, and around which so many blissful associations clustered. Here was the spot where he had made his first avowal of love, and he could almost recall the novel, delicious thrill with which he pressed Edna's hand to his lips. Now the gates were chained and locked, and their lamps broken by vagrant boys; the lodge was tenantless; the marble basin of the fountain choked with dead leaves, and its spouting swans decapitated; the grounds neglected, and the windows of the imposing structure blinded. How sad and deserted an aspect! How changed the place—once the abode of "elegant Eunomia," the goddess of his dreams! He remembered his surreptitious visit and eavesdropping the night of Edna's party. Where were all that youth and beauty now? The sweeping wind answered with a dismal sigh. Was there any omen in this?

His reverie was cut short by the patter of horses' hoofs behind him. It was the four-in-hand of Mr. Nehemiah Gogglemush, a new-comer in Belton, who saluted him with a stare. This man, who seemed ambitious to succeed to the position of the late magnifico, was the inventor of the world-famous "Terpsichorean Ointment," a corn-salve of marvellous virtue, that had brought him a fortune correspondingly marvellous. He had purchased a site on the cliff and reared a gorgeous pile, all turrets, gilt Tudor-flowers and weathercocks, which completely overshadowed Mr. Mumbie's dwelling. Gogglemush seemed to have no end of money and actually dared to set up a drag, while his wife and daughters made shameful exhibitions of themselves in diamonds, point-lace, India shawls; and deported themselves generally in a way that no person in their station, and connected with corn-salve, who had any regard for public opinion, would venture to. Moreover, at church the Misses Adela and Angela Gogglemush, in all their odious finery, monopolized the attention of the congregation, and even the rector was reported to be not indifferent to the attractions of the younger of the two.

Of course it was impossible for the Mumbies to live in constant proximity to such vulgarity, and especially as there was absolutely no one now in the place, except Judge Hull's family, with whom they could associate, as Mrs. Mumbie said, they had been forced to remove to New York.

On his return Mark stopped for a moment at St. Jude's. The sexton wanted to show him the beautiful memorial windows, presented by Miss Heath in honor of her father and mother. Mark peopled the edifice with its old frequenters—with handsome, refined Mr. Heath, dignifiedly condescending, as if he were willing to meet his Maker half way; with Edna's sweet, uplifted, attentive profile; devout, slow-winking Mrs. Applegate, and in the opposite pew, pompous Mr. Mumbie, who occupied one corner with such upright, unvarying exactitude, that he served as a sundial to Mark to measure the service, when the purple ray from a lancet-window moved over the capacious white waistcoat of the portly paper-maker. The new-comers had taken possession of that pew now, for Mark saw in it several richly bound octavo prayer-books, stamped with the name Gogglemush, hideous in Gothic text.

Mark now proceeded to call on Dr. Wattletop. The information in regard to the latter's pecuniary condition, imparted by Mrs. Gildersleeve, troubled her brother-in-law, and he was anxious to offer any assistance that the physician was likely to accept; but when the colonel, after much hesitation and circumlocution, hinted at his desire, Dr. Wattletop cut him short with a "Thanks—thanks, my dear boy, I'm quite easy. You must know that Miss Heath has requested me to accept, at a handsome salary, the position of physician-in-chief to the hospital she is erecting for the county. Noble girl, that—though I don't know after all that she's doing any more than her duty," he hastened to add, fearing that he might have been betrayed into admiration or approval of generosity. "The world, though, is so constituted, so warped from all ideas of justice, that the mere performance of a single act of duty is greeted with applause. Sad commentary, that. Pokemore is associated with me in the management. There was an effort made to foist this humbug Keene upon us. But Pokemore and I at once declared that we would not listen to it, and should consider it an insult and resign at once if this ignoramus and quack were attached in any way to the institution. We carried our point, of course."

Mark reflected on this instance of inconsistency in the doctor. Tolerant and unprejudiced he was towards every system and opinion save one—the one that attacked his professional judgment, and therefore self-love.

The doctor had grown garrulous with age, and gave Mark a long and circumstantial account of the illness and last hours of Dagon; and then branched off into the exposition of some of his theories respecting future existence. All this was listened to with respectful impatience by the colonel, who was eager to return home and prepare himself to take the afternoon train to New York. He was disappointed in this intention, for he found himself obliged to attend a little tea-party that evening, given by Mrs. Sniffen in honor of his return.

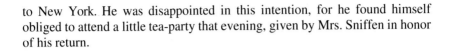

XIX.

The next day Mark arrived in New York. He alighted at the "Albemarle" and proceeded at once to make himself as presentable as his worn uniform would permit, and after a deal of brushing came out almost as smart-looking as a West Point cadet. As the time for the longed-for meeting neared, an unaccountable timidity seized him, and it required more screwing up of his courage to ring the door-bell of Mr. Mumbie's house, than it would to have made him charge a battery. The new residence of the Mumbies was one of those extravagant structures that line the Fifth Avenue, and costly enough to be the domicil of a duke. Mark asked to see Miss Heath. The domestic who answered his ring replied that he did not know whether she were in or not, but would go and see—would the gentleman give his name?

Mark sent up a card and the servant returned with a "not at home."

When would she be in?

Servant couldn't tell—uncertain—didn't know.

The colonel went away, found some brother officers at the hotel, and dined with them. Afterwards he returned to Mr. Mumbie's, but met with no better success; Miss Heath was still "not at home." Disappointed again, Mark returned to his hotel and retired to his room to smoke in gloomy meditation and solitude. He was debating upon the propriety of calling again that day, when his privacy was invaded by one of the officers he had dined with. Being an old comrade of the colonel, he burst in unceremoniously, "Where the devil have you been, Gildersleeve? I've been looking all over for you the past two hours. Want to see you badly. What's the matter, old boy; you look awfully down in the mouth. Not sick, I hope? Here, rouse up; I've got an invite for you to a grand shine to-night. It's a big blow-out, and we'll have some fun."

Mark drew from its envelope an engraved card imparting the information that the pleasure of his company was requested by Mrs. Van Spuytenduyvel at No. —— Madison Square, on that evening.

"What's this, major?" inquired Mark; "Who is Mrs. Van Spuytenduyvel?"

"Don't know the Van Spuytenduyvels! Why, benighted boy, the Van Spuytenduyvels are one of the most illustrious and stupid families in the State, and of the best blood of the Knickerbockers. The wretches wallow in wealth. Where stands yon costly fane was once the ancestral cabbage plantation of the Van Spuytenduyvels. However, that's neither here nor there. The lady is an old friend of mine, and that's enough. Met her a while ago—

mentioned you—told her you were a good-looking boy, battle-scarred, and all that sort o' thing; and she said, bring him along, by all means, and made me promise besides. So don't look so bored; go you must."

"Go, nonsense! Why should I go?" said Mark, in no mood for trifling. "I don't know this lady."

"I told you that I had recorded a solemn vow to bring you, and you've got to go, willy-nilly," said the major, imperturbably.

"But I've no dress suit," expostulated Mark.

"Dress suit, hear the innocent! Not any, thank you. Why, you stupid, you'd spoil all in a swallow-tail coat. What the deuce do you suppose Mrs. V. S. wants of you in black with a white choker? Haven't you sense enough to see that all she cares is to have the proper complement of gilt buttons and straps in her rooms? As for you, my bold soldier boy, you're no account whatever, and she don't just care two pins for your valorous and gallant self; so be sensible—be sensible. Brush up your spread-eagles and prepare; but first get sheared, for you look like a bushwacker with those elf-locks."

The advice was in order, for Mark, in singular contrast with his former scrupulousness in that respect, had become rather neglectful of his personal appearance, and his long black hair floating carelessly down his neck befitted the chief of a band of jay-hawkers better than a spruce Federal officer. "Bestir yourself, Gil; you haven't much time," added the major, as a parting injunction. "I'll call for you at ten."

Ten o'clock came, and with it the major, who found Mark still in the same attitude, unprepared, and ruefully refilling his pipe.

"Now, Gildersleeve, I'll not stand this," exclaimed the lively major. "Go you must. When I say a thing I mean it;" and in spite of his remonstrances the reluctant colonel was borne off to the ball.

Their carriage left them at the carpeted porch of a sumptuous residence fronting Madison Square, and a domestic directed them to an upper room. After a little preliminary adjustment of their toilets, they descended to the parlors, to pay their respects to their host and hostess.

The major presented his friend the colonel to Mrs. Van Spuytenduyvel, a tall dame with massive shoulders and majestic nose, who returned the colonel's bow with becoming haughtiness; and to Mr. Van Spuytenduyvel, a small man, ambushed in the voluminous skirts of his ample consort; and then the colonel and his friend were permitted to pass on and mingle in the festal throng. The major soon found an attractive acquaintance among the ladies, and slipped away, leaving Mark to shift for himself. It was the first time the colonel had ever attended a fashionable party, and the brilliancy of the scene and display of jewels and rich dresses rather dazzled him. A dull pastime, though, for he saw none but strange faces. He looked about him in the vague hope that perchance he might meet the one whose image occupied his thoughts; but apparently she was not present. As he stood staring with an inquisitive and rather bewildered expression, he attracted no little attention. His three years of campaigning certainly furnished an example of how thoroughly not only the mind, but its dial the countenance becomes subdued to what the former works in. He was now the *beau ideal* of a dashing trooper: swarthy and sinewy as an Apache brave, with a decided chin and glittering eyes. The scar on his brow, too, neither softened his sternness nor enhanced his good looks, and he found himself the object of many stares and audible remarks from ladies to their escorts as to who he was, and whether a "regular" or "volunteer," until, embarrassed at the notice he attracted, he threaded his way to a corner secure from observation.

The rooms were excessively crowded, and the atmosphere was heated with the numerous lights, and heavy with the odors of flowers and perfumes. Regardless of all this, some determined dancers were dashing along wildly, and whirling couples carromed like billiard-balls. Mark, inclined to muse, indulged in mental criticism of the company. What struck him most was not the weary, solemn mien of the elder guests, nor the absence of frank joyousness in the young men, but the supercilious nonchalance and worldly-wise air of the young ladies. Here and there was a modest flower, but many wore expressions of bold self-possession, that seemed to his untutored eyes to border on effrontery. Perhaps a harsh judgment on the part of our captious colonel, but it must be remembered that he was still but a child of nature, living in the ideal. His poetic temperament led him to indulge in such exalted fancies of the excellences of the gentler sex, that when taken from his dreams and placed face to face with the sophisticated belles of two seasons, he was naturally discountenanced. To one living outside the pale of fashionable society, its artificiality is painfully apparent. Presently the colonel's soldierly eye was attracted by the erect figure of a young lady, whose back was towards him. Her shoulders and neck were moulded with such perfect grace, that he was desirous to see her face, and changing his position to do so, he beheld a radiant beauty, that recalled a Louis Quatorze marchioness. Powdered hair and a patch enhanced the fairness of her complexion, while bistred lashes gave an unnatural brilliancy to her eyes. Her slender throat was encircled by a diamond necklace, whose pendent cross flashed from a breast of snow, that brought the lines on Pope's Belinda to mind. She was toying with a fan, and chatting with a group of gentlemen who were evidently admiring her, and her beautiful simpering countenance betrayed gratified vanity. Mark scrutinized her closely. Recollections of familiar features arose, and the truth flashed to him that this young person was Edna.

But what a change! Not now the sweet, modest rose of Belton, but an egregiously vain and affected coquette. So thought Mark, in whose unsophisticated eyes the transformation was complete and manifest. He watched her a few moments longer. One of her danglers was made supremely happy by being permitted to button her glove, while another enjoyed the bliss of holding her bouquet. Then a third, a tight-built little fellow, with closely-cropped hair accurately parted in the centre of his round head, a mustache of magnitude, and a crush hat in his hand, gallantly clasping her, led her off in the mazes of a waltz. It certainly was a graceful sight; but Mark saw, or fancied he saw, but another phase of affectation in Edna's posed features and downcast eyes, as she glided around in evident consciousness of the admiration she excited. With a pang of disappointment, Mark shrank away, fearing to be noticed by Edna. He had an undefined dread of being noticed by her there and then, and very soon after, had bidden adieu to Mrs. Van Spuytenduyvel, and left the house.

What bitter emotions filled the heart, and what cynical thoughts the mind, of our impetuous hero that night, it would be difficult to describe. He imagined he had discovered the cause of Edna's neglect of him. She was utterly changed. Other thoughts occupied her mind, and other affections her heart, if she had either, which he was beginning in his bitterness to doubt. Should he make another attempt to see her? No, he would not. She was unworthy of further attention. He should return to his duties at once, and start for the front the very next morning. Such was his decision before he fell into a feverish, disturbed slumber towards dawn. But, as usual, the bright sunlight of morning proved a sedative, and Mark became disposed to be lenient. "Perhaps," thought he, "I have been unjust to her. She has been left an orphan to the care of fashionable people. Could she resist—could any young girl resist the influences of the artificial existence that such people lead? Truth is, I must confess, that I don't know anything about fashion or fashionable people or their ways and manners. I've no doubt that I'm all wrong, and that her heart is all right—that she is as good and kind and candid as ever. But when I think of the dear little artless darling who used to coast down the Academy hill at Belton with me, and laugh so ripplingly when she fell in a snow-bank, and that Pompadour-looking belle playing her eyes at the host of smirking fools around her, I feel as if I could—well, well, she's a warm-hearted girl for all that, and has always been my friend, and I'm a fool" (this was the invariable conclusion arrived at by the colonel in his self-examinations). "At any rate," he continued, "I have no right to judge her harshly. I shall call on her, and her welcome will doubtless efface the disagreeable impression I have received."

XX.

The morrow found the colonel calling again on Miss Heath. Before doing so he took his friend the major's advice, and visited a tonsorial artist in order to present a less savage and more prepossessing appearance. This time he found the young lady at home. As he awaited the return of the domestic who took his card and was about to usher him in, the suspense, the mingled joy and apprehension of meeting, was almost unbearable. He was shown into sumptuous parlors, so filled with paintings and statues that they looked like exhibition rooms, where he found Edna in company with some friends. In a perfectly self-possessed way she came forward to receive him, and she did it so coolly, and introduced him with such an air of indifference to the other visitors present, that poor Mark's heart was chilled. Her appearance, also, surprised and displeased him. She looked, with her fair hair twisted into Medusæan wildness and decorated with broad gold band and dangling sequins; with her delicate ears weighted by Byzantine pendants, and throat circled by a snake-like coil of dead gold,—like an Assyrian princess, beautifully barbaric. But her jaded eyes, and pale cheeks bereft of bloom, told of late hours and departing freshness.

Miss Mumbie was there, and attired much in the same way. There were also two gentlemen present.

"I believe you are already acquainted with Captain Gildersleeve, Ada," said Edna to Miss Mumbie, who bowed rather distantly in reply. "Mr. Jobson— Captain Gildersleeve," she continued, introducing Mark to one of the gentlemen.

"Captain!" exclaimed Mr. Jobson; "why, Miss Heath, this is Colonel Gildersleeve. Didn't I meet him last November when I went down to the front to see my brother? Colonel, of course, delighted to meet you. Don't you recollect Captain Jobson's brother, and the row with your orderly about the shaving brush?"

"Oh, I beg pardon," said Edna, coloring slightly. "I've been away so long that I really forgot Mr. Gildersleeve's present rank."

"Forgot!" returned Jobson, who was a dashing stockbroker, and had all the *brusquerie* of his class; "why, I thought everybody knew how the colonel got his promotion. Why, Miss Heath, he's one of the best known and most serviceable officers in the army. I heard the commander-in-chief himself speak in the highest and most complimentary terms of him; said he, 'That lame devil of a cavalry colonel on H——'s staff is worth all—'"

"My dear sir," interrupted Mark, blushing, and anxious to turn the conversation, though with a secret throb of pleased vanity in his inmost heart, "I remember you now very well. You came up to City Point the day after our skirmish with Hoke's brigade, when poor Archer was shot and your brother wounded."

"To be sure I did," said Jobson; "and some of you fellows at headquarters—I don't say it was you—gave me some of the vilest whiskey, that nearly cut me in two. Why, Miss Heath—"

But Miss Heath was at that moment engaged with the other gentleman, to whom Mark had not been presented. This gentleman, evidently a foreigner, was seated between the two young ladies, whom he was entertaining with some apparently amusing conversation in a subdued voice. Edna, who was reclining regally in an arm-chair, turned her head languidly to listen when appealed to by Jobson.

"Excuse me; I believe I omitted to introduce you, colonel, to Count Borgia—Colonel Gildersleeve;" and the two men bowed stiffly. She then condescendingly addressed a few words to Mark: "Have you been to Belton lately? Dull, stupid place, isn't it? So little society, and what there is is so very inferior. Have you heard about those ridiculous people, those *nouveaux riches*, with that horrid name, who have built near Mr. Mumbie's? Isn't it shameful that such persons are permitted to intrude among respectable people? And they do say Mr. Abbott visits them, and is quite attentive to one of the young ladies. Did you ever hear the like? Dear me, I don't see how any one can live there now. I do so pity Constance Hull. Poor thing, she makes such a martyr of herself, staying there all alone with the Judge, and he is getting so old, and peevish, and cross. Her brother very seldom goes to Belton, I believe, but Constance will stay in the poky old place."

"Perhaps she is one of those persons unfortunate enough to have attachments, and who cling to old associations," said Mark, sarcastically.

Edna seemingly did not heed the thrust, but replied carelessly:

"I don't know really, but it must be very stupid for her."

She spoke with an affected drawl, and drooped her hands from her wrists as a standing dog does its paws. Then turning to the Count, she inquired whether he had been to a certain reception that afternoon, and who were there.

Mark directed his attention to this foreigner, whom he already instinctively disliked. He was a handsome Italian of thirty-five or so, with white teeth gleaming between pulpy red lips partly hidden by a jet mustache with waxed points. He appeared well-bred, spoke English fluently and with very little foreign accent, but minced his words as he displayed his teeth, and smiled so insinuatingly, that Mark's disfavor was intensified at the sight.

The young ladies and the Count began discussing the important subject of a "German" they had attended the previous evening, subsequently to the party at the Van Spuytenduyvels.

"I'm sure, Miss Mumbie, I am right," insisted the Count. "It is exactly as I have said. I did not dance the bouquet figure with Miss Heath; I recollect, with very great distinctness, indeed, that I was leading with the young widow lady, Mrs. Lovett, who has such very charming eyes, and Miss Heath was with—"

"To be sure, Ada, don't you recollect I was dancing with that odious little Herbert Hopper?" said Edna. "Whenever I go to the Pinkertons, I'm sure to meet him invariably, and he never leaves me, so that I have to endure the pleasure of his company the whole of the evening."

"I wish I were in the place of that odious little Hopper," remarked Jobson, gallantly.

"There are others no better," said Edna; "as for Herbert Hopper, I must say that he is a perfect little pest, and I do wish he wouldn't annoy me."

"Say the word, Miss Heath," said Jobson, "and I'll slay him."

"O Miss," deprecated the Count, with a winning air, "do not—do not, I pray you, be so severe with the fire of your indignation on the poor boy. It is not his fault. You do not know what he has to contend with. How can he help it? When we see a parterre of beautiful flowers, do we not all stop and linger around the most beautiful and loveliest of them?" and he added some words in French that caused Edna to smile with evident pleasure, and pout her lips coquettishly.

Mark's feelings underwent a complete revulsion. His bitter disappointment had given place to anger incited by jealousy and the cavalier treatment he had received. Now disenchantment succeeded, and left him very sad. Was it for this he had striven? Where were all those fond illusions and longings, those bright visions of future happiness? Gone in one brief interview with the enchantress that had conjured them. Was this vain, artificial flirt—this heartless girl who treated him with disdain and indifference, the sweet idol he had worshipped so fervently from boyhood? He could stay no longer in her presence, and with a haughty bow to the company rose to leave. Edna bent her head with a dismissive nod, and continued her frivolous conversation with the Count. Jobson sprang up also to leave. "Which way, Colonel? Stopping at the Albemarle, ain't you? Down the avenue, I suppose? I'll go with you. Stop a minute till I look at my watch. By Jove! later than I thought. Ladies, much as I regret it, I must tear myself away. Don't grieve, and I'll promise to return again and heal your lacerated hearts. 'Too late I stayed, forgive the crime, Unheeded flew the hours, How softly falls the foot of time, That only treads on flowers!' With which elegant extract this Child of Affliction begs to subscribe himself on the tablets of your hearts, ladies, as your most obedient and obliged good servant. Ajew—ajew! Parting is such sweet sorrow that I shall say—ajew, till it be morrow. Ha, ha, ha!"

The jocose Jobson then bowed himself out, chaffed the servant in the hall who assisted him on with his overcoat, lit a segar, offered one to the impatient colonel (who was figuratively shaking the dust from his shoes on the stoop), and then hooking his arm in that of the disgusted warrior, walked along with him, chatting with a familiar confidence that rather surprised his companion. Mark examined this new-found friend with some curiosity. Jobson was a tall, spare man, with a good-natured sharp face, keen eyes, a predatory nose, and wispy whiskers. Beneath his drab surtout he wore a brown velvet coat and waistcoat, and his slender legs were encased in cords. A coral splinter-bar pin ornamented his blue bird's-eye scarf, and his watch-chain was composed of miniature snaffle-bits ending in a horse-shoe locket. Altogether he looked the amateur turfman to perfection.

"Deuced fine girl, Miss Heath, ain't she?" he began; "Got the stamps, too— richest heiress in the market. Old man took his death through immoderate use of cold water—fell in the drink over in Jersey, where he owned a whole town; and to think now that this sallow-faced bandit seems to have the inside track. It's a burning shame, I say, that such a smoky-head lazzaroni should be tolerated, when good-looking chaps like you and I, colonel, are around and unprovided for, ain't it?"

The stockbroker's flippant way of treating a subject so near to the colonel's heart grated harshly on his feelings, but curiosity overcame his repugnance, and he inquired, "Who is this Italian—this Count?"

"I'll tell you all I know about him in a few words," continued Jobson. "Throw away that segar first, and take a fresh one—they're Partagas. You see I'm a broker—by the bye, here's my card, and happy to see you down town at my office any time you're that way, or at the club in the evening, whichever is most convenient. Well, as I was saying, I'm a broker, and last year after I closed out the Rock Island pool, out of which I cleared two hundred and forty-five thousand dollars, in less than ninety days, I went to Europe and fell in with the Mumbies. I'm a second cousin of old man Mumbie, you must know, although he never discovered it until I was worth half a million. Anyway Bob Mumbie and I went about together some, and had a good time.

Miss Heath, who, I suppose you know, is a ward of Mumbie's, was with the family, and this feller, this Italian, was their courier. After a while it came out that he was a count, and then they all kow-towed to him as if he were the Grand Mogul. When they got to Italy he showed them his ancestral halls, and all that sort o' thing, and sold Mumbie pictures and marbles enough at five prices to stock a museum, so that the commissions and profits he made on them enabled him to set up for a gentleman, and give up the courier business. But he still froze to the Mumbies, and accompanied them over here. First he made love to Ada, but when he found out that Miss Heath was an heiress, and ever so much richer, he dropped Ada and turned his batteries on the other. Bob Mumbie was also sweet on Miss Heath, but when the Count appeared, poor Bob's pipe was out at once. Mrs. Mumbie is as much magnetized as any of them. She thinks a wonderful sight of high birth, blood, families, and all that sort o' thing, and wants to secure the Count for Ada, though I don't think there's much show for her now. So you see the feller's in clover and, begad, I think he can take his pick of the girls any day he wants to. Can't imagine what possesses our girls to take up with foreign beggars, with handles to their names, when there's lots of their good-looking sensible countrymen to be had, with the rocks to back 'em." Here Jobson threw back the lappels of his coat and displayed his chest. "So it goes," he continued with a sigh. "Some time ago French marquises and barons were all the rage, and now they're running on Italian counts and princes. That Count Borgia hasn't got a red cent. He's passing chips half the time 'round to Morrissey's. Hang me, if I don't think he's a capper, and that's the way he manages to live."

Jobson evidently spoke from warmth of feeling, and the gist of his sentiments found an emphatic indorsement in Mark's breast, who, however, was not disposed to exchange views on the topic, and remained silent. By this time they had reached the Union Club.

"Come in and dine with me?" said Jobson.

The colonel excused himself.

"Well, say to-morrow. I'll call for you in my dog-cart, and we'll take a spin down the Lane before dinner. What do you say?"

The colonel thanked Jobson for his invitation, but said he should leave for the front that evening.

"Sorry, colonel, if you must go. Good-by. Take care of yourself."

Mark promised to do so, and returned to his hotel.

"Henceforth let every incident of my past life, every thought and remembrance connected with her, be dismissed from my mind. Let it be as blank. I blot out every memory of Edna Heath from this moment. No such being exists for me." Such were the colonel's resolves, as he prepared himself to leave. "I can very well understand how men become Trappists. It would take but little to induce me to join the order, provided they permitted smoking. How vain, hollow, and illusory are all our hopes and plans! Vanity of vanities," etc., etc., and he continued in the usual strain of jilted lovers, indulging in gloomy rhapsodies as he packed his portmanteau.

An hour later he was on his way to City Point. Contemporaneously, the object of his animadversions was in her room preparing for the evening's campaign. The hair-dresser had just left, and she remained leaning pensively on her toilet-table. Evidently she was dissatisfied with something, probably with herself. On reviewing the events of the day, and her conduct and attitude towards Mark, a vexing doubt would obtrude that she had perhaps treated him rather shabbily, at least ungenerously, if not unworthily. "After all," she reflected, "it is his fault. He has no one to blame but himself. Why did he not answer my letters? why this unaccountable silence on his part? Perhaps he might have explained it, but then, why is he so intensely haughty, and why does he attempt to overawe me? Am I a child to be chidden and rendered submissive by imposing airs? Still he seemed so joyful when he entered the room—his eyes fairly sparkled. But what could I do? I couldn't fly in his arms or appear demonstrative in the presence of the Count and the others. Still, I might have shown some cordiality. I don't see what possessed me. I did feel like greeting him, but something checked me. O dear! I am so weak and foolish, I presume nothing will do now but I must write a note apologizing like a little goose, and telling him how very sorry I am, and promising never to do so again. No! I won't do that, but I'll smooth it over with a few non-committal sentences, and he will be just as well pleased." Sitting down to her writing-desk, she began penning a formal missive, containing a half dozen white fibs, which, before it was completed, she impatiently tore into bits, and began another which met a similar fate, until at length her feelings found relief and satisfactory expression in the following:

> DEAR MARK:
> Do not leave in anger with me.
> EDNA.

These few words were immediately despatched to the colonel, who, Edna had overheard Jobson say, was stopping at the "Albemarle," and strict injunctions given the messenger to ascertain positively if this were so.

The clerk in attendance at the hotel, unaware that Mark had departed a short time before, replied, when questioned as to whether the colonel were staying there, in the affirmative; and taking Edna's note, flung it carelessly in an appropriate pigeon-hole. It lay there a day; and the next tenant of the room occupied by Mark received it, opened it without looking at the address, and discovering his mistake and the apparent unimportance of the epistle, unconcernedly threw it into the fire.

Accidents seemingly trivial shape our destinies; and this one separated two young hearts forever, and caused a material divergence in their future lives.

Edna, after sending the note, remained at home that evening. She had engaged to go to the opera; but plead indisposition, and grievously disappointed an admirer. She waited in expectation of a swift acknowledgment of her petition. The mask had fallen. If Mark could have seen her now, all his bitterness would have vanished. Old thoughts and recollections had resumed their sway, and her countenance beamed with the latent tenderness of a frank, generous nature. It was not the tristful expression of a love-lorn maiden, for her girlish passion for Mark was indeed gone; but there remained a sincere affection for her old friend and playmate. He came not, neither made he any sign; and Edna retired to her room that night disappointed, and perhaps a little nettled. This feeling very soon passed over; it lasted a day or so, and then with an appeased conscience, and serene conviction that she had made ample amends for her frigid reception of her old lover, she continued to mingle in the whirl of fashionable diversions.

Her wealth and beauty had installed her at once as the reigning belle of the season. Suitors she had without number. Noticeable among them, besides the Italian count, were: the still faithful Spooner, the former dog-fancier, now the Rev. F. Standish Spooner, in charge of a congregation at Roxbury, that he sadly neglected to wait upon Miss Heath, without, however, much hope of success, as his ineligibility as a partner in the dance put him at a woful disadvantage; the dashing stockbroker, Jobson, whom the belle rather disdained, in spite of his horses and yacht, as unrefined and inclined to low tastes; Herbert Hopper, a little fop, with immeasurably more money than brains; a pretty fellow, though, that scores of girls would gladly have taken up with; and last though not least, Percy Brocatelle, a famous leader of the German. Percy's means of livelihood were involved in mystery, and his antecedents humble. He had been a clerk at Stewart's, where his gentlemanly address and good looks had won him many friends and acquaintances from among the fashionable patronesses of that establishment. Under the auspices of the sagacious Sexton Brown, he had forsaken the glove-counter, and made his début as a society-man, gradually rising to eminence in that arduous profession. Envious swells, to be sure, maligned him; sons of successful pork-merchants and stable-keepers blackballed him and refused him admission to their clubs; but Brocatelle rose triumphant over all these obstacles, and was found everywhere—that was anywhere—for who could so deftly tread the mazes of the German as he? Whose head was so round, or hair parted with such precision as his? And who else combined with all this, clothes so faultless, and a mustache so imposing? His taste, furthermore, in ladies' dress —in their laces, gloves, ribbons, and coiffures, was unimpeachable and invaluable. These qualities were not to be gainsaid; and Edna, for one, declared publicly, that she preferred dancing with him to any one else, and dreaded his criticism on her attire more than even that of the great Schmauder. Yet in spite of all these advantages, Percy could make no headway against the Count—the irresistible Count, surrounded with all the fascinating and terrible glories of the Borgia family, whose star was in the ascendant until a prince—a real PRINCE, came along. For it happened in those days that the son of a reigning monarch was making a tour of the States. His mother, who was, naturally enough, a queen, although a queen, bore as irreproachable a character as any matron in her dominions; and as such praiseworthy conduct on the part of a sovereign deserved encouragement, several estimable old citizens of the great metropolis deemed it their duty to manifest their approval of her good behavior, by giving a public ball to her son, out of respect for his august mother. This, to be sure, was but a left-handed compliment to the son, and when a committee of the reverend seignors waited on the prince to tender the proposed honor, he did not evince any lively sense of anticipated pleasure; and after the deputation had bowed themselves off (each one under the delightful delusion that he would be asked in return to drop in at the palace, in a friendly way, on his next visit to Europe) he turned to his mentor and discontentedly said, "Dammit, Grey, must I go to that ball, and be bored by those confounded snobs?"

"No help for it that I can see," replied my lord.

"Well, there will be lots of pretty girls there, I dare say. These Yankee girls are doosid pretty. If they'd only give me a chance to have my fling, and not insist on my leading out a lot of stupid old dowagers, I wouldn't mind it a bit," remarked H. R. H.

Now princeling was to a certain extent justified in his comments, for while the mass of the people had an honest curiosity to see a prince, and rushed to look at him as they would to a unicorn or any other rare sight, there was a select circle who worshipped him as the representative of power and pageantry, and hoped by surrounding him to shine resplendently in the reflected light of royalty. H. R. H. was not an astute lad, but he was probably sharp enough to perceive that all the toadying he was subjected to was due to his rank and trappings and not to him as an individual. That refined snobbery called loyalty has its redeeming side. One can understand the devotion of a good and wise royalist to an imbecile or wretched monarch, because the sentiment may be disinterested, and would still exist were the monarch an exiled mendicant, but the courtiership of republicans is purely selfish and debasing. Most of us, like Thackeray, would jump out of our skins for joy at walking arm-in-arm between two dukes, but it is painful to reflect that we should hardly toss a shilling to either of them the next day if stripped of their titles and reduced to beggary. So Mr. Mumbie, who was abject in the presence of the prince, and ready to prostrate his poor old brown wig in the dust before his royal highness would, in all likelihood, have but grudgingly lent him a dollar had he come in the guise of an impecunious plebeian. But H. R. H. was a good-natured boy and had a part to perform. So he duly attended the ball, was very complaisant, honored several ladies, old enough to be his grandmammas, with his august hand in the dance, and was then allowed to run at large among the younger beauties present. Miss Heath was among those who enjoyed the inestimable privilege of being selected as his partner. Moreover, he graciously flirted with her in the intervals of a galop. He told her that she was a "stunning girl." His Royal Highness had actually said that! Edna thrilled with pleasure. True he had paid the same compliment to the oysters of the country and its cocktails—true he was plain and an awkward dancer, but then he was a prince—a prince of the blood-royal, whatever that might be, and she, Edna Heath, in his princely estimation, was a stunning girl! Was there anything left to live for? Her happiness was complete, but alas and alack! the prince, as princes often do, fluttered away like a fickle butterfly, and she was left forlorn to mourn his disappearance.

Then by degrees the Count—the wily, persistent Count—temporarily eclipsed, arose again and reappeared in the zenith of her favor. At times, when she had leisure to think amid the excitement of her existence, she gave a passing thought to Mark, but she felt absolved from any duty towards him. She had done all that could be required of her, and had gone farther to retain his regard than she would to any other person than so old a friend. It is true she had had a girlish fancy for him, but it was at a time when she was barely more than a child and inexperienced. He could not possibly presume upon that now, especially after the long period in which he had neglected her, and when her letters had remained uncared for. Consequently she felt entirely justified in dismissing him thenceforth from her mind. It is not so certain but that the Count might have shared the same fate, had it not been for an occurrence that turned the scales in his favor.

Mrs. Mumbie, in her anxiety to secure the nobleman for a son-in-law, had watched with much dissatisfaction his marked preference for Edna. This, and the heiress' continued indifference to her son Bob's attentions, were more than her kind, motherly soul could bear. After a long delay and patient waiting, one day Bob ventured to propose. Edna listened with an air of mingled surprise and merriment that rather disconcerted him, and declined the proffered honor. The rejected postulant, chopfallen and sullen, repaired to his mother and related his unsuccess. Mrs. Mumbie could contain herself no longer. The blood of the Skinners was aroused, and her wrath knew no bounds. Rushing in unceremoniously upon the heiress, she overwhelmed her with vehement reproaches. Edna was at first bewildered, and recoiled from the storm of anger so unaccountably directed at her by the usually amiable matron, who raged away incoherently, until at length unburthening herself, the animus of all her fury was very disagreeably revealed. "So, Miss, you have seen fit to insult us—to insult your guardian—to insult the family to whom you owe so much, by refusing my son, who was good enough to honor you by an offer. You hussy! how dare you slight my son—how dare you treat us in this way? This is your gratitude, is it? After all the kindness we have shown you—after all our attention and devotion to you. You precious, artful piece! to think of your eating day after day at our table, sitting at our board with us, looking as if butter wouldn't melt in your mouth, and all the while plotting against the happiness of our children. I don't see how you dare look at me! And the Count—this foreign adventurer whom Ada despises and whom you have encouraged with your advances—this Count has turned your silly head, and I'll no longer permit you to stay in this household."

Edna could listen no longer. With cheeks hot with indignation, and hands to her ears, she retreated into an adjoining room. Mrs. Mumbie, left alone, took to screaming, and throwing herself on the floor, drummed away with her heels in impotent ire. Edna meanwhile put on her hat and shawl, and swiftly leaving the house stood in the street. She drew her veil to hide her agitated countenance, and debated whither she should go. Within a few squares dwelt an intimate friend, a young lady, to whom she repaired and confided her trouble. This done, her pent-up grief could no longer be contained, and she gave way to a long cry. She was very sorrowful. The Mumbies had always been kind to her, and their home was the only one she had known since her father's death. This sudden severance, and Mrs. Mumbie's cruel attack, made her feel very lonely and miserable.

It was not until the morrow that the Mumbie's discovered where their ward had taken refuge. By that time Mrs. Mumbie had recovered her presence of mind, and felt that she had sadly marred her plans by her hasty and intemperate conduct. So Mr. Mumbie was immediately despatched with a verbal apology, and instructions to smooth matters and induce the heiress to return. Mr. Mumbie felt himself rather an incompetent ambassador for such a mission, still he undertook it with zeal having a genuine affection for the daughter of his old friend, and sincerely and deeply regretting his wife's behavior towards her. With what seemed to him subtle policy, he put on sundry tokens Edna had given him, such as a seal ring, a scarf-pin, and a watch-chain which could not fail to open a spring of fond associations that would greatly facilitate his task. He augured well from his reception, for Edna appeared much pleased to see him, and held up her face to be kissed. But when, after a short disquisition on the weather, and some hemming and hawing, he ventured to announce the object of his mission, and, in alluding to Mrs. Mumbie's "peculiar temper," said she "mustn't mind it"—that nobody minded her "peculiar temper" (which was rather a stretch of veracity), as "she didn't mean anything by it," and that the best thing Edna could do was to put on her "things" and go right back with him—the young lady shook her head in a way that caused Mr. Mumbie to lose faith in his powers of persuasion. He tried to appeal to her feelings. "Why, Edna, you can't imagine how we miss you. You know we are a family of strong local attachments. I myself have carried this knife—this"—

He felt in his pockets, rummaged them, searched them over—the knife was gone! Consternation was imminent—when he suddenly recollected that he had, for the first time in his life, left this cherished companion at home. This shock, however, disturbed his ratiocination, and he floundered on rather feebly in his plea.

"As I was saying, Edna, we miss you awfully. If you had only seen us at breakfast this morning, you couldn't stay away a minute. We couldn't any of us eat hardly anything. All I took was a cup of tea and a roll. As for Bob, and you know what a hearty feeder he is, poor Bob couldn't go more than a couple of buckwheat cakes and a chop, and Ada, she just about touched an egg, and kept pointing with her fork at your vacant chair, and saying there's where she used to sit. Last night Will Hull called, and says he, 'Where's Edna?' and Ada didn't know what to say. Now this sort of thing won't do. You must forget and forgive."

"My dear guardian," replied Edna, firmly; "while I shall always retain the utmost respect and gratitude for the kindness you have invariably shown me, and shall always be very much pleased to see you, I never wish to see Mrs. Mumbie again. I could not endure to be reminded of the cruel attack I was subjected to from her."

"Come—come, Edna, you must not talk in that strain. She didn't mean anything by it. I've been through it myself. It's only her peculiar way, you know."

Edna pressed her lips tightly together, and shook her head, in a manner that signified a fixed resolution, and disheartened her guardian.

"Why, Edna, even Blanche has noticed that you have left the house, and goes whining about, and as for the canaries they are dumb and dull as owls," added Mr. Mumbie, at a loss for arguments. But even this touching allusion to the sorrows of the pet Italian grayhound and the singing-birds failed to soften the obdurate ward, and he was obliged to retire baffled.

Then Ada Mumbie came and tried her powers, but with no better success, and Edna's determination remained unshaken.

She stayed at her friend's house, pending the arrival of Mrs. Applegate, who was spending the winter in a distant western city, and with whom she intended to reside in the future.

The moment was a propitious one for the Count. He was aware that some disagreement had arisen between the Mumbies and Miss Heath, but of the nature of it he was in total ignorance. His curiosity was excited. He could learn nothing from the young lady. She of course was silent on the subject, and he had too much tact to appear inquisitive, but Bob—the guileless Bob, in a gush of confidence, inspired by a bottle of Burgundy at the club, imparted the story of his unrequited love, his declaration, and its sequel, to the feeling bosom of a friend, who in turn confided the tale to a dozen other confidential friends. In this way it reached the ears of the Count, who was not slow to perceive the great advantage Miss Heath's present position gave him in prosecuting his suit. Here was a young, inexperienced person, severed from life-long friends, and left almost alone in the world. Naturally she was ready to attach herself to the first sympathetic heart that presented itself in a suitable and engaging way. Craftily the Count played his cards. When Edna went to Philadelphia to reside with her aunt, he followed her there, and had the field to himself. He began by captivating Mrs. Applegate. She bore a striking resemblance to his cousin the Principessa Baldonachi, he said, and had the port and mien of those noble Venetian dames, that Titian loved to paint. He brought her flowers and escorted her to church. The good lady was flattered beyond measure at these unwonted attentions, and pronounced him the most polite gentleman she had ever known. At a favorable moment he took occasion to confide to her, his adoration of her niece—that truly noble young person—for, while he confessed, with a certain reluctance, that he belonged to one of the most illustrious houses of Europe, yet he deemed the only true nobility to be the nobility of the soul, such as Miss Heath possessed; and then, with a sigh, he regretted that the young lady was wealthy. He deeply deplored that. "If she were only a poor girl—if she were entirely destitute—how happy I should be. With what eager joy would I hasten to lay my heart, my title, my patrimony, everything at her feet, and beg of her to accept them. But now, alas! I cannot. No—no—it cannot be—it must not be. The world—the censorious world, would call me mercenary. No—I must suffer in silence. Be still, my poor heart! But you shall be my friend, will you not?"

His visible agitation and moistening eyes touched Mrs. Applegate, who ventured a little consolatory advice. The Count's sentiments and conduct in this manner did him great honor, she said, but she did not think he was called upon to push his disinterestedness to such extremes. For her part, she had always been of the opinion that no considerations of money should be allowed to interfere, where true affection existed, and the happiness of the parties was at stake. The worthy dame already saw herself sweeping down the grand staircase of the Palazzo Baldonachi, on the arm of her noble nephew-in-law.

The Count thanked her a thousand times, for her kind words. She had lifted a load from his heart, he said, and raising her hand respectfully to his lips, the gallant Italian closed the interview.

Having secured the aunt as an ally, the Count redoubled his efforts to please the niece. He surrounded her with delicate attentions. He was pliant, polite, deferential, and at length Edna yielded. What else could she do? How could she, an inexperienced girl, who had never felt, until now, the need of a protector, resist the persistent courtship of a man, handsome, subtle, versed in the vulnerable points of feminine nature, who plied her with ardent protestations of love and constancy. Her aunt approved of it, too, and not long after the announcement was made public, that a marriage had taken place between Count Borgia and Miss Edna Heath, which, naturally enough, created no little excitement among the numerous friends and admirers of the bride in the neighboring city of New York. The match was very frankly discussed at the clubs, rather unfavorably than otherwise, and Jobson freely offered the odds of two to one, in sums to suit, that the Count would either poison or strangle his wife within a year; and odds of ten to one that the extinguishment would take place in less than six months, provided the husband could get a will in his favor by that time—found no takers.

Colonel Mark Gildersleeve read of the marriage in a newspaper, just before the final advance of our army on Richmond. Perhaps his rash bravery on that occasion, when he rallied a broken column against a battery as gallantly as Caulincourt at Borodino, may have been stimulated by the conduct of one who had robbed existence of its charms, and rendered all renown barren.

XXI.

Soon after their marriage, the Count and Countess Borgia sailed for Europe. The latter, before leaving, found use for some of her wealth in liquidating her husband's debts. Not a few of them were incurred at the gaming-table. The Count was in favor of repudiating these, but as the holders of his obligations made application to his wife, she insisted upon paying them. The fact that he proposed to cheat his gambling associates shocked her far more than the knowledge that he had indulged so deeply in the vice. But she was destined to a series of shocks. Having secured the coveted prize, the Count had no longer any object in playing the hypocrite. His true character revealed itself. He was faithless and tyrannous. He attempted no violence towards her, as Jobson had predicted, but his acrimonious temper and bursts of vicious anger, alternating with fits of feigned tenderness, of spurious fawning affection, and his utter dishonesty soon dissipated the little love she had for him; aversion succeeded, and ere the first year of their union had closed, separation took place.

She lives now in Paris, consoling herself in the care of an infant son for the lingering bitterness resulting from disillusion, and the conviction that she was the dupe of a designing knave; while he spends his time between Hombourg, Monaco, and other gambling resorts, squandering the handsome allowance he receives from his wife on condition of never appearing within fifty miles of where she is residing.

———

Mark Gildersleeve, at the close of the war, applied for and received a commission as captain in the regular service. The Government, when granting it, were pleased to convey their appreciation of the efficient and invaluable services he had rendered.

While in Washington, shortly after the receipt of his commission, he met at Willard's, Miss Hull, who had accompanied her grandfather, the Judge, to the capital. Mark had never been intimate with her, but ventured nevertheless to accost her and renew the acquaintance. She received him pleasantly, and he spent several very agreeable evenings in her society. She was not a comely young woman, rather plain, in fact—small, pale, and wearing shell-glasses, but she possessed a fund of good sense and a cultivated mind that were very engaging. Mark discovered that, and found that his wounded heart was now healing, so fast, indeed, that it rather amazed him. "Strange," thought he, "I never noticed how much there was in Miss Hull. I always had an idea that she was a commonplace, in fact, rather insignificant girl. How blind boys are! Upon the whole, I think she's the cleverest and most charming young lady I ever saw; after all, how much more potent are the fascinations of the mind—the graces of intellect, than those of mere physical beauty."

The sequel can be foreseen. Mark's bankrupt heart was now solvent. He fell in love with Constance Hull, and proposed to her. She did not reject him absolutely, but made her acceptance conditional on not being required to leave her grandfather. Here was a quandary. Mark was contented with his profession. He could not bear the thought of resuming his old calling, which he would have to do, in case he returned to live in Belton. One thing was clear: he should have to throw up his commission and leave the army. The alternative was a hard one. Resign his claim to Miss Hull, he could and would not. In this dilemma, and while seeking some way out of it, an event occurred which settled the matter in an unexpected way. Death, the great intermeddler, stepped in and removed the old Judge, and after a proper period had elapsed, Constance Hull consigned her fortunes to the care of Mark Gildersleeve. The latter is now stationed at one of the frontier forts, and he and his wife are as happy as mutual affection and esteem can make them.

Our ecclesiastical friend, the Reverend Spencer Abbott, has also taken unto himself a wife, and is married to Miss Angela Gogglemush, second daughter of the distinguished inventor of the Terpsichorean Ointment. The wedding was the most brilliant affair of the kind that ever took place in Belton, to quote the language of the "Sentinel," and was "got up in a style of Oriental magnificence—the bishop officiated—six bridesmaids—ushers—two thousand invitations—presents innumerable—sixty-two silver tea sets—ten gross butter-knives—one hundred and forty-three salt-cellars—sixty-two bronze card-receivers—diamonds, rubies, pearls, beryls," etc., etc.

Angela is an excellent spouse, and her husband is still in charge of St. Jude's. Not long since, learning that Dr. Wattletop was seriously ill, he went to see him. He found the old physician on his death-bed, and remained with him until the last moment. The rector hinted at repentance and "making his peace with God," but the moribund was apparently as firm in his stoical opinions as ever. To the rector's kind entreaties he shook his head, and replied feebly, "Useless ... useless.... Nothing I say now can cancel one wrong I have committed or any evil done.... The future cannot be at the mercy of chance or opportunity.... Justice, impartial and inexorable, of the Creator. How weary ... weary ... weary.... Death comes so slowly ..."

And the old philosopher felt his own pulse as the current of life was ebbing fast, until like one going to sleep he passed away.

The Mumbies still reside in New York. Ada is not married yet, and Mrs. Mumbie says she rejoices at it when she considers the dangers to which eligible girls are exposed by designing fortune-hunters, and, as a case in point, never fails to cite that of Edna Heath, that "poor unfortunate person," as Mrs. Mumbie calls her, when she expatiates to a friend on the fate of her husband's ward, and relates how her motherly affection was repaid by base ingratitude. "We did all we could," she never omits to add, "to warn her against the intrigues of that foreigner. We expostulated with her, we besought and implored her, but all in vain, and now see the result. I am told, (lowering her voice to a whisper, and with a slight shiver of horror as she bends to the ear of the confidant)—I am told that from the very day they were married he beat her, and on one occasion tried to poison her; she recovered from the effects of it, but her system is a wreck—a complete wreck, and she now drags out a miserable existence, and Mr. Mumbie has actually to pay her husband money to keep him away from her."

The master of the Archimedes Works is now mayor of Belton. The town having attained the dignity of incorporation some two years since, George was chosen its chief magistrate by his grateful and admiring fellow-citizens. He is in no way spoiled by the honor thrust upon him, but, if possible, is more independent than ever; in fact, it would probably, to put it mildly, now require the combined efforts of a drove of hogs on the *Mer de Glace* to exemplify his extreme independence. He and his wife still occupy the small house on Mill Street; and the latter's chief delight is in the periodical visits she receives from her brother-in-law and adopted son, Captain Mark, and his wife, as he never fails to spend the furloughs accorded him in his old home and with his adopted mother.

Our little story is ended. What will probably strike the reader as the most improbable incident in it, will be very likely the one where truth has been the most faithfully followed. We allude to the cause of Mr. Heath's death. The traveller who speeds over one of the railways radiating from the city of New York, may be attracted, when a short distance out from the suburbs, by a fine stone villa surrounded by beautiful grounds and conservatories. It was evidently designed and built by some one of taste and wealth. Some years

162

ago, to the astonishment of all, the owner perished by the act of his own hand. What led him to it was unknown, except to a few. It was remorse created by the discovery that an apparently trivial act of dishonesty on his part, long years gone, had caused the ruin of an innocent boy suspected of the offence. Moral law vindicated itself and became its own executioner.

———————————————

Before parting with the reader, it is meet that we should apologize for having in one instance decked our hero in borrowed plumage. That is, in attributing to him the feat of unspiking the siege-gun. The honor of that exploit belonged to John Stray, a private in the First Regiment N. Y. V. E., and occurred before Fort Wagner. It was done precisely as narrated, and, as an act of nerve and cool courage under circumstances of extreme peril, has but few parallels in our late civil war.

THE END.

———————————————